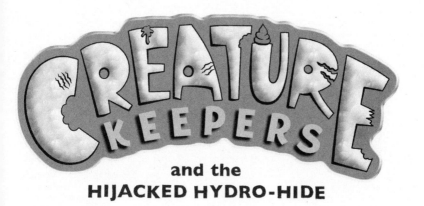

and the
HIJACKED HYDRO-HIDE

and the
HIJACKED HYDRO-HIDE

Peter Nelson & Rohitash Rao

Balzer + Bray
An Imprint of HarperCollins *Publishers*

Balzer + Bray is an imprint of HarperCollins Publishers.

Creature Keepers and the Hijacked Hydro-Hide
Copyright © 2014 by Peter Nelson and Rohitash Rao

Library of Congress Cataloging-in-Publication Data
Nelson, Peter, date, author.
  Creature Keepers and the hijacked Hydro-Hide / Peter Nelson,
Rohitash Rao. — First edition.
    pages cm. — (Creature Keepers ; #1)
  Summary: "Twelve-year-old Jordan Grimsley discovers the
existence of the Creature Keepers, a team of humans assigned to
protect mythical beasts"— Provided by publisher.
  ISBN 978-0-06-223643-2 (hardback)
  [1. Animals, Mythical—Fiction. 2. Secret societies—Fiction.]
I. Rao, Rohitash, author. II. Title.
PZ7.N43583Cr 2014   2014002114
[Fic]—dc23   CIP
                                                             AC

Typography by Alison Klapthor
14 15 16 17 18   CG/RRDH   10 9 8 7 6 5 4 3 2 1
❖
First Edition

For you, Dad. So glad you opened up Kuku Copy and Printing.—P. N.

To Mom, the original Creature Keeper.—R. R.

NO SERVICE.

Jordan Grimsley's very smart smartphone smartly alerted him that he was no longer in an active cellular area. Wi-Fi had vanished about fifty miles back, and now Jordan looked from the tiny, useless screen in his hand to the enormous backseat window of his family's enormous station wagon. The air outside had become muggy and sticky, so all the windows were rolled up. A sign zoomed past. It read: *Now Leaving Leisureville, Florida! Take 'er Easy!*

1

Leisureville was not Jordan's hometown. Florida was not his home state. And nothing about this trip had been easy to take since they left the big city where Jordan lived. The city. Where there was an abundance of Wi-Fi, and cell service roamed free.

Jordan had been riding with his family for two days in an embarrassingly ancient 1972 Pontiac Grand Safari, which Jordan's dad had nicknamed "The Grimsley Family Rambler." Currently, it was rambling the family through the Sunshine State, along a two-lane stretch of broken road called the Ingraham Highway. And according to both Jordan's phone and that sign, they'd just officially blown through the last stop before entering a technological dead zone.

"Dad. There's still no Wi-Fi. And now I lost my signal."

Mr. Grimsley glanced at his son in the rearview mirror, then smiled over at Mrs. Grimsley, sitting beside him in the passenger seat. "You may as well put that thing away for the rest of spring break, Jordan. The Grimsley Clan is off the grid!"

"Clan" was the term Jordan's dad used when they were all doing something he considered adventurous—or worse, character-building. "Off the grid" could only mean one thing: both Jordan, who was twelve, and his fourteen-year-old sister, Abigail, who was sitting beside him, would soon be bored stupid.

Abigail lifted her skull-shaped headphones and glared through dark, mascara-painted eyes. "I still can't believe you made me abandon Chunk while he's going through his first molting period!" She held up a book: *Raising and Caring for Your Reptile*. Jordan noticed a picture of a chubby lizard shedding its skin in a moist, moss-filled terrarium, with a lightbulb hanging over the fogged-up roof. "Auntie Anne better keep Chunk's molting tank at the right humidity level, or she's toast!" Chunk was Abigail's pet iguana, and the only living thing she cared about.

"Don't you worry, Abbie," Mrs. Grimsley said. "Auntie Anne is very reliable."

"You mean she's *old*," Abigail said under her breath. She replaced her headphones and buried her face back in her lizard book. "I can't stand old people."

"Y'know, gang," Jordan's dad said. "If this house turns out to be fixer-uppable, we could open it up as a B and B! That stands for bed-and-breakfast! See, visitors from all over the world come sleep in our beds, and we make 'em breakfast! Fresh-squeezed juice, homemade bread, hand-churned butter, farm-fresh eggs . . ."

As his dad continued a list of basic breakfast items, Jordan turned back to the blur of landscape flying by. The thick, tangled woods on either side of the highway did not look inviting. What they did look was full of nasty insects, mucky water, smelly sludge, and probably more than a few alligators. Jordan hated alligators. *No one from anywhere would ever want to visit here,* he thought.

"It sounds wonderful, Roger," Jordan's mom said. "But let's not get ahead of ourselves. First we have to see what condition this old house is in."

Jordan's parents loved old stuff. Anything worn down or tossed out, they'd fix up and give new life. They still wrote and received *letters,* on actual paper, presumably from other people who also liked old stuff. His dad recently got a letter from a lawyer named C. E. Noodlepen, along with something called a deed. The letter said that Jordan's Grampa Grimsley had left Jordan's dad an old house in the Florida Everglades. The deed made it official.

Jordan knew exactly three things about his Grampa Grimsley: (1) that he died years ago; (2) that they'd never met; and (3) that they never would (see #1). Jordan could now add two more things to that list: (4) his grandfather left his dad a cruddy old house; and (5) Jordan would be spending his two-week spring vacation fixing it up with his family, without Wi-Fi or cell service, bored stupid.

Just as he was thinking all of this, the Family Rambler suddenly jerked and hit something. *WUMP! Scrreech!* His father slammed the brakes, skidding to a stop in the middle of the empty road.

Abigail had bumped her head on the seat in front of her and glared at her dad through raccoon-painted eyes. *"What are you doing?"*

"Roger, what *was* that?" Jordan's mother said in a panicked voice.

"Some animal," Jordan's father said. "It ran out of the woods. I swerved to miss it, but I think it bumped the back corner of the car."

The Grimsley family slowly turned around in their seats. Something big, black, and furry was lying in the middle of the Ingraham Highway, fifty yards back.

"Roger, what is it?"

Jordan peered through the back window. He couldn't make out what it could be, either. But he wondered about something else. "Dad, what if it's—*not dead*?"

"Then it'll be angry," Abigail said. "I would be if

a big, stupid, ugly car hit me."

"We can't just leave it there. Right, Dad?"

Mr. Grimsley looked at his son, then at the black lump lying on the road in the distance, then finally at his wife's worried expression.

"I'm sure it's just an overgrown possum, Betsy," Mr. Grimsley said. "You ladies sit tight." He jumped out of the car and opened Jordan's door. "C'mon, son. The Grimsley men will tackle this challenge together!" Jordan slowly got out, hoping his father didn't mean that literally.

The humid air hit Jordan in the face like a warm, wet towel. It was thick and still as Jordan followed his father to the rear of the car, keeping a sharp eye down the road on the animal lying perfectly still. Whatever it was, that was no possum.

They turned their attention to the back of the 1972 Pontiac Grand Safari. It had a dent in the side panel, and there was a tiny bit of black fur wedged in the bumper. Mr. Grimsley pulled the clump loose and sniffed it. *"Whew,"* he said. "Whatever it is, it sure could use a bath." He offered a whiff to Jordan. The two of them turned to face the animal that had left the stinky clump.

A chill shot up Jordan's back. The creature was gone.

Jordan's heart beat faster as he and his dad walked briskly toward the spot where it had been lying. There was no blood, no fur, nothing—just a sharp odor hanging in the muggy air. "Well, I guess it couldn't have been hurt too badly," Mr. Grimsley said. "So that's good."

"Dad, what was it?" Jordan asked.

"I dunno. Bear, maybe." He sniffed the stinky fur he held between his fingers. "Too big to be a skunk, although it sure smells like a—" He stopped and thought for a moment.

"What's wrong?"

"Nothing." Mr. Grimsley dropped the fur and chuckled to himself. "No, nothing. C'mon. Let's get ramblin' again. I wanna see this house before nightfall."

🐾   🐾   🐾

The last few hours of the drive were silent ones. Mr. Grimsley drove a bit slower and each of them kept their eyes peeled for any critters that might leap out of the woods. As the Ingraham Highway took them deeper into the swamp, the twisting vines on either side of the road gnarled higher and thicker. Jordan felt as if the woods were straining to reach out and grab their Family Rambler.

With the sun sinking behind the thick tree line, the strip of sky above them turned a deep orange. Jordan's dad put on the Rambler's right-turn blinker, even though they hadn't seen a single other car since they passed through Leisureville. They turned onto a new road, passing a sign: *Welcome to Waning Acres: A Retirement Community for the Young at Heart!*

The road immediately became wider and smoother, and the wild, curling, swampy roadside vegetation was suddenly tamed—pushed back behind neat, stone walls, making space for a line of perfect little houses, each with a perfect little lawn. Aside from slightly differing colors, each house was identical to the next.

"Creepy," Abigail said.

"Is it one of these?" Mrs. Grimsley asked.

Jordan stared straight ahead. "No. It's gotta be *that* one."

The street dead-ended at an iron gate, which was cluttered with locked chains and *KEEP OUT!* signs. Beyond the gate rose a front yard thick with weeds, leading up to an enormous house. Completely unlike all the neat, cute little houses, this one stood two stories at least and took up the entire width of the dead end. Its paint was dingy and peeling, its windows broken and boarded up, with black shutters hanging off their hinges.

Mr. Grimsley put the 1972 Pontiac Grand Safari in park and grinned at his family's empty faces. "Here we are." He beamed. "Welcome to Grampa Grimsley's!"

Jordan's dad slid a rusty key into the lock and turned, then pushed open the front door to the old house. The Grimsley family was immediately greeted with a burst of musty air waiting to engulf the first intruder foolish enough to enter. Jordan coughed. It was like breathing through a sweaty old gym sock.

They stepped into the large, empty front hall. There was a dusty staircase on the left, a long, dark hallway straight ahead, and a big living room off to the right. The Grimsleys went right.

They entered what must have been at one time a lovely living room, long before the spiderwebs, mold, smelly carpeting, and peeling wallpaper took over.

Abigail spoke first. "Okay. This place is *totally*—"

"*Perfect!*" Mr. Grimsley exclaimed, stepping into the center of the room, waving his hands around dramatically. "I couldn't agree more, Abbie! It's perfect!"

Jordan and Abigail glanced at each other, then turned to their mother for help. But it was too late. Mrs. Grimsley was grinning ear to ear. "And *totally* fixer-uppable!" she said.

Jordan stared at his parents as they hugged each other in the center of this filthy room. Whatever form of insanity they shared, he hoped they hadn't passed it along to him.

"I can't believe you're going to make us work here on our spring break," Abigail said. "I miss my room. I miss Chunk. I miss—oxygen!" She stepped to a window and ripped open the heavy curtains. The window was boarded up. "Perfect."

"All right, family meeting," Mr. Grimsley said. "Look, I'm beginning to sense that not everyone is as excited as your mother and I about fixing this old place up. But the letter I received from Mr. Noodlepen was clear. We had a short time frame to take physical ownership of the house to claim it as our own."

"We should claim it as a disaster area," Abigail said.

"Look, I know it might need a little TLC—"

"More like TNT," Jordan said, smiling at his sister. She didn't smile back. Abbie never smiled at his jokes.

"But I also know," their father continued, "that a little of the ol' Grimsley grit will turn this place into a palace in no time!"

"I can't believe this is our vacation," Abbie said.

"Anyone can go on vacation," Mr. Grimsley replied. "This is a . . . *renovacation!*"

Making his way down the long hallway, Jordan found numerous doors, each one opening to reveal a small bedroom. The hall continued all the way to the back of the house, leading into a massive dining room. Inside, a long, wide picnic table ran the entire length of the chamber, with benches on either side that could easily seat fifty or more people.

At the far end of the huge picnic table was a swinging doorway, which Jordan pushed through to enter a very large kitchen. Its multiple sinks, miles of countertop, and countless pantries and closets were all just as run-down and dingy as the rest of the house. Jordan tried to imagine the massive meals that could've been prepared here—and wondered who might have sat down at that humongous picnic table to eat them.

There was one last door off the kitchen, which led to the outside. It was jammed shut, and Jordan had to use all his might to push it open. It gave way, sending him stumbling into a thicket of weeds. Lying there, he looked up to see a cracked little face grinning over him. He locked eyes with the stone garden gnome, put his hand over its faded, pink-painted dimples, and pushed himself onto his feet.

The backyard was modest in size compared to the enormous house. It was bordered by a tall ivy hedge on either side, which ran straight back and attached themselves to an even taller concrete rear wall. In the yard were a few rusty old metal chairs overrun with tall weeds. The weeds grew everywhere, but were nothing compared to the monstrous growth towering upon and above the back wall, where a gnarl of swamp trees and vines twisted and tangled like an army of serpents attempting to storm the yard. Jordan couldn't see over the wall but knew it was the only thing keeping the swamp from devouring his grampa's old house—and all of Waning Acres beyond it.

The damp, heavy smell of the swamp wafted

over and past the vines, settling into the backyard and reaching Jordan's nostrils. He shut his eyes, breathed it in, and imagined all the slimy, rotting sludginess that could give off such a dank stench.

"Hey there, pal!"

Jordan's eyes popped open to find his father standing beside him, staring at the swamp-jungle climbing over the wall. "Now there's a Grimsley project! I'll pick up some high-performance hedge clippers and we'll tackle that challenge together!" He pulled out a clipboard and started flipping through pages of tasks. The man actually seemed happy about the impossibly long to-do list he'd created within the first ten

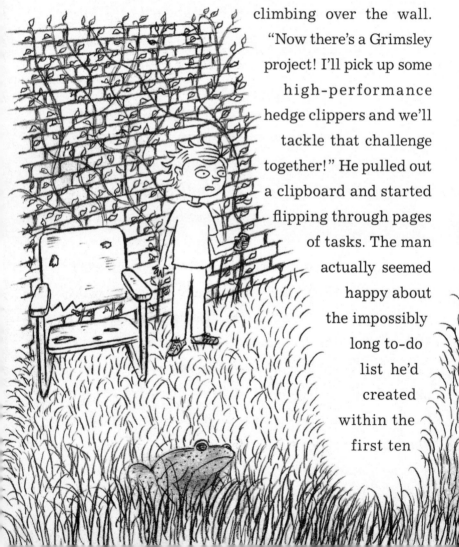

minutes they'd been here.

"Uh, Dad, can I ask you something?"

"Sure, son."

"Why are we doing all this? Why do we have to fix this place up?"

Mr. Grimsley glanced up from his list. He looked out at the sea of weeds leading to the ugly concrete wall barely holding back the swamp beyond it. "Jordan, your mom and I have always dreamed of running a bed-and-breakfast, someplace far from the city, where you and your sister could breathe fresh air."

Jordan inhaled deeply again. The thick, rotten air filled his lungs like a mossy soup. "This place is a swamp, Dad."

"The Okeeyuckachokee Swamp, to be exact! One of the biggest. And it starts right here, in our back-yard. Or ends here, depending how you look at it, I suppose."

He flipped through his to-do clipboard, considering the work ahead. "We've got two weeks to clean this place up, starting with, *hmm* . . ." He flipped through a few dozen more pages of chores. "Rip out carpet in hallway . . . identify sticky brown goo in the upstairs bathroom . . . Here! You can help me set up a few bedrooms so we can all get some shuteye tonight. We've got a big first day tomorrow!" He smacked Jordan on the back, then bounded into the kitchen.

The sun was setting somewhere far beyond the Okeeyuckachokee Swamp, and the thick, curling trees cast long shadows across the yard, straining to reach Grampa Grimsley's house. Like conductors' arms, they seemed to cue a sudden symphony of creaks, croaks, and chirps that rose up from beyond the wall. Jordan moved toward the noise, wading slowly through the tall weeds. He placed his hand on the wall that held back the dark swamp, shut his eyes, and listened for a moment—this time trying to imagine the insects and animals making such a racket.

Suddenly, all went silent. Jordan opened his eyes. He looked up. A dark clump of tree branches was silhouetted against the sunset-streaked sky.

He peered closer. *It seemed to be breathing.* Jordan strained to focus as it swelled. . . . *FWOOSH!* A violent flapping noise broke the silence as the black clump suddenly exploded into pieces, launching from the branches into the air above Jordan's head.

"Aaaaaauuuggh!" He stumbled backward as a flock of blackbirds burst from the branches and took flight. They circled above the old house and flew off, disappearing somewhere over Waning Acres.

Jordan got up slowly. Abigail stood at an upstairs window, laughing at him. Without looking back at the wall, Jordan walked inside.

3

The next morning, Jordan woke with a start. His eyeballs darted around the empty room. He'd been sleeping so deeply that it took him a minute to remember where he was. But when he smelled the musty morning air, it all came flooding back. He got up, put on his clothes, and went downstairs.

He found his father on his hands and knees on the kitchen floor with his head shoved in the large oven. His mother stood over him, holding a large iron skillet rather menacingly. If these weren't his parents, Jordan might've thought he'd stumbled across a complicated murder in progress.

"Okay, the gas is definitely working!" Mr. Grimsley's muffled voice called out.

"Well, then get your head out of there, Roger!" His mother handed the heavy frying pan to Jordan, then bent over and yanked her husband out by his hips. Then she began pulling the groceries they'd bought out of bags and setting them on the counter. Mr. Grimsley stood and lit a burner on the stove with a match.

"Now we're cookin'," Mr. Grimsley said. "With gas!"

"Our first breakfast at our future bed-and-breakfast!" Mrs. Grimsley cooed.

They grinned at each other, then kissed as Jordan stared in horror. "I'm gonna go for a walk, see if I can pick up a cell signal in the neighborhood. I'll be back for breakfast," he said as they continued to kiss. "That is, if my appetite ever returns."

Jordan stepped out the front door and took a deep breath. The morning air was already thick and humid, but smelled a bit sweeter. He walked through the overgrown front yard and past the iron gate. He pulled out his smartphone and looked down at it. NO SERVICE.

He headed down the sidewalk staring at his phone. *WUMP!* Jordan dropped the phone as he slammed into something. It was a rickety table made of old planks of wood. Above it was a sign nailed across two poles on either end. Hand-scrawled in yellow paint it read, *Eldon Pecone's All-Natural Fresh-Squeezed Lemonade.* He stared at the relic for a moment, then looked down and around for his phone. His smartphone lay broken in pieces on the sidewalk.

After gathering it, he stood up to find himself face-to-face with a tall, gawky kid dressed from head to toe in some sort of khaki uniform, holding a small trash can with a recycling logo.

"Greetings, citizen!" the boy said, saluting him by raising his hand in what looked like a clenched monkey paw to the brim of his hat.

"What's that? With your hand? What are you doing?"

"It's the official Badger Ranger Badger claw salute! Say, didja bust your walkie-talkie?"

Jordan stared at this odd-looking kid.

"Badger Ranger rule one hundred and six: 'Be aware, or else beware!'"

"Er, right," Jordan said, rather annoyed. "Good advice. Thanks."

The boy stuck out his hand. "Eldon Pecone. First-Class Badger Ranger, Clan Seventy-Four."

Jordan limply shook his hand. "Jordan Grimsley."

Eldon's wide eyes popped even wider. "Gosh-begollers! Did you say—*Grimsley*?"

"Yeah. Why?"

"There used to be a Grimsley who lived around here, a long time ago. Kinda famous."

"You're talking about my grandfather, George Grimsley. I didn't know he was famous. I didn't know him at all. We're fixing up his house, at the end of the street."

Eldon went white. He suddenly looked like he might throw up into his recycling receptacle.

"You okay?"

"Beg your pardon. It's just—no one's been in that house for a long time."

"Yeah, well, someone's in there now, so . . . I gotta go." Jordan was getting a bit creeped out at the way this kid was staring at him. He gestured over Eldon's shoulder. "Besides, looks like you've got customers."

Eldon snapped out of his daze and turned to see a large group of senior citizens ambling closer, like a band of retired zombies. "Dagnabbit! I'm late setting up my stand! I don't suppose you'd like to help a fellow citizen?"

Jordan looked at the old, rickety lemonade stand, then at the army of thirsty old people dressed in brightly colored sweat suits. "I dunno, what's it pay?"

"Ha!" Eldon pointed to a patch on his sash. "It's part of my Community Service Badger Badge. Folks might bring me zucchini bread or a pot roast, but that's up to them. I could never accept their money!"

"Uh-huh. Well, *Eldon*, I'm afraid I can't accept your kind offer to help. See ya 'round the ol' campfire. Or not."

Jordan turned, then remembered what was in his hand. He tossed the bits of what had been his smartphone into Eldon's recycle can. "Here," Jordan grumbled. "Recycle this."

Storming home in a funk, Jordan passed dozens of residents of Waning Acres as they slowly stepped out of their near-identical houses and shuffled toward Eldon's lemonade stand. Some carried baked goods, some had way too warm-looking knitted scarves, and one old lady had her own *FOXY GRANDMA* mug. But *all* of them were ancient. *Great,* Jordan thought. *Looks like the only people under the age of a million around here are me, Buzzcut Badger-Boy back there, and my stupid, evil sist—*

"Busted, you worm."

Abigail stood just inside the opened iron gate of the house, dressed in her usual black, staring daggers at him through thick eye shadow. "Way to try to weasel out of working. You missed breakfast, when Dad handed out chores. But don't worry—I volunteered you to haul the trash out of the attic. If I have to work, you do." Jordan walked past her, toward the house.

"Where'd you go, anyway?" she asked.

"Just meeting the neighbors. They're like the walking dead. You'll fit right in."

A loud blasting sound came from just inside the front door. Jordan's mom and dad were in the living room, dressed in some kind of space suits, complete with goggles, booties, and gloves. They looked as if they were handling highly radioactive nuclear waste. They attacked the walls and floors with a sandblaster, sending dust everywhere. Although he couldn't see their faces, Jordan just knew they were both grinning ecstatically under their masks.

Jordan climbed the creaky stairs, thankful that at least he'd be alone. The second floor was lined with more small bedrooms. At the end of the hall, Jordan found the pull-down attic ladder and climbed the rickety rungs. The confined space was cluttered with piles of crumpled paper, rags, and cardboard. *Bonk!* Jordan bumped his head on the sloped ceiling that followed the angle of the roof-line. He was at the tippety-top of the house, so it was about a billion degrees. Already drenched in sweat, Jordan tried to open a small window at one end of the attic to get some air, but it wouldn't budge. He pressed his nose against the glass, and gasped at what he saw.

High above the backyard wall, Jordan stared out at the vast Okeeyuckachokee Swamp. It stretched as far as he could see, its tangled roof of treetops and thick vines keeping whatever lay beneath hidden from view.

From that angle, he could also see down into the tops of the tall hedges lining the sides of the backyard. Where one of the hedges met the back wall, he noticed a large, cracked opening. It opened to the Okeeyuckachokee. And it looked big enough to walk through.

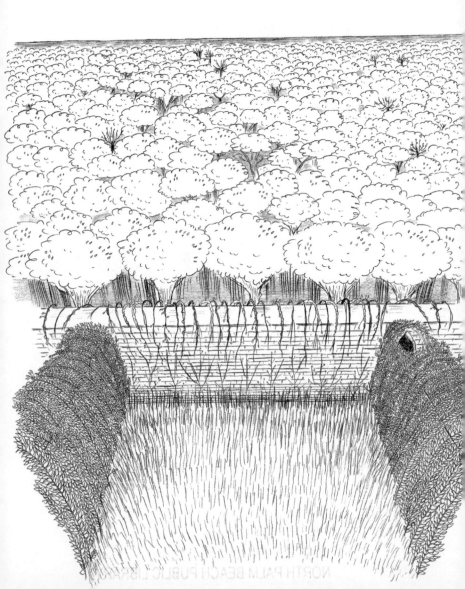

From the ground, the secret opening Jordan had spotted was completely hidden within the hedge. Jordan walked to the point where the hedge met the back wall, then pushed through the thick greenery. He found himself standing in a hollowed-out center of the hedge. And there before him, as he stood in the sunlight filtering through the branches above, Jordan saw the passageway.

He approached cautiously and leaned out of the dappled sunlight, closer to the shadows on the other side of the opening. The air felt cooler inside, and the strange swamp noises were quieter and more distant sounding. If it weren't so creepy, it would've been peaceful.

"Jeepers, this is some secret fort!"

"Aaah!" Jordan spun around. Eldon's head was poking through the hedge, grinning at him. "What are you doing, sneaking up on me like that?"

"I didn't mean to spook you," Eldon's head said. "I have something for you." Outside the hedge wall, Eldon fished for something in his khaki pocket. "Your walkie-talkie. You asked me to recycle it. So I did." Eldon's hand jabbed through the hedge and handed Jordan his smartphone. The pieces had been crudely slapped together with wood, wire, and a few rusty screws. It was a FrankenPhone.

"Wow. Thanks, I guess."

"Happy to help." Eldon grinned proudly. Then

he noticed the wall. "Say, you're not thinking of going in there, are ya?"

"I was just curious."

"Well, curiosity killed the cat, Jordan."

"Thanks, but I'm not a cat, *Eldon*."

"Ha! I know that." He pointed to a patch on his sash. "Animal Classification Badger Badge, Level Four. So I think I can accurately differentiate between *Felis domesticus* and *Homo sapiens*, thankyouverymuch."

"Okay, Mr. Level Four, so what kinds of animals live in this swamp?"

"Mammals: Florida panther, marsh rabbit, rice rat, Florida black bear—"

"That must've been it."

"Must've been what?"

"My dad hit something big, black, and furry yesterday. Stinky, too. Had to be a black bear." He peered back into the opening. "Hope the poor thing is okay in there."

Eldon looked at Jordan. "Boy, your grandfather sure wouldn't have thought it was a bear."

"What do you mean?"

"From what I've heard he was supposed to have been . . . y'know, *crazy*."

"*What?*"

Eldon looked at Jordan's angry expression. "Oh. I'm sorry. I thought you—"

"You just said my grandfather was crazy! Take it back before I give you a badger patch in getting a bloody nose!"

"Badger *Badge*. And I said I was sorry. I thought you knew what everyone knows. That your grandfather went—well, cuckoo."

Jordan felt a rush of heat go to his head. He dropped his smartphone and made a fist. The next second, his fist flew through the air. *KA-POW!* Eldon's head popped back out of the hedge, and Jordan heard him hit the ground outside. Jordan caught his breath. He'd never hit anyone before in his life. He stepped out of the hedge and onto the sidewalk outside.

"Gosh! Now what'd ya do that for?" Eldon sat up, pulled out his Badger Ranger hanky, and held it to his bloodied nose. "*Very* poor citizenship skills!"

"That was for calling my Grampa Grimsley crazy. Don't do it again, *got it?*"

Eldon studied Jordan. A tiny smile peeked out from behind his handkerchief. He got up, turned, and walked off. Jordan watched him go, his hands still shaking.

A rustling noise behind him caused the hair

to stand up on the back of his neck. Jordan slowly approached the hedge, then, mustering his courage, stepped back inside. He peered through the opening to the swamp. Standing a good distance inside was a shadowy figure. It seemed to be staring at him. Jordan stared back, waiting for it to move. Finally, he shouted, "WHO'S THERE?"

The shadow didn't move. Jordan leaned as close to the opening as he dared. *Maybe it's just my imagination,* he thought to himself. He turned to step back out but remembered something. He looked down to pick up his FrankenPhone and froze. It was gone. He looked back into the swamp. The shadow, whatever it had been, was gone, too.

Hauling the trash out of the hot, muggy attic soon had Jordan dripping with sweat. With each trip back from the garbage bin in the front yard, he'd stop and take a peek out the tiny attic window at the swamp below. And each time he'd wonder what creature beneath that endless canopy of tangled treetops had his FrankenPhone.

His last load was one he'd avoided all day—a large pile of nasty-looking rags wedged deep in a far corner of the attic. He crawled on his belly across the grimy floorboards, then reached out into the crevice and grabbed hold of the rags. One pull told him they were snagged on something. He tugged harder, then repositioned himself for leverage—and heaved as hard as he could. *WUMP!* Whatever was holding the rags was hard and heavy, by the way it felt when it bonked into Jordan's head. He dragged it out of the crevice and pulled the nasty coverings off. It was a small suitcase. It had been wrapped in a sheet and jammed into the attic corner, then hidden under the mountain of rags.

The suitcase was worn and beat up, and above the plastic handle were two gold initials: "G.G." Jordan placed his thumbs on the latch-release buttons. The latches popped open with a *click!* He flung open the suitcase and screamed.

"Aaaahhh!" A horrible black, eyeless gorilla head grinned up at him. It took Jordan a second to realize it wasn't a gorilla, or even a head. It was

a mask—cheap and furry, with rubber teeth, rubber ears, and a pair of eyeholes. Jordan tossed it aside to see what the menacing monkey mask was guarding.

First, he found the rest of the costume. There was a white stripe running down its back, but otherwise it looked like a typical adult-sized ape suit. Jordan set it aside as he found something even stranger—a large, apelike rubber foot, attached to a stick.

He set down the foot. All that was left was a bunch of old newspaper clippings lining the bottom of the suitcase. One of the clippings showed a blurry picture of a large, black shape walking behind a swamp tree. Jordan picked it up. The headline read: *LOCAL MAN GETS GLIMPSE OF FLORIDA SKUNK APE IN OKEEYUCKACHOKEE SWAMP!*

Jordan scanned the article. Then another. And then another. Each one was from the *Leisureville Daily News* and was dated from the summer of the same year. Or as they all described it, *SKUNK APE SUMMER!* Jordan was amazed at how many sightings of a large, black, stinky creature there were. As he read headline after headline, he noticed the story line begin to change. As that summer wore on, more and more people claimed to have seen the creature, and not just in the swamp. By the end of that summer, the sightings had grown quite common within Leisureville:

LOCAL PICNICKERS SNAP PHOTO OF LEGENDARY SKUNK APE IN DOG PARK!

Skunk Ape spotted going through mayor's trash cans.

LEISUREVILLE LAZYBOYS BASEBALL GAME INTERRUPTED WHEN SKUNK APE RUNS ONTO FIELD! Z-Boys go on to beat the Pompano Pelicans 6-4

Soon, the articles began to report that the Skunk Ape might be a fraud:

LEISUREVILLE COMMUNITY COLLEGE SCIENCE DEPT DOUBTS SKUNK APE REAL

Leisureville police dept looking for Skunk Ape hoaxer.

FED UP COMMUNITY TO BOGUS SKUNK APE: ENOUGH ALREADY!

And finally, an article claimed proof that Skunk Ape Summer had been a massive hoax.

This one included a picture of an old man wearing the black furry suit with no mask, being led away by police. The caption hit Jordan like a punch in the gut: *Eighty-year-old George Grimsley is accused of fright-*

'DISTURBED' LOCAL RETIREE SUSPECTED IN SKUNK APE HOAX

80-year old George Grimsley is accused of frightening the community, disturbing the peace, and impersonating a Skunk Ape.

ening the community, disturbing the peace, and impersonating a Skunk Ape.

"So it's true," Jordan said to himself. "Grampa Grimsley *was* crazy."

"THAT'S RIGHT! AND NOW THAT YOU'VE DISCOVERED MY HORRIBLE SECRET, I WILL PEEL YOU AND EAT YOU LIKE A BANANA! AAAAAARRRR!"

Jordan looked up at his sister standing over him, wearing the mask. "That's not funny."

Abbie pulled it off and tossed it at him. "Whatever. Come down for dinner, chimp bait."

SLAM! Jordan dropped the old suitcase on the giant dining-room picnic table, nearly upsetting an entire pot roast his mother had just set before the family.

"Moving out so soon?" Mr. Grimsley asked.

Jordan popped open the suitcase. He pulled out

the Skunk Ape costume, then the large foot-on-a-stick. Setting them on the table, he laid out the newspaper clippings in front of his parents, holding up the last one, with the picture of his grandfather being arrested, in his father's face.

"Give it to me straight. Was Grampa Grimsley crazy?"

Jordan's parents traded worried glances. His father took a deep breath. "I think a nicer term would be *obsessive.*"

"Sure," Abbie said, looking at the picture. "Obsessed with running around in public dressed like a crazy ape-man. Can we eat?"

Mrs. Grimsley began serving up pot roast as she eyed her husband carefully. Jordan's father took a deep breath. "Even as a young man, your grandfather had been obsessed with *cryptons*—"

"*Cryptids,* dear." Mrs. Grimsley corrected him. "He was a *crypto*zoologist."

"Right," Mr. Grimsley said. "That's right. Cryptozoologist."

"That sounds made up," Jordan said.

"You're not far off," Mrs. Grimsley said. "Cryptozoology is a pseudoscience. The study of and search for creatures whose existence has never been proven."

"Like, vampires?" Abbie said with a sudden gleam in her eye.

"Vampires are mythical creatures," Mr. Grimsley said. "They're different."

"Yeah, different because they're *hotties*. And they might be real. Scientists don't know."

"They pretty much know." Mrs. Grimsley sighed. "Eat your pot roast."

"You mean Bigfoot and stuff," Jordan said.

"Yes," Mr. Grimsley said. "Bigfoot, Loch Ness Monster, Yeti, all the ones you've heard of, and a lot more you probably haven't."

"Did Grampa Grimsley ever find any of them?"

"No," Jordan's mother said coldly. "Because they're not real."

"And that made him go crazy," Abbie said. "End of story. Pass the rolls?"

Mr. Grimsley cleared his throat. "Growing up, I didn't see much of my father. He'd wander off into the world, searching for his cryptids, leaving us for months. Then one day . . . he didn't come back at all."

"What'd you do?" Jordan asked.

"As strange and sad as it sounds, I'd gotten used to my father not being in my life. So . . . we went on with our lives. The years went by, your grandmother passed away, your mom and I met, married, had Abbie . . . and right around that time your grandfather suddenly reappeared. Quite unexpectedly."

"Quite inconsiderately, too," Jordan's mother said. "Abbie was a toddler and I was pregnant with Jordan. We had to drop everything and rush down here."

"You've been here before?" Jordan asked.

"How cute was I as a baby?" Abbie asked.

"Not Waning Acres," Jordan's dad said, picking up the newspaper article. He had a sad look in his eye as he stared at the picture of the old man in the ape suit.

"Leisureville," Mrs. Grimsley said. "Where the police picked him up. He gave them our name and told them where they could contact us. He'd obviously kept track of us over the years, even though we had no idea where he was."

"So what was with Skunk Ape Summer?" Jordan asked. "Why'd he fake all that?"

"I suppose after spending his life hunting for proof of his beloved cryptids," Mrs. Grimsley said, "he finally decided to make some proof of his own."

"Of course we were so happy to hear from him," Mr. Grimsley continued. "The local police dropped all charges and released him to our care. We were going to bring him back to the city, where he would live the rest of his days with us."

"So what happened?" Jordan said.

Mr. Grimsley stared sadly down at his pot roast. Mrs. Grimsley put her hand on his shoulder. "Your grandfather refused to leave. He said his 'life's work' was here. He begged us to release him into the swamp, like some old reptile."

"He sounds kinda cool," Abbie said.

Mr. Grimsley looked up from his plate. "He begged me to come with him. He kept saying how he wanted to show me something. He said he had a secret to pass along to me. I'll never forget the look in his eyes when I told him I couldn't do that."

"We were set to drive back up to the city the next morning," Mrs. Grimsley said. "But that night, he ran away. In his pajamas." Mrs. Grimsley patted her husband's shoulder. "His mind had gone. There wasn't anything anyone could've done."

"It stormed cats and dogs that night," Mr. Grimsley said. "Thunder, lightning. Heavy rain. The next day there was an all-out search for him. They found footprints and were able to track him. He must've walked all night. We weren't surprised when we heard where they found him."

Jordan looked at the ape foot-on-a-stick. "The

Okeeyuckachokee Swamp."

"The poor old fool wandered straight into an alligator's nest," Mrs. Grimsley said. "All that was left of him were torn bits of his pajamas. Just horrible."

"Whoa," Abbie said.

Jordan looked at his father. "I'm sorry, Dad."

"Thanks, son," he said, brightening. "But it was a long time ago. The real tragedy is how your grandfather searched the ends of the earth in vain for nonexistent cryptids, and in the end he missed out on meeting two of the most amazing creatures in the world—his grandchildren."

Sniff! The family turned to Abbie. Her thick eyeliner was smudged and running down her face. *Sniff!* She wiped away a black, clumpy tear and got up quickly. "I'm having an allergic reaction. Must

be the mold in this stupid place!" She ran out and stormed down the hall, leaving a quiet hush over the table.

Mrs. Grimsley broke the silence. "Well, your grandfather's 'life's work' may have been a sad waste, but he ended up leaving us something special—this great old house, which we'll fix up and bring comfort to travelers from all over the world!"

"And breakfast!" Mr. Grimsley said. "Right, Jordan?"

Jordan sat in silence for a moment, staring down at the Skunk Ape mask. "What if Grampa Grimsley was right about cryptids? What if he wasn't crazy? What if his life's work wasn't a waste?"

"That's a very nice notion," Mrs. Grimsley said. "And I know it's fun to think about imaginative creatures, but that's just what they are—*in your imagination*."

"It's not just my imagination." Jordan grabbed the Skunk Ape costume and held it up. "Dad. Look at this. Remember that thing you hit on the highway?"

"That was a bear, Jordan. Or possibly a possum."

"I thought that, too! But today I think I saw something. Something that definitely wasn't a bear or a possum. In the swamp."

"You were in the swamp?" Mrs. Grimsley was on her feet. "Roger! I told you to tell him to stay out of there!"

"I didn't go in," Jordan said. "I was just—looking in. But *something* was there. Or at least I think it was. I mean, I know it was. Because a second later, it wasn't."

Mrs. Grimsley shot her husband a look as she cleared a pile of dishes and carried them into the kitchen. Mr. Grimsley looked at Jordan thoughtfully. "Son, that swamp is not a place to play near. There are lots of dangerous things in there. Not imaginative creatures, *real* ones. Gators, snakes—"

"Skunk Apes?"

He smiled. "There's no such thing as Skunk Apes. Or Bigfoots, Loch Ness Monsters, Yetis, or—I'm sorry to break it to your sister—hottie vampires. The world is small, and it's crowded with people. Lots of people. Some are like your grandfather, obsessed with the idea of hidden, secret creatures. And y'know what? The world is a better place for having dreamers like him. But the things they seek aren't real. They can't be. If they were, how would they ever remain hidden?" He stood up and gathered some dishes. "You've had a long day. Go and get some sleep. Tomorrow I'd like you to chisel all those gravy stains off the ceiling."

Mr. Grimsley pointed up at the brown-splotched ceiling before carrying the dishes into the kitchen, leaving Jordan alone. Jordan stared down into the dark, empty eyeholes of the Skunk Ape mask. It stared back at him with a big rubber-toothed grin.

The next morning, Jordan rose early. The house was quiet, and he assumed everyone else was still asleep. This was not the case, of course, as his father had been up for hours, planning the day's chores. Jordan found him standing in the front doorway, clipboard in hand, inspecting some rusted hinges.

"'Scuse me, Dad."

"Jordan!" Mr. Grimsley said, a bit startled. "Getting a jump on your daily project?"

"Kind of. I met a kid yesterday and thought I'd go get to know him a little. If there's a chance we might move here, I may as well try to make a friend."

"That's great, son! But it's awful early. You sure this friend of yours is up?"

Suddenly, a single, sour-sounding bugle played off in the distance. It was hard to tell, but it sounded vaguely like a horribly off-key military wake-up song.

"Trust me," Jordan said. "This kid's up."

"Well, don't be too long. You've still got your to-do chore to do."

"Scrubbed the dining-room ceiling last night. Cleaned the walls and floors, too. I couldn't sleep. See you at dinner."

Mr. Grimsley smiled as he watched Jordan make his way past the fence and down the street. "Up and out and done with his chores before breakfast," he said to himself as he pulled out his list and crossed the items off. "Well, he *is* a Grimsley."

Jordan found Eldon setting up his stand, carefully squeezing lemons into an enormous pitcher of water, preparing an oddly large batch of lemonade.

He approached him slowly, unsure how to begin. "Hey," he finally muttered.

Eldon looked up from his sugar-to-water ratio. "Oh. Hello."

"How's the nose?"

"Minor fracture," Eldon said. "But I had my first-aid kit handy, as I always do."

"Of course." Jordan smiled. "Listen. I'm really sorry. I don't normally go around punching Beaver Scouts in the face."

"Badger Ranger." Eldon pointed to a large patch on his shirt. "First Class."

"Right." Jordan studied Eldon's sash, filled with Badger Badges. "Did it take you a long time to earn all those?"

"Yessirreebob. Anything worthy of the uniform is worth earning."

Jordan peered closer. "You sure have a lot of 'em. I'll bet you know a whole bunch of stuff."

Eldon's face suddenly lit up. "Holy smokies! Are you interested in becoming an official Badger Ranger?" Before Jordan could answer, Eldon was talking a million miles a second. *That's terrific! You'd have to start out as a Runt, of course, but with a lot of grit and my expert guidance, you could be a Fifth-Class Ranger by the end of next year, easy* peasy, lemon squeezy! Here, hold still for a moment."

Eldon whipped a measuring tape off his utility belt and began measuring Jordan, presumably for his uniform size. Jordan took a step back and Eldon stopped. "Whoa. Listen, that all sounds *super-duper* and all. But . . . I'm not looking to join."

Eldon's measuring tape snapped shut, and his face drooped a bit. Jordan gestured to the dozens of colorful Badger Badges pinned to his sash. "I was asking because I wanted to know if any of your buttons there were for hunting or tracking."

Eldon's grin slowly returned. He puffed up his chest and stuck one of the badges close to Jordan's face. It was green, with a small trail of little brown prints running across it. "Official Badger Badge, First-Class Spooring. They don't just give out these humdingers willy-nilly."

"Great!" Jordan said. "Uh . . . what's *spooring*?"

"Spooring is the most ancient tracking method known to man, used by the earliest hunters to find animals by reading subtle clues from their natural environment."

Jordan peered at the badge. "Oh, yeah. I see the little brown footprints there."

Eldon chuckled. "Those aren't footprints, Jordan. You see, in the hands of an experienced spoorer, an animal's *scatalogical leavings* are like a road map."

"You mean those are little—"

"Droppings. Dungbombs. Doo-doo."

"Wow. That's some patch."

"It's a scratch-and-sniff, too. Go on, try it."

Jordan looked at Eldon. He really didn't want to, but seeing as he needed his help, he forced a grin, leaned closer, and scratched the tiny poop badge. Then he put his nose to it. *Sniff-sniff* . . .

"*Ha!*" Eldon burst out laughing. "Boy howdy,

Jordan! Too bad they don't give out Badger Badges for gullibility! You'd be First-Class in no time!"

Jordan nodded and smiled. "Ah, okay. You got me. Good one."

"That was for the bloody nose, neighbor." Eldon smiled. "We're even."

"So as an expert spoorer, do you think you might be able to help me?"

"You betcha! What'd you have in mind?"

"I want to go into the Okeeyuckachokee Swamp and track the Florida Skunk Ape."

Plop. Eldon accidentally dropped a whole lemon into the pitcher. "Uh, Jordan, I'm always up for an opportunity to keep my spooring skills sharp. But that sounds kinda *craz—*" He stopped himself, remembering how much his nose hurt.

"It's okay, you can say it—crazy. Just like my grandfather. I know all about him. I found his Skunk Ape hoax kit. I read the old newspaper articles. But what if there *is* something out there— he just couldn't prove it? I might be crazy, too, but I have a feeling there's proof in that swamp that will show everyone that my Grampa Grimsley's life's work wasn't a waste."

Eldon looked Jordan over carefully. "Jordan, the Okeeyuckachokee is dangerous. There are a lot of very real creatures in that swamp. Ones your grandfather did find. Ones that killed him."

"Fine." Jordan poked Eldon's sash. "I get it. You don't wanna dirty up your pretty little badges by actually using any of your skills."

"Jordan—"

"Hey! While we're young!" A grumpy old lady plopped down an apple pie on the counter. Behind her, other elderly residents were shuffling up to the stand. "Fresh baked, with lots of cinnamon, just the way you like it. Pain in my butt to make. So are you open, or what?"

"Uh, thank you, Mrs. Fritzler," Eldon said. "You didn't have to go to all that—"

"Zip it, pup tent." Mrs. Fritzler was staring at Jordan. "Who's this? The new help? 'Cause he looks about as helpful as a girdle on a hippo."

Jordan held out his hand. "Jordan Grimsley, ma'am."

"Grimsley?" The old woman gasped, followed by others behind her. She leaned in and studied his face. As whispers murmured down the line of old people, she leaned back again. "Yes, I see the resemblance. You have his nose."

"You knew my grandfather?" Jordan asked.

"We all did," shouted an old man in a tattered bathrobe from the back of the line. Jordan looked down the mob of elders waiting for lemonade. Every single one of them was staring at him.

"Great!" He shouted so they all could hear. "Then maybe one of you could tell me about George Grimsley's life's work!"

There was a moment of silence. *"Hwaaah-hwaaah-hwaaaah!"* They all burst out laughing. Some leaned on one another for support. A few fell to the ground, rolling around on the grass.

"What's so funny?" Jordan yelled at them.

"Life's work?" Mrs. Fritzler said through tears

of laughter. "Ol' Georgie boy may have been a generous man. *But he was nuttier than an elephant turd!*"

As they continued to laugh uncontrollably, Jordan shot Eldon a look. Then he spun around and stormed down the sidewalk, back toward his grandfather's house.

7

Jordan burst into the hedge and stood fuming as he peered at the shadowy swamp on the other side of the hole in the wall. He looked down at his feet and tried to convince them to do their job. "C'mon, guys. I bet it's not as scary in there as it looks from out here." He took a deep breath. "We can do this. One . . . two . . . *oof!*"

Something shoved Jordan through the cracked opening in the wall, landing him face-first in a puddle of brown, gooey sludge on the squishy, swampy floor. He lifted his head out of the muck and looked back through the opening. Even with a face full of swamp crud, Jordan could make out the silhouette of Eldon's stupid-looking ranger hat. The

Badger Ranger stepped through the opening and stood over him, staring nobly out at the shadowy terrain.

"What'd ya do that for?" Jordan said.

"Payback. For the bloody nose."

"You said we were even!"

"So I did." Eldon offered his hand. "Then I suppose I should apologize."

Jordan scooped a handful of muck from under his butt before slapping his hand into Eldon's with a *SPLAT!* "You said it was too dangerous in here when I asked for your help," Jordan said gruffly as he pulled himself up.

Eldon calmly pulled out a fresh Badger Ranger official handkerchief, wiped his hand, and offered it to Jordan. "But I never said no, did I?" He seemed more serious as he peered through the swamp into the darkness beyond. "Hmm . . . which way do you think we should go?"

Jordan wiped his face and looked around. He was wrong about what he'd told his feet. The swamp looked much scarier on this side of the wall. Every direction offered a tangle of trees hanging heavy with long, stringy vines. Overhead some daylight broke through, but rather than extinguish the shadows, the light splintering through the mist only made the place feel more like another planet. "You're the expert," he finally said.

Eldon looked down at his Badger Badge–filled sash. "So I am," he said. "C'mon." He stepped past Jordan and began walking deeper into the swamp. Jordan rushed to catch up.

"What made you change your mind, anyway?"

Eldon stopped and yet again pointed out another badge on his sash. "Community of Caring Badge," he said. "'*A Badger Ranger shall not knowingly allow a civilian to wander into his or her own grisly death.*' I looked it up in the manual. Rule sixteen point four dash C." He smiled at Jordan, then turned and continued slogging into the Okeeyuckachokee.

Following closely behind, Jordan was distracted by the croaks, chirps, gurgles, and groans all around him. Some sounded distant, others disturbingly nearby, and potentially hungry. It was making him nervous. "Well, are you gonna start spooring, or what?"

"Righty-o!" Eldon stopped and looked around. He put a finger in the air, then crouched down and sniffed a clump of moss. He stood up again, shut his eyes, and took a deep breath. His eyes popped open. "This way."

As they trekked deeper into the swamp, every so often Eldon would stop and inspect something only he could've thought suspicious. A scratch in the bark of a tree trunk, a strange indentation in the mud, a foul-smelling clump lying in their path. In each instance, Jordan would grow excited about finding a clue to locating the Skunk Ape. But in each instance, Eldon would consult his well-worn *Official Badger Ranger Spooring Guide*, study the clue in question, then shake his head. "Markings of a swamp possum," he'd say. "Classic sleeping pattern of a Key Largo wood rat." Or, "Just as I suspected. Gopher tortoise turd."

After what felt like hours, Jordan had had enough. "What are you doing?" Eldon looked up from the field-guide index, where he was reading about something called "migratory toad mucous."

"I'm spooring. What does it look like?"

"It looks like you don't know what you're doing. What's with the book?"

"The *Official Badger Ranger Spooring Guide* is

the last word on tracking and identifying animals in the wild."

Jordan snatched the weathered old book out of Eldon's hands. "Look at this antique! If it's the last word, no one's written anything about spooring since 1967!"

Eldon took it back. "Let me remind you that if not for my Community of Caring instincts, you would be out here alone—totally unprepared and very likely lost—wandering in circles trying to find some silly, nonexistent mythical creature."

"Cryptids aren't silly. And they're not mythical, either. They're creatures whose existence has yet to be proven. Or isn't that in your ancient guidebook?"

Eldon stepped forward—and jammed yet another badge in Jordan's face. "See this one? Species Classification Badger Badge. I had to research, study, and memorize all the animals of the world to get this badge. Trust me. There's no such thing as a Skunk Ape."

Jordan looked at Eldon, then out at the shadows. He shut his eyes and took a deep whiff of the dank, muggy swamp air. He opened his eyes and pushed Eldon's book back at him. "Keep it," he said. "And keep your stinking badges. I'm gonna find proof, my way." He headed off in a different direction, deeper into the swamp. "Follow me and you'll see there's more to this world than what you read in field guides or manuals. Or the *Leisureville Daily News*, for that matter."

Jordan ducked under vines, hopped over puddles, and sidestepped mucky pools. When the swamp became too overgrown with trees for him to keep walking, he stopped to let Eldon catch up. Looking back, however, he saw that Eldon wasn't behind him.

Jordan backtracked to the place where he'd last seen him. Eldon wasn't there, either. But something else was. Wide and flat, with five massive toes, was a footprint in the muck. It was three times the size of Jordan's own foot. *And it stank.*

"Skunk Ape!" Jordan was so excited he nearly forgot that Eldon was missing—at least until he noticed something else in the mud: a much smaller set of footprints, these made by a pair of standard-issue Badger Ranger hiking boots.

A horrible realization struck Jordan.

"Eldon!" He ran as fast as he could, following the two pairs of footprints deep into the swamp.

They ended at the base of an enormous tree, where Eldon's prints suddenly vanished. Jordan walked around the massive tree trunk, looking for any trace of him. Circling back, he looked up, hoping to see Eldon sitting safely in the tree's branches, ready to apologize for ever doubting him. The branches were filled with hundreds and hundreds of ripe, yellow lemons—and exactly zero frightened, apologetic Badger Rangers.

Jordan backed away and slumped his body against a dark, mossy lump, not caring that his butt was in the muck again. He gasped for air as his mind raced and terror gripped him. He was all alone and definitely lost. But worse than that, he feared something awful had happened to Eldon. He was no master spoorer, but even he could add up the evidence: the Skunk Ape had chased Eldon to this giant lemon tree, where it caught him and— Jordan couldn't even finish the awful thought of what might have happened next.

He had to calm down and think. He caught his breath and inhaled deeply through his nose. As he did, an overwhelming stench assaulted him, followed by a horrible realization: the Swamp Ape was still out here, probably very close and possibly still hungry. As this thought gripped him, he began to slowly stand. He immediately felt a heavy, horrible force hold him down. A large, black, furry paw was planted firmly on his shoulder. The dark, mossy lump he'd been leaning against was no mossy lump at all.

Jordan opened his mouth to scream, but no sound came out. Panicked, he rolled out from under the Skunk Ape's grip and scrambled across the swamp floor toward the tree. The Skunk Ape rose up slowly, towering over him. It was black and furry, with wide shoulders, an enormous head, and wild, staring eyes. In a single step, it loomed over Jordan, cornering him at the base of the tree. It raised its massive, hairy arm. But instead of smashing him, it reached up, clutched a branch jutting out of the tree trunk, and yanked it like a lever. The moss beneath Jordan gave way. A trapdoor in the swamp floor opened up, and Jordan felt himself falling, falling, falling into pitch-blackness.

Jordan slid down a long, dark slide until he finally tumbled out onto a soft surface, landing with a *WHUMP!*

He slowly stood and looked around. He was all alone in a room that reminded him of a fancy study or library reading room. The lower walls were dark, caramel-colored wood panels with large bookcases built into them. Above those, the walls turned to dirt, with thick, strong roots burrowing in and out, forming a web of natural support beams. It was one of the strangest and most beautiful places Jordan had ever seen.

Mounted prominently on one panel above the hole he'd slid out of was a large wooden shield, like

a family crest, with the letters *CK* carved on it. On the opposite wall at the far end of the room was a large portrait of an old man, staring down at the entire room. Jordan recognized this man immediately. It was his Grampa Grimsley.

He walked toward the portrait and stopped at a small, square wooden table in the center of the room. Perched atop the table was what looked to be a shiny golden bowl or trophy.

This was no trophy. It was an urn. These were his grandfather's remains. He reached up and slowly lifted the lid. Inside, the gray ashes looked soft and cool. They reminded Jordan of a picture he'd once seen of an astronaut's footprint in the dusty surface of the moon.

Footprints! A sudden thought struck Jordan. If he'd fallen down here and survived, then maybe, just maybe—

"Jordan!" A familiar voice spun him around. "About time you got here!"

"Eldon!" He rushed to the grinning Badger Ranger. "I'm so happy to see you! I thought you might've been eaten by—" He stopped short and looked around anxiously. "Listen to me," he said in a whispered tone. "I saw it. I saw the Florida Skunk Ape. He's alive! He's real! But you must know that. I saw your footprints, then I didn't. What happened? Did it chase you? Did it hurt you? Where is it now? What is this place? Why aren't you freaking out like I am?"

Eldon said nothing. He just stood smiling at Jordan.

"Okay," Jordan continued. "You're in shock. You've gone mad with fear. Didn't you hear what I said? The Skunk Ape is real! Tall, dark, and stinky! It used a trapdoor contraption to capture me, which means it must possess some level of intelligence—"

WHUMP! A large mass of black fur came flying out of the slide behind Eldon. It belly flopped onto the red rug and tumbled past them, landing on a large couch. Slowly, it rose from the couch and stared directly at Jordan. It was the Skunk Ape.

"Sorry. I couldn't help but overhear," it said in a calm voice with a slightly refined accent. "Regarding my intelligence. Thank you so much. The tall, dark, and stinky bit I didn't appreciate, but I've decided to let it slide. Get it? Slide?"

Jordan stood frozen in terror. Eldon calmly stepped past him, walking right up to the giant, smelly beast and putting a finger in its face. "Speaking of which, it wasn't too intelligent, tumbling in like a big, fuzzy wrecking ball. How many times have I told you, you're too big for the slide? Use the elevator, for Pete's sake!"

Jordan pointed at the Skunk Ape in the room. *"It t-t-talks!"*

"Name's Bernard," the giant creature said in what was really a lovely-sounding voice. "And the proper word choice in that context would be 'speak,' not 'talk.' And yes, I do both."

Eldon and Bernard traded concerned glances as Jordan began breathing very fast. He jerked his head around like a chicken. He noticed there were no doors to this room, and immediately began to feel those beautiful, bookcase-adorned, wood-paneled walls closing in on him. He backed up against one of them, his eyes the size of golf balls. "You stay away from me, *both of you*! I mean it!" Jordan ran full speed toward the only way he knew to get out—the same way he came in. Eldon and Bernard calmly watched as he dived, frantically trying to scramble up the slide. He slid back down—this time landing in the arms of Bernard. The huge, smelly creature looked down at him like he was a new kind of tree fungus he'd come across.

"If I may, I'd like to insist you try to calm down, my friend," he said to him.

"*Aaaaaaauuuuuuuggghhhh!*" Jordan twisted his way out of Bernard's arms and dropped onto the soft carpet. He crawled across the floor to a nearby coffee table and curled up beneath it, hoping to wake from this very strange nightmare.

Eldon glanced at Bernard and whispered, "Perhaps you should make us some hot cocoa."

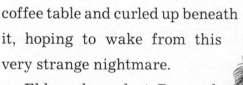

A few moments later, Jordan found himself sitting across from Eldon in a comfy chair in the cozy room, eyeing a ten-foot-tall Florida Skunk Ape as he gently handed them each a warm cup of hot chocolate.

"Thanks, Bernard," Eldon said. "If you don't mind, I think it'd be best if—"

"Of course. If you'll both excuse me." Bernard quietly crossed to the far side of the room, leaving Eldon and Jordan sitting alone.

Eldon cleared his throat. "Jordan, I'm not sure you're ready for what I'm about to tell you. It's probably gonna seem a little . . . well, *crazy.*"

Jordan's shaking hand lifted the cup from its saucer. "I was served a hot cocoa by the Florida Skunk Ape. Try me."

Eldon took a sip. "You were right about your grandfather. His life's work wasn't a waste. And he wasn't a failure. He created all of this, and a lot more. Your grandfather, the great George Grimsley, found the Florida Skunk Ape."

As this sank in, Jordan gazed up at his grandfather posing nobly in the portrait. He looked much more heroic than he did being hauled away in an ape suit in the newspaper pictures. "I knew it," Jordan said softly.

Eldon smiled. "But he didn't just find one Skunk

Ape, Jordan. He found more."

Jordan's gaze returned to Eldon. "There's more than one Skunk Ape?"

"*Pff*—you wish," Bernard said from the other end of the room. He was dusting a large, built-in bookcase.

"Bernard's the only Skunk Ape." Eldon stood and crossed to where Bernard was dusting. He pointed to a book on the top shelf. "If you wouldn't mind," he said.

Bernard easily reached up for the book. Eldon walked the book back to Jordan and set it on the table in front of him. It was large, thick, and leather-bound and had the title embossed in gold letters on the cover.

"A Skunk Ape is a cryptid," Eldon said. "Which, as you know, is a very rare creature. They live for a long, long time, and there's only one of each type. But

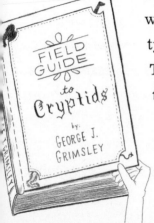

what your grandfather discovered was that there are many different types of cryptids in this world. This is his personal account of all the cryptids he encountered."

Jordan reached out to open the great book, but Eldon put his hand on the cover, stopping him. The Badger Ranger smiled at him as he held it closed for one more moment. "Jordan, your grandfather didn't just find these cryptids. He befriended and protected nearly all of them. *That* was his life's work."

Dun-dun-DUN! Dramatic music suddenly punctuated the moment, startling Jordan. Bernard sat in a chair at the far end of the room, playing a tuba. Eldon shot the cryptid a stern look. "Bernard, could you please go into another room to practice your tuba?"

Bernard shrugged, stood up, and pressed a panel. One of the bookcases opened like a large door. He and his tuba exited through it.

Jordan slowly opened the field guide. Page after page was filled with old photographs of his grandfather, over many decades, standing and smiling alongside the most incredible creatures Jordan had ever seen. "*Tasmanian Globster . . . New Jersey Devil . . . Fiji Mermonkey . . . Southwestern Giant Desert Jackalope . . . West Virginian Mothman . . . Florida Skunk Ape . . . Pacific Northwestern Sasquatch . . .*" Jordan stopped. He looked up at Eldon, his mouth hanging open in disbelief.

"My grandfather *knew* Bigfoot?"

"Syd? Everyone knows Syd. Terrible poker

player. Can't bluff to save his life. But you can bet your bottom dollar your grandfather met him first."

Jordan chuckled as he flipped back to the very first picture in the book. It was an old Polaroid photo, quite unlike the others. More of an action shot than a posed one, it was labeled *Chupacabra, Puerto Rico, 1977*, and showed a horribly vicious doglike creature, its eyes glowing red. The thing looked enraged by the flash of the camera, like it was about to attack whomever took the picture. "Where's my grandfather in this one?"

"Holding the camera, probably about to run for his life. That was his very first encounter with a cryptid. The Latin American Chupacabra. Like I said, your grandfather befriended *nearly* all of them."

Jordan flipped ahead of the disturbing image to the later pictures again, this time focusing not on the incredible creatures, but on the incredible man standing beside them. He looked so happy, so alive. "Tell me about him," Jordan said.

Eldon stood and stepped beneath the giant portrait of George Grimsley, looking up at it admiringly. "Your grandfather turned his back on the stuff most men strive to attain. He'd found a higher calling, and didn't care that the outside world might think he was a failure, or worse, crazy. See, the outside world could never know his secret, sacred mission—to protect and keep hidden the most rare and legendary animals mankind has never known. Under the noses of men who would have exploited his amazing discoveries for fame or profit, he created a secret society of guardians responsible for keeping the mysterious creatures of the world just that—a mystery. He created the Creature Keepers."

Jordan's mind was racing as he tried to take everything in. "But, you're revealing it all to me. You dragged me through the swamp, scared the daylights out of me, and dropped me in the middle of this place. Why?"

Eldon stepped over to the shiny, golden urn. "I suppose so we could see just how much of your grandfather you had in you."

"We? Who's 'we'?"

Eldon smiled. He stepped to the urn and knocked on it the rhythm from some dorky, old-fashioned tune Jordan had never heard before: *"Shave and a haircut, two bits!"*

The gonglike ringing of the last two knocks vibrated throughout the room. The panel beneath the portrait of Grampa Grimsley rumbled and rattled clumsily, lowering like a drawbridge. As it did, the portrait slid up. The two moving objects separated, creating a passageway the size of an open garage door. Jordan stood in amazement as he took in what was on the other side.

"Jordan, welcome to Creature Keeper central command."

Shoooo-PAHHHH . . . Shoooo-PAHHHH . . . A horribly mechanical, heavy breathing sound suddenly rattled throughout the chamber. Just inside the passageway, Bernard stood in a washtub filled with water. He wore too-small swim fins stretched over a few of his toes, a diving mask tightly wedged on his face, and a tiny air tank on his hulking back. He stopped his creepy breathing and turned to them, his voice muffled through the fogged-up mask.

"Sorry, did you tell me to go practice my *tuba*, or my *scuba*?"

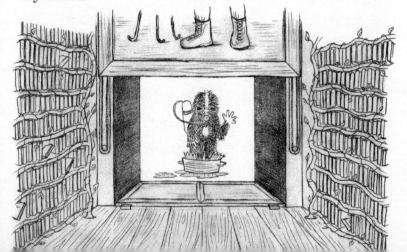

The room was much larger than the library, with
its high, root-burrowed dirt walls reaching far
overhead from a factorylike floor cluttered with
large worktables, rows of desks, and huge maps
mounted on rolling easels. Like the library room
Jordan had tumbled into, this larger cavern seemed
like it was from another age—all wooden furniture
and very old, very clunky-looking machinery.

But unlike the library, this space was clearly
built for business, not comfort. Seated at the wooden
tables, chairs, desks, and workstations were dozens
of kids, all about Jordan's age. Many wore old-
timey radio headsets, tuning in to radio signals
at old-timey switchboards, tapping out messages

on old-timey telegraph machines, and reading printed messages off old-timey ticker-tape printers. It looked like a set from a movie—an old-timey movie. Jordan wondered where all the computers were.

The worker kids wore khaki Badger Ranger uniforms and were taking their responsibilities very seriously. Still, Jordan noticed they were as interested in him as he was in them. As Eldon led him around, each kid would stop whatever strange task he or she was doing and size him up before returning to work.

"This nifty gang of go-getters makes up Creature Keeper central command. They're the main support center for the Creature Keepers we have in the field. They provide us with essential research, sighting surveillance, crisis control, everything we need to run a smooth operation, all day, every day, in real time."

"Kinda like online tech support for my home

computer," Jordan said. Eldon stared blankly at him for a moment, and a few of the nearby kids looked up at him with equally confused expressions. "Uh, never mind."

"From this base," Eldon continued, "the CKCC monitors and assists our heroic Creature Keepers all over the world, as well as the cryptids each one is responsible for."

"And what do the Creature Keepers do, exactly?"

Eldon turned and pointed above the passageway door behind them. "Basically, all the stuff on our official banner up there."

Jordan turned and looked up at the massive tapestry hanging over the doorway.

"So when do I get to meet a Creature Keeper?"

Eldon stuck his hand out, just like when they first met. "Eldon Pecone. Chief Creature Keeper, Skunk Ape Division. I kind of run things around here, but my primary responsibility is to protect and preserve a certain local cryptid."

BRAAP! Bernard was still standing in the bin of water with his mask on, but had replaced his snorkel with his tuba, which he used to blast a deep, offensive-sounding note. He gave them a nasty look, stepped out of the tub, and stormed out of the room in his swim fins. *Flop-flop-flop.* "Did I say something wrong?" Jordan said.

"No, I did. Most cryptids think they don't need their keepers. Some more than others. A consequence of our work to keep them hidden is that some have forgotten how dangerous the world is." He directed his words very loudly at the door Bernard had just flopped through. "THEY FORGET THAT WITHOUT US KEEPERS, THEY'D BE HUNTED DOWN, THROWN IN A CAGE—*OR WORSE*!" He glanced at Jordan, slightly embarrassed to have lost his temper. "Sorry you had to see that. Not very Ranger-like of me. C'mon."

Making their way down a long, narrow staircase and through a series of hallways and passageways,

75

Eldon and Jordan passed more kids in Badger Ranger uniforms.

"So, this central-command crew. Are they all Badger Rangers, too?"

"Ha! No. There aren't Badger Badges for the top secret work they do."

"So what's with the uniforms?"

"I just think it's a nifty look. Don't you?"

As they descended deeper, Jordan was trying to keep his millions of questions from bursting out all at once. "Are the Creature Keepers kids, too?"

"Uh-huh."

"You said the cryptids would be hunted if men found them. Is that why?"

"That's one reason. But not the only one."

"But who are all these kids? I mean, where are their families?"

"This is their family. Many of them were abandoned and forgotten when they joined us—their parents and friends long gone. They needed protection, too."

"But those creatures in the book—how can they be cared for by just kids?"

"They're special."

"Of course they're special. So how can you trust them to just some orphan kid—"

76

"No, no. Not the creatures. The *Keepers* are special. Their age doesn't really matter. They have an ability to connect, to earn trust, because their hearts are young and pure. And cryptids can be taught to sense that. There were many years, long before the Creature Keepers came along, when cryptids weren't always so well hidden. Once humans spotted or discovered them, stories were told and passed along for centuries, describing horrible monsters and demons. They learned that men would hurt them and couldn't be trusted. Your grandfather was the first human to establish trust with a cryptid. Then another, then another. It became the purpose of his life. It took sacrifice, patience, and kindness—as well as another discovery he made right here, in this swamp."

Eldon stopped at a doorway and allowed Jordan to enter. It was a laboratory. Tubes, vials, and

beakers were spread out over a long lab table. At the far end of the room a few kids in goggles and lab coats were gathered around a hole dug in the dirt floor. One of them climbed out of the hole holding a large soup ladle filled with a clump of damp soil. He turned to the end of the table and plopped it into what looked to Jordan like a clunky waffle iron. The iron clamped down on the clump of muck. Steam seeped out the sides as it squeezed the lump until— *bing!* The lab-coat kids leaned in closely and peered at a thin, glass tube connected to the bottom of the muck squeezer. A small amount of brownish liquid trickled through the tube. As it slowly made its way along a series of vials and beakers on the long table, the lab-coat kids followed it, manning the labyrinth of tubes, filters, and flames.

By the time the liquid reached the other end of the table, the few drops squeezed from the clump of mud had been boiled and purified into a single, tiny crystal droplet. It dripped off the end of the last glass tube like clear syrup, landing in a waiting tiny little bottle with a faint . . . *ploink!*

"*Yaaaaaaaayyyy!*" The lab-coat

kids burst into cheers and hugged one another as if they'd just landed the first Skunk Ape on the moon. Once the celebration subsided, they scurried back over to the hole at the other end of the room where another kid took the ladle and descended into the hole.

"What's going on?" Jordan whispered, turning back to the tiny bottle. "What is that?"

"A purified elixir. Your grandfather discovered a unique nutrient in the soil of the Okeeyuckachokee. We figured out how to refine it into a sort of medicine. We use it to protect the cryptids, to keep them healthy, happy, and hidden."

"It's such a small amount. How can it possibly help such giant creatures?"

Eldon led Jordan through a gigantic vaulted door. The walls rose up high above him, and were filled entirely with tiny cubbyholes. In each slot was a tiny bottle of the elixir, sparkling like diamonds embedded in the walls of a mine.

"Whoa," Jordan said. "It must've taken years to fill all of these!"

"Don't forget distribution. Once a year they're delivered to Creature Keepers all over the world. Kinda like Santa Claus. You still believe in Santa, don't you?"

"At this point, I'd say anything's possible." Jordan stared up at the sparkling walls of elixir, rising as high as he could see. His question from before was still burning in his mind. "Eldon," he finally said. "You said you brought me here to see how much Grimsley I had in me. But tell me the truth—why are you showing me all of this?"

"Because you are a Grimsley," Eldon said. "And we Creature Keepers need your help."

10

Jordan followed Eldon along torch-lit halls that steadily grew longer and more twisting, as if dug by a giant earthworm with a horrible sense of direction and design. There were steep inclines Jordan climbed with the help of roots jutting out of the packed dirt walls, followed by sudden dips that he had to slide down on his butt.

After a while, he wasn't sure if they'd gone deeper underground or had climbed closer to the surface. But he was very glad to be done walking through the creepy obstacle course as they reached a door marked: *CRISIS ROOM—TOP SECRET!*

Jordan glanced at Eldon. "I thought this whole place was top secret."

Eldon opened the door and gestured for Jordan to enter. "Think of this as top secret *within* top secret."

The room was long and narrow, with a rounded ceiling and just enough space for a wooden conference table and surrounding chairs. Bernard was stuffed into one of the chairs, sitting quietly with a notepad and pencil. Beside him was an anxious-looking girl about Jordan's age.

Eldon gestured for Jordan to sit down across from them, then he began. "All righty, gang. Here's what we know—or what we think we know. A while back, Doris here received a distress radio signal from our Creature Keeper in the Scottish Highlands, Alistair MacAlister—one of the best we've got."

They all looked to the girl. She nodded dutifully, then pulled out a folded-up piece of paper. She cleared her throat and began to read in her best attempt at a Scottish brogue. *"Strange intruder . . . STOP. Floated away into fog . . . STOP. Musta spooked ol' Haggis-Breath, she's gone missing . . . STOP. Will report back as soon as I find her."* Doris looked up, concluding: *"Full stop."* She folded the paper back up, popped it into her mouth, chewed a bit, and swallowed it.

They all stared at her for a moment.

"Er, top-notch work, Doris," Eldon finally said. "Very, uh, thorough."

"I really thought her accent brought it to life," Bernard whispered to Jordan.

Eldon continued. "We've had radio silence from Loch Ness ever since."

"Loch Ness, Scotland," Jordan said. "Are we talking about who I think we're talking about?"

"Nessie," Eldon said. "Haggis-Breath is Alistair's code name for her."

"Whoa."

"Only he dares call her that," Bernard added. "She hates it, self-important diva that she is."

"Be nice, Bernard," Eldon said. "She could be in danger."

"*Please*. You know she thinks she's too fabulous to be cooped up and hidden from the world. She's probably flopping around on some beach, *desperate* to get spotted. Trust me, there's no reason at all for you to go check this out."

"She wouldn't really do that, would she?" Jordan said, trying his best to hide his amazement at all of this.

"Think about it," Bernard said. "Ever seen pictures of her?"

"Sure. Everyone has. But I assumed they were all hoaxes."

"That's thanks to Alistair," Eldon said. "Hoaxing is one of the most important responsibilities a Creature Keeper has, especially in response to a potential sighting. Pull off a few obvious, goofy-looking hoaxes, and people tend to lump the real one in with the fakes ones. Then they move on with their lives. And Alistair's one of the best hoaxsters we've got."

"He oughta be," Bernard sneered. "He's had to do it enough to cover her blubbery butt."

"C'mon, she's matured a lot," Eldon said. "She's taking her responsibilities much more seriously nowadays."

"What responsibilities?" Jordan asked. "The Loch Ness Monster has responsibilities?"

Eldon turned to Jordan. "All the cryptids are special. But there are three who are *especially* special." He reached over to an easel and pulled down a rolled map of the world, divided into three equal parts. "Even though their powers affect the entire planet, the Big Three are spread across three separate sections of the world—"

"Mostly because their egos could never fit in the same time zone," Bernard scoffed.

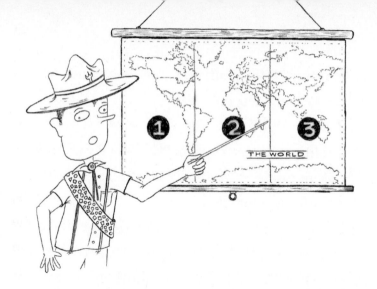

Eldon pointed to the center section. "Zone Two, Greater Europe, is Nessie's domain." He pointed to the section on the left. "Zone One, covering the Americas, is Syd's territory."

"Syd."

"Sasquatch," Bernard said. "Wendigo. Nuk-Luk. Bigfoot."

Eldon pointed to the last section of the map. "The third is Wilford's area. The Yeti. He resides here, in Asia. Himalayan mountains, to be specific."

"I said Nessie was a nightmare," Bernard said. "Wilford's unbearable."

"A nicer word would be *unsociable*," Eldon said.

"Or maybe . . . *abominable*?" Jordan suggested. "As in 'snowman'? Okay. So, Nessie, Syd, and . . . *Wilford*. They live in different parts of the world. I got that. What are their powers?"

"Oh, that. They control water, earth, and wind," Bernard said. "Respectively."

"Excuse me?"

"I told you how cryptids have lived here a long time," Eldon said. "They've kind of bonded with the planet—and its elements."

"So, like, Nessie can affect the weather and stuff?"

"She keeps all the Earth's waters in balance," Eldon said. "So in the highly unlikely event that something dreadful has actually happened to her, there could technically exist a slight possibility that the Earth's oceans, tides, and currents could potentially be thrown into total and complete chaos."

"That would be *so bad*," Doris chimed in. The others had kind of forgotten she was there, and her sudden, shrill voice startled them. Doris was a bit weird.

"Yes, it would be, Doris," Eldon said. "Thank you."

"Listen," Jordan said. "Just a few hours ago, like the rest of the world, I thought Bigfoot, the Yeti, and the Loch Ness Monster were a bunch of myths and hoaxes. So I know I'm new to all this, but wouldn't a missing six-ton water lizard be a bad thing for your operation?"

"So bad," Doris repeated.

"So why aren't you guys at DEFCON one, or CryptoFreakout four, or whatever?"

"Quite honestly, with Alistair being a bit of an eccentric, and Nessie being a bit of a"—Eldon glanced at Bernard—"*free spirit*, we were hoping that no news out of Scotland was good news. Then Doris picked up a local newscast and transcribed for us a troubling turn of events."

"Thanks, Eldon." Doris was now speaking in a newscaster's voice, or what she thought that should sound like. She held her papers in front of her and wore a small piece of brown yarn as a fake moustache. "And good evening. Our 'Weird Wide World' report tonight comes all the way from across the pond, in merry old Scotland! It seems the little lakeside towns of Inverness, Fort Augustus, and Drumnadrochit have been evacuated because of severe flooding. Now, what makes this 'Weird Wide World' worthy is that the lake in question is actually a *loch*, and the loch in question is actually—you guessed it—*Loch Ness*! Uh-oh! Let's hope there aren't any certain famous monsters causing trouble for the evacuated townsfolk up there! From all of us here at the WLVL Leisureville Local News team, I'm Truman Sinclaire. Back to you, Eldon."

"Wow, Doris," Eldon said. "Again, really terrific work." Doris pulled her moustache off. Bernard burst into applause.

Eldon turned to Jordan. "Something's fishy. People think the waters of Loch Ness are tranquil, but that's only because Nessie has been there for centuries, keeping them that way. So I'm going to fly there and do some emergency spooring. Bernard wanted to come, but I can't rightly fly across the Atlantic with a giant Skunk Ape as a copilot. And that's where you come in."

"*Yes!*" Jordan jumped onto the table and pumped his fist a few times. "*Yes, yes, YES!*" He hopped back down and hugged Doris. "Of course I'll come with you!" He began talking faster and faster as he plotted aloud. "I'll have to give my parents an excuse—I can make up some story. Will I need a sleeping bag? Do you want me to steal my dad's car? Hey! Can I drive?" He stopped and looked at them with a crazy grin. "I

can't believe this! I'm gonna help you guys find *the Loch Ness Monster*!"

Jordan suddenly felt a familiar weight on his shoulder as Bernard's paw gently pushed him back down into his chair. "Calm down, junior," he said. "He just wants you to babysit me."

Jordan looked up. The grin on his face faded as Eldon handed him an old, worn-out book. The cover read, *Raising and Caring for Your Skunk Ape.*

"I need someone to keep watch over my creature while I'm gone. It's a rare and sacred request, and I'm proud to ask it of the grandson of George Grimsley. Will you accept?"

Jordan was stunned. "Why me? This place is crawling with kids who could watch him. . . ."

"But you're the only one who has your grandfather's heart. His spirit. His—"

"You've got his *name*," Bernard said. "I told him the only way I'd agree to be left behind was if he recruited an *actual Grimsley* to stay with me. I never thought he'd find a way to do it."

Eldon gave Jordan a sheepish smile. "I sure as shootin' didn't, either. I was desperate, so I'm afraid I sent a letter to your father, letting him know that he had rights to the old house."

"Wait. *You're C. E. Noodlepen?*" Jordan said.

"It's not in the Badger Ranger code to pass one-self off as someone else, but in this case it was an emergency. Also, I was technically doing a community service, since your father was unaware that the deed had been left to him. The time constraint I totally made up to get you down here quickly."

"But *C. E. Noodlepen?* Where'd you come up with the name?"

"It's an anagram. For my own name. I just re-arranged the letters."

They all sat in silence, jumbling the letters in their heads. Bernard wrote down both *Eldon Pecone* and *CE Noodlepen* on his notepad. A moment later, they had all figured it out, more or less at the same time.

"Aah. Right. Okay," they all said.

"You sneaky little badger," Jordan added.

"It got you here, and so I'm happy I did it. And now I'm hoping you'll run the lemonade stand for me *and* take care of my Skunk Ape."

"Pff." Bernard pouted. "I do not need a baby-sitter."

"This from the cryptid who just the other day went out wandering around in broad daylight, only to get *hit by a car.*"

Jordan swallowed hard as Eldon winked at

him. He decided it best to pretend to act surprised. *"What?* No way. Drivers nowadays!"

"Please," Bernard scoffed again. "They were dim-witted *humans*. Probably thought I was a bear or something. Besides, it was just a scratch."

"You see what I have to deal with?" Eldon said. "Honest to goodness, Jordan, he's such a stubborn brat, I wouldn't blame you if you said no. Of course, I really hope you'll say yes."

Jordan looked at them. He broke into a wide grin. "Are you kidding? I'm in!"

The tiny elevator creaked with every pull as Bernard tugged a rope running through the center of the rickety wooden box. Jordan and Eldon were stuffed up against him, and Jordan strained to look past the Skunk Ape's smelly armpit through the hole at the top, hoping to catch a glimpse of a pulley or some sign of the top of the elevator shaft. All he saw was darkness.

"Are you sure this thing is safe?" Jordan asked Bernard.

"Of course. It's old, but strong, reliable—and doesn't need tending to. Just like me."

At the top, Eldon opened the door and stepped off. Jordan followed, happy to be out of the tiny

death trap. "Although I insist that I don't need your supervision," Bernard said, "it has been a pleasure meeting you, and I suppose we'll be seeing each other again soon." He took his paw off the rope to shake Jordan's hand and—*WHOOSH!*—the car and its oversized cargo dropped, disappearing down the shaft. Jordan and Eldon heard a *CRUNCH!* that echoed up the dark shaft, followed by Bernard's voice. *"I'm okay . . . !"*

"Yeah," Eldon said sarcastically. "He doesn't need anyone to watch him."

Eldon and Jordan approached a door with a knothole above it, which let in a stream of sunlight.

Eldon peeked out the hole, then swung open the door. The thick tangle of overgrown vines told Jordan they were back on swamp level.

"Are you coming back to Waning Acres?" Jordan asked.

Eldon shook his head. "I have to stay here and prepare for my trip tomorrow. I'm leaving first thing in the morning. But if you walk straight in that direction, you'll reach the wall. Okay?"

Jordan nodded, and Eldon handed him something. "In case you lose your way." It was a clear crystal or glass ring, with a small red bead on top. "If you press the center, it emits an olfactory signal into the air. Bernard will receive it, and he'll come find you, wherever you are. But I really don't like to give Bernard a reason to wander, so please use it only if you're lost, or about to be eaten, or something like that."

"So it's kinda like Skunk Ape GPS."

"You're off by two letters."

Jordan studied the ring closely. It was smooth and see-through, with a Creature Keeper insignia etched into it, along with the letters *GJG*. Jordan looked up at Eldon. "This was my grandfather's."

Eldon smiled. "He was Bernard's original Keeper. It makes sense that you should have it."

Jordan slipped it on his finger. "I won't let you down," he said.

"I know. And I'm sorry this isn't the big adventure you'd hoped it was. But being a Creature Keeper isn't about big adventures. We do little stuff, for a bigger cause. Remember the three *H*s on our banner: Helping, Hiding and—most importantly—*Hoaxing*. The greatest skill a Creature Keeper has. To pull off a just-fake-enough-looking hoax makes humans think what they saw wasn't real, that it was another human playing a trick on them. That seems like a small and silly thing, but without skilled hoaxsters, the cryptids would've been discovered long ago."

"Thank you." Jordan turned and walked a few yards away from the tree trunk, but was still under the long branches of the great lemon tree when Eldon's voice stopped him.

"Oh, one more thing you'll need. Hold out your hands." Eldon reached up and thumped a low-hanging branch with his fist. A half dozen lemons fell out of the tree directly above Jordan, landing in his open arms. "Remember to run my lemonade stand while I'm gone, will ya? The folks in Waning Acres need a glass a day or they get cranky. Badger's honor?"

Jordan looked up from his armful of lemons and smiled. "Badger's honor," he said.

12

Jordan was so excited he couldn't sleep. He stared at the ceiling, listening to the swamp sounds drift through his bedroom window. Somehow they didn't sound as strange and alien to him as they did before. They seemed to be calling out to him now, like a chorus of friends.

The dank, mysterious odors were now more inviting, too. He shut his eyes and inhaled deeply through his nose, taking it all in. The nasty stench that suddenly invaded the other smells hit him like a stink pie in the face. He knew that smell. *Bernard.*

He sat up and took another big whiff. He couldn't see the Skunk Ape, but he was out there, all right. And he was close.

Jordan's mind raced. Maybe he was being tested. He could imagine Eldon, who was all about passing tests and earning badges, running a mock drill to see how Jordan might handle an AWOL Skunk Ape. If there was a mock sighting, Jordan might even be expected to pull off a mock hoaxing. He grabbed his grandfather's suitcase containing the Skunk Ape hoaxing stuff. *Best to be prepared,* he thought as he crept out of the house in his pajamas.

Or maybe Bernard was sneaking out on his own. He was very stubborn, and not at all happy about having to be watched. It might be like him to do something dramatic, just to show that he wasn't going to behave himself if he was left with an inexperienced non-Keeper.

Jordan tightened his grip on his grandfather's old suitcase as he ran through the cool night air. Either way, he was going to prove himself, just like a real Creature Keeper.

He stopped where the hedge met the wall. One big whiff told him Bernard was on the other side. He pushed through the hedge and stepped into the swamp.

The swamp at night was a very different place. Every sound and smell seemed more intense, every shadow more dark and creepy. Jordan thought of his grandfather running through this same swamp in his pajamas, just like him. This made him stop in his tracks. He realized he'd lost Bernard's scent. He'd also lost his bearings. He wasn't sure which direction the wall was. He thought again of his grandfather, and how that turned out. *Crrrooooaaak!* Jordan's head snapped in the direction of the sound. It could've been a bullfrog, or it could've been an alligator. *It could be the alligator that ate Grampa Grimsley!* Jordan *really* didn't like alligators. He clung to the case as he began running, barely able to see in front of him. His stomach felt cold, yet his neck felt prickly and hot. Sweat was beading on his face and he could barely swallow as he ran around a large eucalyptus tree.

WHUMP! He slammed into something large

and bounced off, falling backward and dropping the hoaxing kit. He sat up and focused on the black mound in front of him, and the nasty but happily familiar smell that filled his nostrils. He never thought he'd be so happy to sniff such a stanky stench. He smiled as Bernard helped him to his feet.

"What in the devil are you doing out here?" Bernard whispered.

"I could ask you the same thing!" Jordan shot back.

"Well, I was looking for you."

"And I was looking for you!"

They stared at each other for a tense moment. Bernard smiled. They both burst into laughter. Bernard fell backward, his giant butt flopping in the marshy muck. This made the two of them laugh even harder. They were both in tears, and Jordan forgot all about alligators.

Moments later, Bernard was carrying the suit-case, escorting Jordan home through the swamp. "I must say, running out here in your pajamas just to find little ol' me? Impressive."

"I didn't want to let Eldon down. I really do want to help out the best I can."

"I'm glad to hear you say that. I know Eldon thinks the way for you to help is to take care of me.

But it's him who we need to protect right now."

Jordan glanced up at Bernard's face. He looked sincerely troubled.

"Eldon thinks I like to just go out wandering around," he continued. "And I do. But that has nothing to do with why I wanted to accompany him to Scotland. Something's going on over there. I'm worried it may be more than he can handle."

"But you said Nessie probably just wandered off, to get spotted."

"I thought that at first, but it's been weeks, and there hasn't been a hint of that chubby diva. She's not subtle—we'd have seen something by now. I was just saying that, hoping he wouldn't go. I'm worried. And I'd like you to go with him."

"What?" Jordan stepped back. "I can't! He's counting on me to take care of you!"

"Trust me, he needs you far more than I do. I'll be perfectly safe here on my own."

"I saw you fall down an elevator shaft just today! And yesterday you were hit by a car!"

Bernard thought for a moment. "The elevator incident wasn't my best moment. But as for the car, you guys didn't hit me—I hit you."

"You knew it was us?"

"I'm not proud of it, but I was desperate. I'd made

a deal with Eldon that the only way I'd stay is if he got a real Grimsley to watch me. When he wrote that ridiculous Noodlepen letter, I figured I'd better keep a lookout for any Grimsleys. And sure enough, there you were. I thought if you got spooked, maybe you'd all turn tail and head home."

"So you hit our car? How did you know it was us? How did you know we were Grimsleys?"

"It's hard to explain, but a creature can sense its Keeper. It's a bond that lasts a long, long time. I have it with Eldon, and I felt it, a tiny bit, as you and your family got closer. I just knew."

In the dark, Jordan felt the ring on his finger. "Because of my Grampa Grimsley. He was your first Keeper."

"That could explain it. That or the horribly ugly car you were driving. It's just like what your grandfather might've driven. Probably did, at one point. He had no taste in the finer things."

Bernard reached down and gently lifted Jordan onto his shoulder. He took a deep breath, and continued walking. "It was a long time ago. I'd been running and hiding from men for centuries. In the early days it was sticks and rocks. Then spears and arrows. As time advanced, so did their weapons and methods. They even trained their own creatures to track me. Between the shotguns and the bloodhounds, the swamp grew smaller, with less room to run and fewer places to hide."

Jordan looked out at the dark swamp, imagining it swarming with hunters and hounds.

"Luckily, your grandfather found me first. He said if I wanted to survive, I should go hide in the great lemon tree. I climbed to the very top, and hid within its bursting lemon blossoms. Its thick, white petals kept me hidden from the men's guns, and its sweet, heavy fragrance kept me hidden from their dogs. When he came back, he offered me a more permanent safety—a fortress beneath the tree I'd hidden in, deep underground, sheltered by its roots. Your grandfather invited me to stay forever. So I did."

Jordan thought for a moment. "What was my grandfather like?"

"He was all alone. He'd been estranged from his family after spending his life traveling the world, finding incredible creatures that he didn't dare tell anyone about. But he could tell me. He told me about every one. Every adventure, every amazing place he'd been, every amazing cryptid he'd discovered and met."

"His life's work," Jordan said.

"Not quite. What he wanted was to offer them the safety he'd given me. So we worked on a way. But men were still sniffing around the swamp, and he feared they'd ruin everything. Something had to be done to lure them away, once and for all. So that summer, he did it."

"*Skunk Ape Summer.*" Jordan looked up. As they reached the wall, Bernard set him down, along with his grandfather's Skunk Ape kit. Jordan clicked open the suitcase. Bernard chuckled as he pulled out the rubber face and held it up to his own.

"He'd wear this suit and let himself get spotted, each time farther away from the swamp. Every sighting drew the attention closer to Leisureville, farther from the Okeeyuckachokee Swamp—and the future base of the Creature Keepers."

Bernard took another deep breath. "Of course, for it to really work, for it to get people to give up on the notion entirely that I was real, one more thing had to happen. And your grandfather was the only person to do it. He let himself get caught. He allowed himself to look like the local fool. But he didn't look nearly as foolish as the people who'd claimed to have seen an *actual* Florida Skunk Ape. Suddenly no one believed I was real—it was just a crazy old man in a costume. I never saw him after that. I understand that he tried to make it back after getting caught, but—" He blew his nose—*SKRONK!* "After all the incredible creatures he'd tracked over his lifetime, it was a boring old alligator that did him in. I found his pajamas strewn all around the gator's nest. Then I found the gator. It had died from a bad case of indigestion. I guess you could say your grandfather didn't go down easy."

Bernard smiled as he placed the mask back in the suitcase. "But what was done was done. I couldn't get a dead alligator to uneat your grandfather, so I cremated them both. Your grandfather and a scaly old swamp creature, man and beast, all mixed up together in that urn. I like to think it's the way he'd have wanted it."

Bernard clicked the suitcase closed and stood up. "Your grandfather wasn't just my first Keeper. He taught me everything I know, including how to sense humans who have hearts that are young and pure. That's how I knew to trust Eldon when he dropped into my life, and probably how I knew your ugly car contained a Grimsley or two. But more than anything, your grandfather sacrificed his life to save mine. And that's why I can't let another one of my Keepers get hurt, ever again."

Jordan picked up the case. "I'll help you, Bernard. Tell me what to do."

"Just be ready tomorrow morning." He gently took the case from Jordan. "And if you don't mind, I'd like to keep this. You won't be needing it where you're going."

"It's yours anyway," Jordan said. "In a way, he made that hoax kit for you."

Bernard smiled. "Oh, that reminds me." He held something out to Jordan. "This belongs to you." It was Jordan's FrankenPhone.

13

Early the next morning, Jordan was startled out of a sound sleep by his father, calling to him from downstairs. "Jordan! Get down here! Someone to see you!"

He jumped out of bed and headed down the stairs. His heart was beating fast—then it nearly stopped. In the front hall at the bottom of the staircase, his parents were standing in their bathrobes talking to what had to be the weirdest-looking Badger Ranger he'd ever seen. Looming in the doorway, stuffed into a uniform, was Bernard, grinning nervously. The poor creature had done a horrible hack job on himself trying to shave his body, leaving his rashy-pink skin with random clumps of black fur in spots he must've had a hard time reaching. His arms hung a foot past the sleeves of his uniform, and his bulky legs seemed to be bursting out of the khaki shorts like two stubbly, overstuffed sausages. Jordan wasn't sure if he should laugh or scream. But the grin on his father's face quickly made him breathe easier.

"Jordan! You never told us you were interested in becoming a Badger Ranger!"

"It's wonderful, sweetie," his mother said. "We're so proud of you."

"Ranger Master Bernie here was just telling us how you wowed the local clan yesterday." His father beamed. "And you said you were going out to make a 'new friend.'" He smiled slyly, then suddenly gave

Jordan the official Badger claw salute. *"Mission accomplished, son!"*

"Uh, yeah," Jordan stammered. "Eldon Pecone. He's a Badger Ranger, too. He made it seem so . . . cool."

"Mr. and Mrs. Grimsley," Bernard said, startling Jordan. It was unsettling to see a shaved Skunk Ape address his parents. "First-Class Badger Pecone is one of our top-notch Rangers. He brought your son to our, er, *clubhouse*. Thought he had potential. And he was right."

"Ha!" A cynical laugh burst from the top of the stair. Abbie stood smirking down at Jordan. "Congratulations! You're officially a *first-class dork*!"

Bernard studied Abigail a moment, then calmly turned back to face Jordan's parents. "Mr. and Mrs. Grimsley, the only thing left in Runt Ranger Grimsley's initiation is to partake in our Badgeroobilee. It's a three-day campout, and I assure you there will be plenty of adult—"

"Yes!" Mr. Grimsley blurted out. "Take four days! Teach my son how to make a shelter out of leaves and an old shoe! Show him how to start a fire with a few twigs and a burp! *Go! Go!"*

"*What!?*" Abbie yelled down. "The runt gets to *leave*?"

"This is so great!" Mr. Grimsley continued, ignoring his daughter's evil glare. He stepped up to Bernard and spoke in a low tone, his eyes suddenly glassy with emotion. "Y'know, my mother wouldn't let me become a Badger Ranger. She was afraid I'd run off in search of adventure like my—" He stopped suddenly, gathering himself. Mrs. Grimsley took his hand. "Anyway, thank you, Ranger Bernie. Thank you for accepting my boy. I couldn't be happier."

"Believe me, we're happy we found him." Bernard shot Jordan a wink.

Mr. Grimsley said to Jordan, "You up for tackling a character-building adventure, son?"

"I'll go get my stuff!" Jordan bounded up the stairs, past his fuming sister and down the hall toward his room.

"Start talking, you insect." Abbie stood leering at Jordan from his doorway. "You might've fooled Mom and Dad with this Badgeroobilee bullcrud, but not me. What're you up to?"

Jordan flung the backpack over his shoulder and grinned. "You heard Dad. I'm going on a character-building adventure."

"Please. Camping? Without a DSL connection or Java-encrypted computer whatevers, you'll lose it.

You're doing this just to get out of working." She stepped dangerously close to him. "And if you don't have to help them fix up this smelly old mold factory, then neither do I."

Jordan smiled as an idea popped into his head. "You're right. And you won't. I can get you out of working inside this musty house all day. All you'll need are those charming people skills of yours. And those lemons." He pointed to the fruit Eldon had given him, piled in the corner of his room. "Grab 'em, follow me downstairs, and try not to say anything."

Moments later, Mr. and Mrs. Grimsley were standing on the front doorstep of the old house, waving as Bernard and Jordan hiked off, up the street. "I knew coming here for spring break would be a positive experience," Mr. Grimsley said. "But I didn't think we'd see the effects so quickly!"

"For both of them!" Mrs. Grimsley said. "Who would've expected Abigail to be the community-service type? Running a lemonade stand? It's *wonderful*!"

They waved to Abbie in the distance, standing somewhat cluelessly beside Eldon's lemonade stand with her arms full of lemons,.

"Bonus to all of this," Mr. Grimsley muttered

under his breath as they waved and smiled. "Now we can *really* fix this house up without having to quality-control those two."

"Let's get to it!" Mrs. Grimsley said. The two of them dived inside as Bernard and Jordan doubled back, sneaking toward the entrance to the Okeeyuckachokee Swamp.

14

The thousands of waterways, inlets, and small bays making up the western coast of southern Florida linked the swampy wetlands to the Gulf of Mexico. Within the Okeeyuckachokee Swamp, the Creature Keepers' great lemon-tree hideout lay just inland from one such inlet, known as Ponce de Leon Bay.

A tangle of trees and vines hung over the edges of the bay, a natural curtain of greenery for the small boathouse and a dock hidden within. Eldon Pecone was busy at the end of that dock, loading supplies onto a rickety-looking old seaplane floating on pontoons in the brackish water. He smiled to himself as he heard the familiar thumping footsteps of Bernard's oversized feet.

"I'm glad you came to see me off. I was worried you'd be pouting somewhere." Looking up, Eldon nearly fell off the dock at the sight of the sheared Skunk Ape in a tightly fitting Badger Ranger uniform. "Good gravy!" Eldon shrieked. *"Why are you disrespecting that uniform?"*

Bernard cleared his throat and spoke in a very solemn tone. "I wear the trappings of this organization in protest, as a symbol of my being, um, trapped here, against my will."

"Take it off. Not only do you look ridiculous, you'll stretch it out."

"I most certainly will not," Bernard huffed. He began doing deep squats, just to drive Eldon a little more crazy.

"Hey! Stop that this instant! And why are you all shaved? What does that symbolize?"

Bernard looked down at himself. "Oh, that. I had to do that to get into the shorts."

Eldon stared at him for a moment. Then he started to giggle. Then he lost it. He laughed so hard he nearly fell off the dock again. As he rolled around in hysterics, Bernard rushed to him, taking the opportunity to signal a nearby bush. Jordan popped out with his backpack and tiptoed past them, toward the plane.

"I can't believe how stupid you look!" Eldon squealed through fits of laughter. He wiped a tear out of his eye. Jordan was still making his way toward the plane behind him. Thinking quickly,

Bernard scooped Eldon up. *"Hey!"* Eldon was suddenly swung around in a great Skunk Ape hug and carried away from the plane toward the boathouse.

Bernard glanced back to see Jordan toss his backpack into the seaplane and scramble inside. The Skunk Ape set Eldon down inside the boathouse. Parked there was a rickety-looking fan boat, as well as an old wreck of an open-air, glass-bottom tourist boat once used for swamp cruises. Eldon eyed Bernard. "What was that all about?"

"I'm just going to miss you, that's all," he said, picking up the last box of supplies. He and Eldon walked back out and down the dock to the seaplane. Bernard tossed the box in the rear of the plane. *"Unh!"* A faint grunt came from inside, as the box landed on Jordan's head.

"Oh, don't make a fuss," Eldon said to his big friend. "I'll check things out and be back in a few days." He saluted Bernard and boarded the seaplane.

BANG! Smoke shot out from the engine as the propellers sputtered to life.

Eldon slipped his goggles down over his eyes and gave a thumbs-up. The plane coughed as it moved slowly out onto the bay. Bernard stood at the end of the dock and watched the old seaplane pick up

speed, gliding across the water. It lifted into the air unsteadily, then circled over the tree line, disappearing out of sight.

Bernard exhaled. "He's gonna kill me when he gets back."

Abbie plunked a pile of lemons down on the lemonade stand, looked down the street at the old people slowly making their way toward her, and thought of her brother. *I'm gonna kill him when he gets back.*

She opened a rickety wooden cabinet beneath the bar. There was a pitcher, mixing spoons, paper cups, a bag of sugar, and a stained, folded-up piece of paper. Hand-lettered across the top of the weathered sheet of Badger Ranger official stationery it read, *Eldon Pecone's Old-Fashioned Homemade Lemonade Stand Instructions*. Beneath that was written a basic recipe for lemonade, as well as a checklist for setting up the stand.

"Great. Another to-do list," she sighed. "I miss Chunk. He's the only one who gets me."

She thought about her pet iguana as she followed the recipe. She loved that lizard. He was wrinkled, scaly, and indifferent. Reptiles seemed ugly to most people, but they didn't care what people thought. And Abbie felt that made them beautiful.

"Where's Eldon?" a croaky voice suddenly barked at her. She looked up. Standing there before her was an old, wrinkly woman in tattered bunny slippers who'd ambled up to the stand.

"Didn't know it was Halloween," another, older neighbor chimed in. "Who are you supposed to be, the Bride of Dracula?" This one was a dude, and not only was he still in his bathrobe, he hadn't bothered to close it up. He wore big, baggy boxer shorts pulled way up over his belly button. They had lobsters printed on them.

As they both glared at her, Abbie knew she should be angered, offended, or at least irritated by these rude old people. Instead, she started laughing.

She laughed right out loud, then poured them the first cups of lemonade of the day.

A few hours into the flight, Eldon reached into a bag on the seat beside him and pulled out a peanut-butter-and-banana sandwich. He rechecked his flight instruments, sank his teeth into his lunch, and broke into song.

"Oh, give me a home, where the Skunk Ape don't roam! Where the Yeti isn't hunted by men . . ."

From where he was hidden, Jordan could hear Eldon's song all too well. A giggle in his belly began fighting to get out.

" . . . Where humans won't see, Mothman or Ness-ieee! And Bigfoot's never spotted agaaaaain!"

That was it. The giggle would not be tamed. *"Haw-haw-haw!"*

Eldon spun around as he coughed up a big bite of peanut-butter-and-banana sandwich, spraying it all over the seat behind him. "Who's there?" he yelled. He put the seaplane on autopilot, and stood staring at the back of the plane in a fighting crouch position. "Whoever you are, you should know that I happen to be a First-Class Badger Ranger with a Level-Six Badger Badge in self-defense!"

Jordan slowly stood up from behind the last seat.

"What are you doing here?" Eldon screamed at him.

"I thought you might need a little backup." He snickered. "Maybe we could sing duet."

"Very funny." Eldon plopped back into his seat and turned the autopilot off. "I'm turning this plane around and taking you back."

"No! Please. Look, I'm sorry I snuck onboard," Jordan said. "But Bernard thought—"

"Bernard!" Eldon spun around so quickly that he forgot he was controlling the seaplane. It veered violently for a moment, and Eldon turned back and righted it. "I'm gonna kill that Skunk Ape when I get back."

"Listen, I know I disobeyed you. But Bernard was really worried about this mission. He had me worried. He thinks there might be something fishy going on."

Eldon stared straight ahead at the clouds for a good, long time. Finally, he reached over and picked up a large, leather-bound map book off the copilot seat and nodded to it. Jordan smiled as he scrambled to the cockpit and sat down next to him.

WUMP! Eldon dropped the book in Jordan's lap. "This was not part of the plan. But since you're here, you may as well make yourself useful and navigate." Eldon nodded at the book. "We're looking for Loch Ness. It's in Scotland. Under *S*."

The sky outside grew dark as the tiny plane began its descent into the Scottish Highlands. No sooner had they entered a thick layer of fog, their craft was suddenly slammed by a strong wind. Jordan and Eldon jerked violently in their seats.

"Hold on," Eldon said. "This could get bumpy."

Jordan looked out the window. Through the fog he caught glimpses of craggy hills and rugged peaks. "Eldon, there isn't any flat land!"

"We're in a seaplane. We don't need flat land; we need flat water. There." He pointed at a dark blotch below. "That must be the loch!" Eldon pushed forward on the control stick. The plane nosedived; Jordan's belly flopped. Eldon yanked back again, and the plane leveled out.

SPLASH! They landed hard, tossing Jordan forward, and then jerking him back in his seat.

An instant later they skimmed to a stop, bobbing gently up and down. Eldon turned off the engine. "And thanks to Nessie, the loch is *always* flat."

Jordan looked down at the open book in his lap. He ran his finger along the rocky topography of the Scottish Highlands, stopping on a strip of deep green on the hand-drawn map. He looked out the window at the dark water beneath him and smiled.

Jordan was floating in the middle of Loch Ness.

15

Thwack! The sound outside the plane startled Eldon and Jordan. *Thwack!* They jumped out of their seats. Something hit the plane. *Thwack!* The windshield cracked. They peered closely at it. Nothing there but a small mud stain. Eldon hit a switch and the seaplane's wiper wiped away the mud. *Thwack! Thwack!* Two more, just outside the door.

Jordan jumped up and moved toward it. *Thwack! Thwack!* These hit one side of the plane, then the other. *Thwack! Thwack! Thwack!* Jordan lifted the latch and cracked open the door. Outside, the water was flat, still, and black as coffee. Tiny mud stains spotted the side of the plane. *Thwack!* Jordan ducked just in time as something flew past his head, bounced off the plane, and hit the water with a *splash!*

Jordan stared down at the water. A large, shimmery shape shifted just beneath the surface of the loch. *Nessie?* The shape disappeared into the murkiness. Jordan turned to face Eldon. "I think I found her! *I found the Loch Ness Mons—*"

Thwack! Thwack! Thwack! Thwack! Thwack! Thwack! Shards of silver suddenly exploded from the water, attacking the plane. Something hit Jordan in the head. *"Ow!"* He reached back and lost his grip, falling straight into the thousands of projectiles erupting from Loch Ness.

"JORDAN!"

Thwack! Thwack! Thwack-thwack-thwack! The plane was being pummeled with small silver objects. Eldon rushed to the open door. He slipped on something on the seaplane floor and glanced down—dozens of tiny, spiky-backed fish flopped around at his feet. *Thwack! Thwack-thwack! Thwack!* They were now hitting the plane from all sides. Eldon peered out the door into the blinding hailstorm. He didn't see Jordan. He took a deep breath and flung himself into the water.

"Jordan!" he cried out, splashing around. The fish were flying past his face. One wriggled up the pant leg of his Badger Ranger shorts. *"Aaah!"*

"Eldon! Over here!" Eldon spotted Jordan through the fish blizzard. He was standing and waving at him. *Standing?* Eldon stopped thrashing around and stood up. The water was only waist deep, and getting lower by the second, as if some force was sucking the water backward. He felt the current rushing by him and grabbed the side of the plane.

"Hold on!" The water continued to flush past them toward the far end of the loch. The seaplane began to drift with it, until the water grew so shallow it grounded itself in the mucky bottom, surrounded by tiny fish flapping around in the dark mud.

"What's going on?" Jordan shouted from the other side of the plane.

"I'll tell ya what's goin' on, laddies!" A thick, Scottish brogue answered him. They both looked up to see a burly, barrel-chested kid in a plaid raincoat, floppy rain hat, and rubber waders trudging toward them through the fish-filled mud. *"Yer about to get flushed away with them sticklebacks, if ya don't hop back onboard that flyin' boat a yers!"*

Jordan looked where he was pointing, in the direction where the water was flowing. It was the

far end of the loch, where they'd flown over for a water landing. He didn't remember that large, smooth, black mountain in the distance, which now seemed to be rising up like the back of a giant. Jordan froze, then looked down at the mud. The loch hadn't drained—it had *ebbed*. And that mountain in the distance wasn't a mountain—it was the water of Loch Ness, pulling back and gathering into a giant wave that was about to come crashing back down, right where they were stuck.

"Oi! Quit yer sightseein'!" The rubber-booted Scot grabbed Jordan and swung him around the other side of the plane, then shoved him and Eldon inside. He climbed aboard, slammed the door behind them, and spun around. *"Strap yerselves in! We're about to go fer a Loch Ness sleigh ride!"* He jumped in the pilot's seat as Eldon and Jordan buckled up behind him. A rumble from behind grew louder. *Then louder. THEN LOUDER.*

KERRRRSPLAAASSSHHH! The seaplane jerked

violently as it was swept up by the crashing loch water. Their Scottish pilot moaned and grunted, gripping the wheel as he struggled to right the seaplane. The tsunami of black water tossed them like a bath toy. Nearly toppling tail over nose, they rode the giant wave as it crashed into the empty canyon, refilling the loch. He wrestled the controller and they careened straight ahead along with the mighty water.

"Yeah!" Jordan yelled.

"You did it, MacAlister!" Eldon added.

"MacAlister?" Jordan said, glancing at Eldon. "You *know* this madman?"

"We're not outta this yet, laddies!" the Scot yelled back.

"Dead end, dead ahead!" Eldon shouted. They all turned to the windshield and saw the same thing—rushing toward them was the sheer face of a rocky cliff. The other end of the loch. They stared in horror at the wall of rock looming directly in front of them. At the last second, MacAlister jerked the controls. The three of them screamed as the seaplane veered across the downward slope of the wave, diving straight at the left side of the narrow canyon. Carving to the side as the wave continued to push them forward, MacAlister steered for

a cave opening in the side wall. In a half second, the cave entrance would be underwater. MacAlister leaned on the wheel with all his might, and they slid down and across the wave, straight at it. MacAlister pushed as hard as he could, threw his head back, and let out what sounded to Jordan like some sort of Scottish war cry.

"Odelidehleheeeeiiillllll!"

The plane skimmed into the side entrance, which led to a shaft curving in and then straight upward. The loch water rushed in behind and beneath them, refilling the underwater cavern, lifting the seaplane like a cork in a bottle. They rose higher and higher in the dark shaft until the water leveled out, and all was suddenly calm.

Jordan opened his eyes. The plane bobbed up and down, floating gently inside a massive cave. It was as if a great hydro-elevator had lifted them to the penthouse floor, and now they were floating on the surface of its indoor pool. The boy Eldon had called MacAlister unbuckled and jumped out first. Eldon and Jordan followed him, hopping from the edge of the plane onto the wet cave floor.

The cave was enormous, housing not only the pool created by the vertical tunnel filled with the loch water, but a series of side tunnels, a cozy fire pit, and various pieces of handcrafted knobby wooden furniture. Taking it all in, Jordan was drawn toward an arch of sky at the opposite end of the cave. He walked to the opening and gazed down at the now peaceful waters of Loch Ness, far below.

"Whoa."

"Quit gawkin' at the view and help me save yer bucket o' bolts!" MacAlister had tied a rope to the plane's pontoons and was tugging away like an ox. "That there loch's gonna flush back out again, and when she does—*whoosh!*—yer little plane's gonna get flushed down with it like a *wee turdlet!"*

The three of them pulled the seaplane out of the pool and onto the slippery rock floor, then stood at the mouth of the cave and waited, staring down at the darkening loch. As night fell and the moon rose over the distant cliffs, they watched the great waters of Loch Ness begin to recoil again like a monster waking from a peaceful sleep.

GUUUURRRRGLE! A loud sucking sound echoed behind them. The pool where their plane had just been bobbing peacefully began to swirl faster and faster, forming a violent whirlpool until—*FLUUSSSSHHH!*—it dropped out of sight.

Jordan and Eldon looked back down at the receding waters of Loch Ness. Shimmering in the moonlight below were thousands of the silvery fish, gleaming and sparkling as they flopped around in the mud. "Sticklebacks," MacAlister said, pulling off his rain hat. A mop of bright red hair tumbled out. "Poor things are so confused with the water comin' and goin.' Bet they miss ol' Haggis-Breath gobbling 'em up. Bet they miss her . . . almost as much . . . *as I do!*" *SPLORF!* He blew his bulbous nose and began bawling like a baby.

"There, there, Alistair," Eldon said. "We'll find her."

"Her," Jordan whispered. "You mean . . . *the Loch Ness Monster?*"

"*DON'T CALL HER A MONSTER!*" MacAlister's ruddy cheeks were suddenly in Jordan's face. This boy was shorter than Jordan but nearly twice as wide. Standing up on tippy-toes, he was nose-to-nose with Jordan and had a wild look in his eyes.

"Sorry," Jordan said. "I didn't mean anything by it."

Eldon stepped between them. "I know you're upset, Alistair, but he's here to help. I'm the one who was hoping this wasn't a true emergency. I see now how serious it is. It was Jordan here who figured I'd need assistance. And he was right."

Alistair stepped back, eyeing him suspiciously. "Jordan, eh?"

"Jordan *Grimsley*," Eldon said. "It's okay. He's George Grimsley's grandson."

Alistair froze. His eyes grew wide. Then they

refilled with tears, and he dropped to his knees. "I'm so sorry! Your grandfather would be ashamed to call me a Keeper! I hate meself! I'm a big, fat Creature *Loser* is what I am! Please forgive me!"

"No, of course!" Jordan glanced at Eldon. "I never actually knew my grandfather, so I really don't know what he'd think, but I'm sure he'd understand. . . ." Jordan helped the blubbering Scot to his feet. Alistair looked at him. His nose twitched. His eyes grew wider. He opened his mouth to say something and—*Waahaahhhhh-TCHOO!*—a sneeze exploded in Jordan's face, blasting it so hard it blew his hair back.

"Thanks for that," Alistair said with a sniffle. "It helps, it really does." He pulled off his raincoat to reveal a green-and-red tartan kilt. He kicked off his waders and plopped down.

As Jordan wiped the Scot snot off his forehead, Eldon leaned in gently. "Jordan, why don't you go and grab the supplies out of the plane. We'll light a fire, dry off, and have some cocoa."

Jordan took a torch from Eldon and made his way toward the plane. He noticed a side cavern off the main cave and decided to check it out. Inside was a large, plush sleeping area—like a doggy bed for an over-pampered, oversized poodle. A *very* oversized poodle. It was the size and shape of an aboveground swimming pool. He approached the curved edge of the enormous bed. It was wet to the touch, and rippled as he made contact with it. It was a water bed in the true sense of the word, made from a sponge-like material that *oozed water*. Jordan caught his breath. This was the perfect resting place for a giant, amphibious, cryptozoological creature after a long day of keeping the earth's waters in balance. This was Nessie's bed.

A large tartan cover of the same green-and-red pattern as Alistair's kilt hung over the bedside. Jordan smiled as he thought of the big, tough Scot sitting in his cave, knitting a blankie for his Haggis-Breath. He reached up to pull it, and the blanket slid off the wet bed, covering him. He struggled to free himself and when he did, he found clumps of white fur stuck to him. He brushed off as much as he could, then looked closer at it. He looked around the room. This fur didn't come from the blanket Alistair had made, and it wasn't the color of his fiery red hair. And although they hadn't met yet, Jordan was pretty sure silky-blond fur wasn't something shed by the Loch Ness Monster, either.

16

"It was a foggy night. Thickest fog I'd ever seen." Alistair MacAlister stared into the fire as he wrapped his short, stubby fingers around a steamy mug of hot cocoa. "Perfect night for ghosts." Unfortunately for Jordan and Eldon, their host only had one green-and-red tartan kilt. As Eldon and Jordan's clothes were drying nearby, they sat in their damp underpants.

"I woke up before dawn, sneezin' like crazy. Dunno if it was the sneezin' that woke me, or the strange squealin' noises. Horrible, high-pitched sounds. No animal I'd ever heard. I checked on Haggis-Breath, and found her gone. Somethin' was wrong. She'd just gotten home from the Black Sea, and had gone right to bed."

"Hold up," Jordan said. "The Black Sea?"

"Oil spill," Alistair said. "She went in and slowed the currents to keep it contained 'til the cleanup crew got there. So she was dead tired."

Eldon noticed Jordan's confusion. "That shaft we came up isn't the only tunnel in this cave," he explained. "There are a series of complicated underground waterways, linking Loch Ness to water systems all around the world."

"Only Nessie has the instincts and ability to navigate 'em," Alistair said. "From here she swims for days underwater. Goes wherever she's needed, uses her power over currents and tides to keep the seas clean and in balance."

"What would happen to the seas if . . . she didn't?"

The two Keepers glanced at each other. "You saw Loch Ness," Eldon said.

"Picture the waters ebbin' and flowin' violent like that, but to the whole Atlantic Ocean," Alistair said. "Without my Nessie keeping order to things, what you saw today would be a drop in yer cocoa." He swirled his mug, spilling a small splash into the fire. It hit the flames with a smoky *tsssssssss. . . .*

"Maybe she's out working," Jordan said. "She could be in the North Pacific, the Indian Ocean, or patrolling the Baltic Sea or the Bering Straits."

"The loch is growing more and more violent. They evacuated all the coastal villages. My Nessie wouldn't let that happen. Something's wrong. Something in . . . *the spirit world.*" His hand trembled. He took a deep slurp of cocoa, his eyes darting around the dark cave.

"I love telling ghost stories around the fire as much as any Badger Ranger," Eldon said. "But they're just stories. They're not real." He picked up his Badger Ranger official notebook and pencil. "Let's get to the facts. You heard squealing noises?"

"Aye. Coming from right here, near the lookout. That's when I saw the apparition. Thought he was mortal at first, just an odd little man, standing there smiling at me. He acted like I should know him, but I'd never seen him in my life."

"What'd he look like?" Eldon asked.

"Weird old geezer," Alistair said. "Barely a hair

on his head, bit hunched over. All in white. Shiny white suit. And his skin—ghostly white."

"Did he say anything to you?" Eldon said.

"He called me by my name, as if we were old mates who bumped into each other in the street. 'Hello, Alistair,' he says. He's got this large cage on wheels, but covered up. Whatever otherworldly

beastie he's got inside is thrashing around, making them horrible noises. He looks like he might let it loose on me, so I grab me pokin' stick. I say, 'You let that thing out an' I'll poke it somethin' fierce!' He says, 'I don't think you would.' I says, 'Try me!' I was sneezin' like crazy, but I figured I could still handle this intruder."

"Then what?" Jordan asked, his eyes growing wide.

"Then—it gets weird," Alistair said.

"*Then* it gets weird?"

"He grins at me with that creepy, milky-white face of his—and pushes the cage over the edge! I rush him with me pokin' stick, but he just steps backward, *right off the edge himself.* That's when I see he's from the spirit world. He just floats there a minute, in the fog, *in midair*! I can hear his caged beast floatin' behind him, goin' crazy, squealin' somethin' awful, no doubt because it realized it wasn't gonna get to chomp on a nice, juicy Alistair MacDrumstick that night. As he drifts off, disappearing into the fog, he says, 'So long, Creature Keeper.'"

"Impossible," Eldon said. "You must've heard an engine, a propeller, *something.*"

"Just the awful squealin' of his horrible beast and the ghostie's high-pitched gigglin'. An' the sounds of my own sneezes, of course."

"Stealth chopper," Jordan said. "Computer-controlled NOTAR blade-modulation system, most likely synched with a shrouded tail rotor. Military-grade." The other two stared at him.

"I was thinking a hot-air balloon," Eldon said.

"Or that," Jordan added.

"This old man must've had something to do with Nessie's disappearance."

Alistair was suddenly on his feet. "It wasn't no old man! It was a ghost! The highlands are filled with ancient spirits! This specter came for me with his demon-creature as a warnin'! He scared off

Nessie, an' left me all alone with a horrible curse!" *AAAH-TCHOO!* He exploded in another sneeze, then slumped back down and sobbed into his cocoa.

"Gosh, Alistair," Eldon said gently. "There's no such things as ghosts." He looked at Jordan for help. "Isn't that right, Jordan?"

Jordan thought about this. Two days ago, he would've said there were no such things as Skunk Apes or Loch Ness Monsters, either. Who knew anymore? Eldon kicked him. "Uh, yeah! I mean no. Of course not."

"Then how'd he know my name? How'd he know I was a Keeper? Only a member of the spirit world would have that kind of knowledge."

"Or a member of the Creature Keepers," Jordan said. "Think about it. Who else would know to come here? How to get in? This had to be an inside job."

Eldon shook his head. "It can't be. None of ours would harm a creature—or threaten a Keeper." He stood up. "Okay. Show us where you saw Nessie last. Her bedroom, right?"

"NO!" Alistair MacAlister was back on his feet. "You can't go in there! You'll get the *ghost sneezin' curse*, like me!"

"Sorry," Jordan said. "'Ghost sneezing curse'?"

"Aye. The ghost put a curse on me. Why do you

think I sneeze like I do all the time?"

"Because you live in a damp cave in Scotland, and always have a cold."

"No! It's the ghost sneezin' curse! It started that very night! An' it's double-worse whenever I go into her bedroom!"

Jordan thought of something and glanced down. Stuck to his arm were a few strands of the mysterious silky-white fur. He picked them off and flicked them in the direction of Alistair.

AAAH . . . TCHOOO! Alistair burst into a fit of sneezes. "See? Even talking about it brings the ghost sneezin' curse back! I say we get out of this cursed cave and don't ever come back!" *AAAH . . . TCHOOO!*

"Alistair," Jordan said slowly, "do you have any allergies?"

"Aye. I'm allergic to hares," he said. "And *ghost curses*, apparently."

"Hares. You mean like rabbits. Are there any in these parts?"

"Mountain hares are common to the highlands, but they don't come around."

"Maybe because you have a giant water lizard for a roommate," Eldon said.

"Had," Alistair replied sadly.

"Did Nessie wear any sort of fur coat that night?"

Despite the dire situation, Alistair couldn't help bursting out laughing. "I know my Haggis-Breath has a reputation as being a bit of a diva, but she ain't no fashion model, laddie! The only coat she has is her Hydro-Hide, but it sure ain't made outta fur!"

"Nessie has a very special outer skin," Eldon explained. "It's the source of her power. Her coat is made up of millions of moveable scales that she controls with great precision—and great force. It's how she manipulates the water. It also enables her to swim at superspeeds. She can even use them to reflect her surroundings, to help her appear invisible."

"Not that she ever does," Alistair said. "My Haggis-Breath isn't shy about being seen. Makes my job a challenge but—" *Sniffle!* His big eyes were welling up with tears again. "She was worth all the trouble, and a million times more!" The redheaded Keeper lifted his kilt and blew his nose loudly into it. *SPLORRRFF!* "And she's certainly *not made of fur,*" he said to Jordan.

"That's what I thought." Jordan suddenly bolted toward Nessie's bedchamber.

"*Oi!*" Alistair shouted. "Where do you think you're going?" He and Eldon ran after him, past the seaplane, around the deep shaft that was the indoor pool, and into Nessie's bedroom. Jordan stood in front of the huge water bed, holding up a corner of the enormous tartan blanket crumpled on the floor.

"You leave her blanky alone!" Alistair shouted. "I crocheted that for her meself!" Furious, he stormed up to Jordan and grabbed it out of his hands. His eyes started to water, but not from sadness. His nose twitched. Eldon and Jordan stood back and gave him plenty of room. *Ahh . . . aahh . . . AAAH . . . TCHOOO!* His massive sneeze exploded and he dropped the blanket, stepping away. "Y'see? I told ya! It's *the ghost sneezin' cur—*" *TCHOOO!*

"It's not a curse, Alistair!" Jordan picked up the snot-sprayed blanket and pulled something from it. "It's a clue to who our traitor might be!" He turned to Eldon. "In my grandfather's field guide to cryptids, there was something called a Giant Desert Jackalope. That's a creature that's half stag and half hare, right?"

"Yes," Eldon said. "That's right."

Jordan held out his hand and showed Eldon a clump of the mysterious fur.

"I don't suppose he has white fur, does he?"

Eldon studied the fur, then looked up at Jordan. "He's not a he, he's a she. And yeah—as a matter of fact, Peggy's a sandy blond."

17

As the morning sun slowly rose over Loch Ness, Jordan, Eldon, and Alistair stood watch over the steadily rising water. They'd managed to push the seaplane up to the mouth of the lookout cave, and were waiting to shove it over the edge at just the right moment.

"Okay, this is it," Alistair said to Eldon. "Remember, you only have a few seconds to climb into the cockpit and grab that stick, then yank it, hard as you can."

Jordan glanced at Alistair. "Are you sure about this?"

"That rogue wave got your plane in here. Now it's gonna get us out."

"I won't have time to start the engine," Eldon said. "But the momentum from the fall should give me time to position us so the pontoons hit the wave like a ramp."

"Bet there isn't a Badger Badge for that," Jordan said.

Gurgle! The pool behind them had filled again during the night, when the loch tide came rushing in. Now it was heading back out, and the water began to swirl and flush.

"All right, lads, that's our mark. Five . . . four . . ."

Jordan looked out at the loch below. The water pulled back like a scorpion getting ready to strike. "Three . . . two . . ." It began to form a watery hill beneath them as it rose up. *"ONE!"* As the hump of

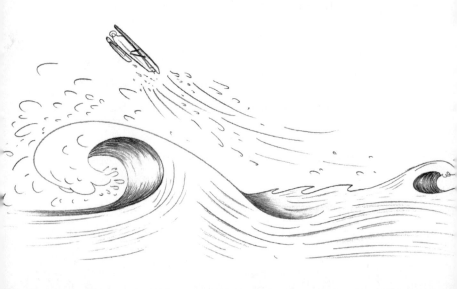

water swelled, the three of them shoved the plane over the edge and quickly scampered inside. It plummeted like a stone toward the receding water as Eldon dived into the pilot's seat, grabbed the control stick, and yanked back as hard as he could, pulling the plane out of its nosedive.

SPLASH! The seaplane leveled just in time for its pontoons to meet the growing hump of water. Like a car caught on a rising drawbridge, it began gliding backward down the wave. Keeping his hand on the stick, Eldon hit the ignition and gunned the engine. The propellers whirred and the tiny plane began to climb back up the rising water, gaining speed as its ramp grew steeper. Eldon pushed the little plane for everything she had. Her engines roared, and she

zoomed forward, shooting off the cresting edge of the watery ramp, straight into the sky.

"*Yeeehaaaaaw!*" Eldon shouted.

Jordan looked out the window at Loch Ness far beneath him. He could just make out the sparkle of the poor little stickleback fish as they flopped in the mud. Eldon pointed the little plane westward, toward the Atlantic Ocean, and Jordan shut his eyes. He smiled as he listened to Alistair chuckling and cheering Eldon on for a job well done.

"See? Nuthin' to it, just like I said!"

"And we've got just enough fuel to make it to our next stop," he heard Eldon say. "The Chihuahuan Desert in West Texas—jackalope country!"

Something about this announcement didn't sit quite right with Jordan, but he was too tired to put his finger on it. He laid his head on his backpack and drifted off into a deep sleep.

"There she is, boys! Dead ahead!"

Alistair's voice jolted Jordan awake. The Scottish Creature Keeper was sitting in the copilot's seat with the big map book in his lap. Jordan peered out the window. They were over the desert, with nothing but sand for miles and miles.

"There's the little town," Eldon said excitedly.

"And not a moment too soon—we're nearly out of fuel." Jordan saw in the distance a town with what looked like a single road and just a few small buildings. The road dead-ended at a fenced-off clearing.

"And look," Alistair said to Jordan. "Some o' them high-tech military helio-choppers you were talking about!"

Bobbing in the desert air, parked in the clearing, were five hot-air balloons anchored to the sandy ground. "Very funny," Jordan said.

"The giant jackalope's burrow should be just outside of town, due east," Eldon said. "I say we set her down on Main Street and investigate on foot."

Jordan's feeling that something wasn't quite right returned. He looked out at the desert, and suddenly realized what it was. "Hey, guys," he said. "I dozed off for a while, there. What's the plan for landing a seaplane in the desert?"

Eldon and Alistair stared straight out the window in silence for a moment. Jordan got up and joined them in the cockpit. "Guys? I think you just passed the town." The plane suddenly shuddered, and died. A red light lit up on the panel. They all looked at the fuel gauge: *EMPTY*.

"*Aaaaaauuuuuuggggggghhh!*" Eldon jumped out of his seat. "Jordan, take the controls! Keep her steady, and keep her *in the air!*"

Jordan did as he was told. Eldon ran to the back of the plane and began rummaging around the cargo hold.

"What are you doing?" Alistair yelled. "This is no time for a snack!"

"Parachutes!" Eldon hollered back. "I'm looking for parachutes!"

Jordan's hands felt sweaty as he gripped the wheel. The plane was eerily silent as it drifted above the desert. It was steadily losing altitude. Jordan circled it back toward the little town, hoping to catch a breeze to glide on. He kept his eye on the five hot-air balloons in the distance.

Eldon returned to the cockpit with a single parachute and a strange look on his face. "Found one," he said. "Just the one. Jordan—you take it."

"What?" Alistair squealed. "Why him? *He's not even a Creature Keeper!*"

"Because I got him into this, and he's not going to die on my account," Eldon said. He pushed it toward Jordan, who shook his head and pushed it back.

"No. I'm not taking it. I'm not leaving this plane without you."

"Well, there you have it! Very noble!" Alistair blurted out, grabbing the chute. "That's friendship for ya! You two really have something special—I could sense it right away!" He began yanking at the parachute, trying to stretch it over his big, round back. "I don't wanna be a third wheel, so I'll just step outside, let you two have some privacy, and—" *RRRIIIIP!* The parachute suddenly split open, its silky insides spilling out like guts. "Oops."

Jordan couldn't keep the seaplane in the air for much longer. He stared out at the parked hot-air balloons in the distance. "I've got an idea," he said. "Strap in. This is gonna make our takeoff feel like a roll in Nessie's water bed." Eldon and Alistair buckled up as Jordan aimed the descending plane straight for the hot-air balloons.

The seaplane came in low and fast, slamming into the first balloon—*KA-BLOOM!* It burst as they hit it, and its thick material got jammed up in the plane's pontoons, flaring out behind them, catching the wind. This slowed them down as they careened into a second balloon, which didn't pop, but got stuck under the plane's wings. The thick material covered the windshield as Jordan tried to aim them into a third balloon. *BLOOOMPH!* This one didn't pop, either, but stretched and spread beneath the plane like a cushion.

BA-BOING! The balloon-padded seaplane hit the

ground, and bounced over the fence. *BA-BOING! BA-BOING!* It continued bouncing away from the little town, into the open desert. Jordan, Eldon, and Alistair bounced around inside like rag dolls.

The rollicking ride ended as the seaplane finally slid to a stop behind a large, red rock—one of many jutting out of the desert. Balanced on the last balloon, it slowly tipped, leaning ever so slightly against a single, pointy cactus standing alone.

POP! Sssssssssss... Their giant air bag deflated, lowering the seaplane and its passengers gently to the desert floor.

Jordan turned to face his passengers in the back. Eldon was pale and Alistair was green. Neither of them looked hurt. "Thanks for flying Totally Insane Airlines." Jordan smiled. "Take 'er easy!"

Eldon unlatched the door, swung it open, and stepped outside first, followed by Alistair, who fell to his knees and kissed the sandy ground. Jordan stepped out last and looked around. Alistair stood and slowly approached Jordan. The overgrown Scot raised his arms and grabbed Jordan off the ground, giving him the second-biggest hug he'd felt in as many days. *"Ooof!"*

Alistair set him back down. *"What a ride!"* He grinned. "You *are* a Grimsley!" He chuckled as he pulled something out of his kilt pocket. "Here. I want you to have this. Whittled it myself. In case you need it." He slapped a knobby, wooden sling-shot into Jordan's hand, then stepped back onboard the plane.

"Thanks," Jordan said, admiring the handiwork.

"Great job, Jordan," Eldon said. "I probably should've said this before you saved our skins—but I'm really glad you came."

Jordan smiled. "Thanks. Me too."

Eldon peered around the large rock, back at the town in the distance. "Now let's just hope nobody in that little town spotted us."

"We crash-landed a seaplane into a bunch of hot-air balloons, popping them as we dragged their brightly colored pieces across the empty desert floor. Astronauts orbiting the Earth probably spotted us."

"I dunno." Alistair stepped back out, reading the old map book. "Last log says here the town is pretty much deserted."

"We'll find out soon enough," Eldon said. "Peggy's burrow is out here somewhere. The book should provide the whereabouts. Let's just hope she's in it. If Jordan's theory is correct, her Keeper may have abandoned her."

Alistair scanned the pages, his lips moving

slightly as he read. "Okay. Says here her burrow lies under a sort of bunny-shaped marker. Now how are we supposed to find that?" He and Eldon scanned the desert horizon. Jordan, however, looked up.

"You mean, like this one?"

The giant rock towering over them was shaped like a chocolate Easter bunny. Suddenly, the sand beneath them began to vibrate. A scratching sound came from beneath the base of the rock, and sand kicked out from under the rock bunny's rear end. Then two small tree branches seemed to be emerging from beneath the rock, until Jordan saw the massive, fluffy head they were attached to. The Giant Desert Jackalope squirmed the rest of its enormous body out of its burrow and sat up. It was nearly half the size of the massive rock it crawled out from, and towering at least twenty feet above them.

"Whoa," Jordan said.

"Great Scott," Alistair added.

"No." Eldon smiled. "Great Peggy."

Peggy tilted her antlered head and shook her floppy, silky-white ears, sandblasting the three of them below.

"We must've woken her up," Eldon said. "Don't make any sudden noises or moves. We've got to very carefully get her to go back into her burrow, or she'll run."

"Got any giant carrots?" Jordan muttered.

The Giant Desert Jackalope sat with a dazed, empty look in her eyes. She sniffed the air, then lifted a leg to scratch herself. She sniffed again, then yawned.

"Just move very slowly, and remember—*no sudden noises*," Eldon repeated.

Peggy lifted her giant leg and scratched again, this time right below her neck. A flurry of fur floated down over the three of them. Jordan and Eldon looked over at Alistair. He was holding his nose. Which was about to explode.

Huhph . . . huhph . . . HWAHHH-TCHOOO! A violent sneeze blasted from his face. Peggy shot straight up into the air. They all looked up but lost her in the sun.

"Gesundheit," Jordan said.

"Thanks," Alistair said.

BOOM! The ground shook again, this time from the other side of the rock. The three of them ran around it and stopped dead when they saw what Jordan imagined to be a Creature Keeper's worst nightmare: Peggy the Giant Desert Jackalope was hopping full speed across an open desert in broad

daylight, straight for an unsuspecting little desert
town.

"Gentlemen," Eldon said. *"The bunny has
landed."*

18

Jordan's sneakers filled with sand as he raced behind Eldon through the hot desert sun, a sprint made even harder as every ten yards or so he was forced to run down and then up one of Peggy's sofa-sized footprints.

When they finally reached the small town, they found it oddly quiet for a place where a Giant Desert Jackalope had presumably just bounded through.

"Where is she?" Jordan panted. "Where is anybody?"

Eldon looked up and down the empty, dusty road. "Peggy's very shy, but she spooks easily. One of the easier cryptids to keep, actually, so long as you don't send her off in a blind panic. If we're lucky she'll jump at the first person she sees and flee back to her burrow. That's why I had Alistair stay behind."

Jordan's lungs burned as he tried to catch his breath, and he wished he had gotten to stay back. He pictured Peggy having a cozy water bed like Nessie's, and Alistair napping on it in the cool shade of her burrow.

"Can I help you folks?"

A friendly, laid-back voice startled them half to death. A leather-faced, middle-aged woman, with skin the color and texture of an old tangerine, smiled a crooked-toothed grin at them. "Dang! Didn't mean to spook y'all! You two jumped higher than a jackrabbit on a desert rock!" She stuck her hand out. "My name's Bertha. Bertha—*SWEET SCREAMING BLAZES*!"

"Interesting name," Eldon muttered to Jordan. "Must be Native American. The Tarahumaran tribe was indigenous to this region." He reached for her leathery hand. "Nice to meet you, Ms. Sweet Screaming Blazes."

"No, you buzzard brain! Look!"

Jordan and Eldon spun around, half expecting to see Peggy eating someone. All they saw were two semi-inflated balloons bobbing lamely in the sun.

"Hey! Balloons," Jordan said, trying to sound

innocent about it.

"Exactly! Those balloon-thievin' swine swiped my dirigibles again!" She sprinted down the road, yelling back to them. "There used to be six, then there were five, and now there's only two! That's three more that are gone!" Eldon and Jordan followed, keeping a sharp eye out for Peggy.

"Lotsa things disappearing around here," Jordan said.

Bertha stopped in her tracks and turned around slowly. She eyeballed the two of them, and didn't like the way they were glancing around nervously. "Where'd you two come from, anyway? I ain't never seen you around here before."

"Ma'am, do you live alone in this town?" Eldon said, ignoring her suddenly suspicious stare.

"Just me and my husband, Milo." She backed up slowly until she reached a little balloon-rental shack. "Milo ain't here now. Went to Midland to pick up some tourists. But he'll be back any minute, so don't try any funny stuff—" She suddenly pulled a shotgun from the shack and aimed it at them. *"Balloon burglars!"*

"Please, ma'am," Eldon said. "You're mistaken. I can explain."

"Eldon," Jordan whispered. "It doesn't matter.

Let her think we took 'em. Remember why we came here." He spread his fingers behind his head like antlers and began to hop up and down.

"What's he doing?" Bertha said. "Tell him to stop or I'll shoot. It's weird."

Eldon turned to Jordan. "I'm a Badger Ranger, First Class," he whispered. "I will not allow a fellow citizen to think I stole her private property."

"Okay," Jordan whispered back. "Then go ahead and explain how we crashed our seaplane into her 'private property' and dragged it across the desert!"

"Y'all did what now?" Bertha said. "What're you two whisperin' about?"

"Ms. Sweet Screaming Blazes," Eldon said, straightening his Badger sash. "As a full-fledged First-Class Badger Ranger, I can assure you that I would never—"

"Oh, shut it, Ranger Rick," Bertha said. "You two show up outta the blue with no car, no truck, and expect me to believe you had nothin' to do with four of my hot-air balloons gone missin'? You think I'm stupid?"

"You said you already lost one. When did that happen? Did you get a glimpse of the thief?" Eldon pulled out his Badger Ranger official notebook and pencil. *Click!* He looked up to see the shotgun cocked and aiming right at his nose.

"Don't you reach in yer pockets again!" she said tensely. "And as for getting any glimpses, I'd say I'm lookin' at the dirty, rotten balloon snatchers right now. . . ."

"We don't have time for this," Jordan said, pushing the barrel away from Eldon's face. "We're on official cryptozoological business and—"

KABLAM! The shotgun went off, blasting into the sky, sending Jordan and Eldon diving into the dust and Bertha flying backward onto her bottom.

RUMBLE! The ground shook. Bertha looked down at the sand beneath her feet, then up at a very odd sight. A mound of sand was coming right at them. Bertha raised her shotgun at the approaching wave of sand. She got ready, took aim, and . . . *CRASH!* The incoming dune exploded before she could fire, knocking them all back and spraying everything with sand. Jordan saw a soft, white underbelly fly overhead, followed by a large, cottony tail. He sat up beside Eldon and turned around just in time to see Peggy land on the little rental shack in the balloon field, flattening it with a *SMASH!*

"Great horny toads!" Bertha stared in shock for a moment, then leaped to her feet and ran straight toward the giant jackalope, shotgun in hand. Eldon

and Jordan scrambled to their feet and raced to save Peggy, who was staring mindlessly at a silver hubcap lying in the sand.

"No! Wait! Don't shoot!"

"Stay back! This here devil bunny's been stealin' from my balloon park! Prob'ly thinks it's some kinda giant radish farm!" Bertha aimed between Peggy's sleeping bag–sized floppy ears. "An' now it's gonna git what it deserves. . . ."

She cocked the gun, closed one eye, and squeezed the trigger. . . . *Click*.

Bertha turned the gun upside down. A stream of sand poured out of the barrel, onto her boot.

Bertha tossed the gun away. Fuming, she stormed straight up to Peggy and began throwing a tantrum, kicking sand and yelling horrible names, trying to get the creature to fight. But Peggy stared off vacantly, her antlered head tilted slightly, transfixed by the shiny hubcap.

Jordan started giggling. "Wow," he said. "Good thing there are no witnesses to this."

"Yeah," Eldon added. "Thank goodness Mr. Sweet Screaming Blazes is in Midland."

Kzzzrrt! "Bertha, it's the Milo-Mobile, holler back, over?" The crackly voice came from under Peggy's butt. Specifically, it came from a crushed CB radio that had somehow survived a Giant Desert Jackalope's butt landing on it. *Kzzzrrt!* "I'm about a half mile out, got me a bus full of Bulgarian tourists with their eyes on the skies—and they got cash! Be there in a few minutes, so prep the balloons! Milo-Mobile out!"

"Oh, no," Eldon said. Bertha turned toward the two of them and smiled.

"Hear that? Your freaky, furry friend here's in trouble now!" She cackled. "My Milo's the best desert-critter wrangler in all of Texas! He'll hog-tie this here mutant zombie rabbit and we'll charge five dollars apiece for a picture with her! We're gonna be rich!"

Jordan and Eldon shared a look. Off in the distance, a sky-blue bus was making its way toward town, followed by a big trail of road dust.

Eldon grabbed Jordan. "C'mon!" They bolted past Peggy and Bertha, toward one of the last two balloons in the field. Eldon kept stopping and picking up small stones and tossing them away.

"What are you doing?" Jordan asked.

"Aha!" Eldon exclaimed as he handed Jordan a triangular stone. He pointed to one of his Badger Badges. "Native American studies," he beamed. "That's a genuine Tarahumaran arrowhead. As I said, they were indigenous to this region."

"Yeah, but is now really the best time to collect samples?"

Jordan followed Eldon into one of the hot-air balloon baskets. Eldon gathered a rope, tying one end to their basket, and fashioning another into a lasso. He looked at Jordan. "Okay! Use the Tarahumaran arrowhead to pop the balloon!"

Confused, Jordan reached up and started stabbing their balloon with the dull arrowhead stone. "Not ours!" Eldon yelled. "That one!" He pointed to the other balloon, parked about twenty feet away. Jordan looked at him like he was crazy. Then he remembered something. He reached into his back pocket and pulled out the slingshot that Alistair had given him. He placed the arrowhead in the sling, pointy side out, and took aim. He took a deep breath, pulled back, and let go. The arrowhead sailed through the dry desert air and pierced the other hot-air balloon.

PHHHHLLLLLTTT. . . . The air escaping from the hole in the balloon made a loud, long farting noise. Its sound snapped Peggy out of her trance. She leaped into the air and dashed across the field toward the open desert, straight for home, which also meant straight at Jordan and Eldon in their balloon. Eldon was ready for her. He swung his lasso as the giant jackalope approached, and hurled it, snagging Peggy's antlers. Their balloon jerked into the air, snapping the anchor rope and yanking them over the fence. Peggy raced for her burrow, with Jordan and Eldon in tow.

Sailing through the air behind Peggy, Jordan glanced back. Bertha stood at the fence, looking astonished as she faded in the distance. Farther behind her, the sky-blue Milo-Mobile pulled to a stop as Jordan and Eldon soared away from them, across the desert, like parasailers.

As Peggy approached the bunny-shaped rock outcrop marking her home, it didn't seem she had any intention of stopping. She'd had a very traumatic day, and was now running in a blind panic, way too fast. Eldon and Jordan sensed this, and didn't know what to do. They couldn't jump out of the basket without getting severely mangled. But even if they could abandon their bunny ship safely, Jordan knew Eldon wouldn't. As head Creature Keeper, he could not allow a cryptid running around free without supervision. Who knew where she'd stop to blankly zone out? At this rate, she might run all the way to New York City, just to stare at the shiny buildings.

As the bunny rock loomed closer, they began

yanking on the lasso to try to slow her down. Nothing was working.

Then they heard the booming sneeze of Alistair MacAlister. *HWAAA-TCHOOO!* "OI! UP HERE, YA HAREBRAINED HARE!"

Peggy glanced up, then immediately skidded to a stop in the sand. The basket drifted past her, floating gently to a stop near the top of the bunny-shaped rock. Standing atop the outcropping was Alistair, holding a shiny silver object over his head.

Jordan and Eldon slid down the rope, and then down Peggy, who stood motionless beside the rock, as if she were posing for a sculpture of herself.

"Nice little joyride, fellas?" Alistair jumped off the bunny-shaped rock, continuing to hold up

a shiny cluster of silver spoons held together on a giant key ring. Peggy stayed mesmerized, following the spoons with her beady eyes.

"Sorry to interrupt your fun, but along with this little knickknack, I found some other stuff in that burrow that I thought you might wanna see."

Jordan stared up at the zombified-bunny. "How'd you know to do that?"

"Oh, yeah. Found this, too." Alistair pulled a beat-up old book out of his kilt and tossed it to Jordan: *Raising and Caring for Your Giant Desert Jackalope.*

"Nice work, Alistair!" Eldon exclaimed. "Can you get her into the burrow? We might have company soon."

Alistair winked at them. "Check this out." Peggy followed as he jingled the keys toward the bunny-shaped rock. "Okay, girl! Go get 'em!" He tossed the keys into a narrow space hidden at the base of the rock. Jordan heard them jangle as they fell somewhere deep below the desert floor.

Peggy dived, disappearing into her burrow, squirming and kicking sand at the three of them. She also buried the object she'd been sitting on the entire time she was staring at the keys. Their trusty little seaplane was now a pancake.

Alistair gestured to his partners. "After you, gentlemen."

Jordan entered the dark space where Peggy had disappeared and slid down a steep, sandy slope, landing on a cool floor deep beneath the bunny rock. The burrow was a large, circular, dug-out space with no corners or sharp edges. It was like being inside an enormous egg room—the perfect shape to house a gigantic, clumsy rabbit with sharp antlers and a habit of crushing things with its butt. Cracks in the rock above allowed narrow beams of sun-light in, as well as air. But not enough air, as Jordan immediately noticed—it smelled like a petting zoo on a hot day.

Peggy was snuggled up at the far end of the egg-shaped room, on a large pillow-bed. Upon closer

inspection it appeared to be hand-knit, completely from silky, white bunny fur. Jordan noticed many things made from the fur: wall hangings and area rugs and even furniture, including a couch and a lovely end table.

Alistair hung the spoons on a hook in front of Peggy. She stared at them, then tucked her giant fuzzy face between her soft paws and drifted off to sleep.

"What a dump," Jordan said. He sat down on a dark brown, slightly squishy stumplike seat. He sank into it a bit as he looked around. "Stinks in here, too."

"Uh, especially where you're sitting, I should think," Alistair said, chuckling. Jordan and Eldon looked at him. "That's no stool, I'm afraid—*that's a stool!*"

Jordan looked down and sniffed. He was sitting on a giant bunny pellet. *"Eww!"* He leaped out of the chair and began scooting his butt along the sandy floor like a cat in a litter box. "This place is disgusting!"

"What do you expect?" Eldon approached Peggy, reached out his hand, and gently stroked her nose. "Poor girl. Abandoned by her Keeper, she had no one to take care of her or keep her burrow clean."

"Shameful," Alistair said. "Doesn't deserve the honor of being called a Keeper."

"Who *was* her Keeper?" Jordan asked.

"Harvey Quisling, age thirteen," Eldon said. "Fully trained and experienced First-Class Creature Keeper. I have no idea why he'd leave his post."

"This might help explain." Alistair stepped to a messy desktop. Among the clutter, Jordan and Eldon saw a cross-Atlantic wind-pattern map, an ad for Milo & Bertha's Hot-Air Balloon Tours, a calendar with dates circled in red, and a sketch of a flyer for something called *Quisling's Zoopendous Crypto-Zoo.*

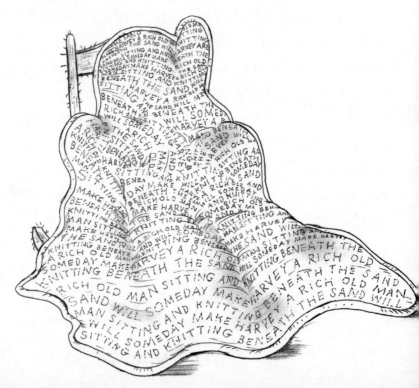

"Looks like he was quite a tailor," Jordan said, noticing an old sewing machine beside the desk. "As well as a knitter."

"I'd say more of a nutter," Alistair concluded. "Check out the cozy little psycho-blankie he was workin' on." He held up a massive quilt draped over a fur-lined rocking chair. On it, the same stitched sentence ran across the quilt over and over again: "SITTING AND KNITTING BENEATH THE SAND WILL SOMEDAY MAKE HARVEY A RICH OLD MAN..."

"Okay, so it looks like Harvey Quisling went a little quilt-crazy down here," Jordan said. "But it doesn't explain who showed up the night Nessie disappeared."

"No," Alistair said, "but check this out." He handed them a letter written in curvy, inked handwriting on fancy parchment paper. "This is what I wanted you lads to see."

To: Mr. Harvey Quisling
Chihuahuan Desert Burrow,
West Texas

From: Señor Areck Gusto
Mexico City, Mexico

Dear Mr. Quisling,

This letter confirms the terms of our agreement. I,

ARECK GUSTO,

shall design, construct, and fully fund one (1)

CRYPTO ZOO

facility, to be built in the northern Everglades, off the west coast of Florida, USA. You,

HARVEY QUISLING,

shall be responsible for the capture and confinement of one (1)

LOCH NESS MONSTER

for public presentation in said zoo. All ticket sales, gift shop and snack bar proceeds shall be shared equally between us.

I very much look forward to our partnership.

Sincerely,
Señor Areck Gusto

"Impossible," Eldon said, looking more upset than Jordan had ever seen him.

"Florida Everglades," Jordan said. "It can't be a coincidence."

"We can't let this happen. Not there. Not any-where."

"Trust me, it won't!" Alistair scoffed. "D'you two really think my Haggis-Breath can be caught by a loony bunnysitter and his rich grandpappy? Transferred to some swamp-zoo on the other side of the Atlantic, then kept in a tank just to be gawked at! Please—I know her better than anyone. There's no bleedin' way she'd go without a fight!"

"Let's hope you're right," Eldon said.

Peggy's ears suddenly sprang straight up in the air. The two fluffy antennae tilted toward the entrance to the burrow. The others strained to listen as well.

"I don't hear anything," Alistair said.

"You're not listening with those things." Jordan pointed to Peggy's ears.

"They're coming," Eldon said. "They'll see the balloon outside. They'll find her. We have to do something." He turned to Alistair. "Mac, I need you to stay here with Peggy. Jordan and I are going to go see about this crypto-zoo."

"Not on yer life," he said. "I'm her Creature Keeper. I'm comin' to Florida."

"I need you to remember your sworn vow—to all cryptids."

"Help, hide, and hoax," he muttered.

"You take care of the first two. Jordan and I will cover the third. We'll lure ol' Bertha and Milo far away from this rock."

"But hoaxing is the funnest one."

Eldon smiled at him. "There'll be plenty more hoaxing in your future, Mac. I promise."

"Just find her," Alistair said. "And stop whoever's done this."

Eldon smiled at him. "Creature Keeper's honor."

Alistair turned to Jordan. "You're no Keeper— not yet, anyway. But you're definitely a Grimsley. Just listen to Eldon, and do everything he says. He's the best there is."

"Funny, that's how he described you." He smiled at Alistair, then turned to Eldon. "Okay. I'm ready for my first hoax."

"Good," Eldon said. "Now grab a couple of those giant bunny turds and follow me."

20

Abbie poured the last cup of lemonade and handed it to Mr. Norris, a wrinkly old man in a shiny blue tracksuit. "There you go, Mr. N," she said. "My last cup."

He gulped it down, crushed the paper cup, and slammed it onto the counter. "Mm-mm! That's some good sarsaparilla!" he exclaimed. He turned and skated off on Rollerblades toward some elderly neighbors setting up a pair of roller-hockey nets.

In the yard next door, another group of retirees was playing a vigorous game of volleyball. Mrs. DeMartelli leaped four vertical feet and spiked the ball, sending it bouncing over a hedge. Mrs. DeMartelli was at least eighty-six years old.

Across the street a half dozen old folk pulled folding chairs out onto the lawn, joining Mr. Hirschberg, who was sitting quietly. "That's more like it," Abbie said to herself. "That's what old people do." Suddenly, they began to somersault, one by one catapulting themselves into the air, landing in handstands on their chairs, stacking themselves on Mr. Hirschberg's shoulders like circus acrobats.

Abbie's customers were all involved in some feat of strength or dexterity. She looked down at the empty pitcher in her hand. "Must be something in the water."

"You look like him, too, y'know," an old woman's voice croaked from behind.

Abbie spun around to find the old woman with the bunny slippers standing behind her. "Mrs. Fritzler! Don't sneak up on me in those rat slippers of yours!"

"Got more of a sassy mouth than him, though."

"Who are you talking about?"

"Your grandfather. George." She scowled. "You *are* George Grimsley's granddaughter, aren't you?"

"Yes."

"Well, all right, then," she said, picking up a rag and bumping Abbie out of the way. "Don't make me explain everything to you like you're a brainless guppy." Abbie smiled as Mrs. Fritzler wiped the counter. *Brainless guppy,* she thought. She'd have to remember to use that one on Jordan.

The sky-blue bus rumbled across the scorching desert, straight toward the bunny-shaped rock. The Bulgarian tourists bounced in their seats, snapping pictures of nothing much out the window, looking a bit confused as to where they were being taken, or when they might get lunch.

"Y'see?" Bertha yelled into the ear of a large, bearded man in the driver's seat. "Y'see those tracks, Milo? I told ya! A giant bunny rabbit stole our balloons!"

"Bertha, sit back down and stop talkin' crazy," Milo said. "There ain't no such thing as a giant desert bunny. And besides, if our balloons was dragged out here, we'd see 'em by now. Them balloons are huge."

"I told you, this ain't no *ordinary* giant desert bunny! He's got antlers, Milo. Big ol' antlers! I bet he used 'em to pop our balloons! Makes total sense!" She turned to the tourists. "Am I right?" They nodded, more out of polite confusion than agreement.

"Antlers? All right, I've heard enough. I'm turnin' around and headin' back—"

Bertha suddenly gasped. "MILO! DEVIL BUNNY, TWELVE O'CLOCK!" Milo looked up and slammed the brakes, sending the Bulgarians into the seatbacks in front of them.

The tourists scrambled off the bus to find Bertha grinning as Milo stared at the odd-shaped rock in the distance. Something stirred behind it. Something big. And white. And puffy.

"What in the name of heckfire?" Milo mumbled.

"I told ya," Bertha whispered back. "Now you'll see. You'll see I ain't crazy. . . ."

The large, whitish blob moved slowly out from behind the bunny-shaped rock. It looked to have big, floppy ears, a sort of round, puffy face, and a big, blobby belly. It was still too far away to make out much detail, but it was definitely huge, definitely bunnylike in shape—and most definitely on the move away from the bunny-shaped rock.

"Well, I'll be an armadillo's uncle," said Milo.

"I told ya." Bertha grinned.

Click-click-whir-zzzt-click-click, went all the Bulgarian tourists' cameras.

"EVERYBODY BACK ONNO EL BUSSO!" Milo suddenly shouted. "EL NOW-O!" They all piled back on and Milo gunned the engine, roaring in hot pursuit across the desert.

Bertha was screaming at her husband as the white bunny-blob disappeared inside a steep, rocky ravine. "Faster, Milo! He's gonna get away!"

"Relax, honey," Milo said. "We got him. That ravine dead-ends. There's no way out 'cept the way he hopped in." He gunned the engine. The Bulgarian tourists grinned nervously at one another, hoping they were racing toward lunch.

The bus rolled into the ravine and stopped, blocking the entrance. A few hundred yards in front of them sat the huge, white bunny, bobbing gently with its enormous back to them. They all slowly piled off the bus and began sneaking up on it. The creature had a blobby butt that drooped over brown feet; a big, white back; oddly shaped lumps for ears atop a lumpy, featureless head; but—

"Hey," Milo whispered to his wife. "Didn't you say he had big ol' antlers?"

Bertha looked up at the top of the devil-bunny's head, bobbing and swaying high above the desert floor. "Wait a cottontail-pickin' minute," she said.

Click-click-whir-zzzt-click-click! went the Bulgarian tourists' cameras.

Bertha and Milo waved the tourists back and approached on their own. As they got closer, the bunny's blobby butt bobbed up and down, exposing its feet to be wooden, or *wicker*—like a basket— and a good six feet off the ground. They reached up under the great bunny's butt to grab a wicker foot, and two heads popped out.

"Bombs away!" Jordan yelled. They both unloaded the huge Peggy turds, which hit the ground with a stinky *SPLORT!* They just missed Milo and Bertha, who dived to take cover behind a rock.

Click-click-whir-zzzt-click-click! The Bulgarian tourists snapped wildly, turning their cameras upward as the basket began to rise. *SPLORT- SPLORT! SPLORT!* Jordan and Eldon dropped a few more giant pellets. With each turd-bomb, they rose higher into the air, lifting skyward, up, up, and out of the ravine.

When it was safe, Milo and Bertha crawled out from the rock they were hiding behind and looked up at their hot-air balloon, which had been expertly

roped into the shape of a giant devil-bunny, thanks to some good ol'-fashioned First-Class Badger Ranger k n o t - t y i n g know-how.

Click-click-whir-zzzt-click-click!

As the lumpy dirigible drifted eastward, Milo noticed Bertha staring off with a crazed, empty expression on her face. "Bertha, I think we need to get outta the desert for a spell. Whaddya say we go on a nice, long cruise together?"

"Yeah . . . ," she faintly whispered, "I think I'd like that."

21

The rolling desert hills below drifted by silently as Eldon studied a map he'd found in Peggy's cave. He checked his compass, put a finger in the air, then jotted a note in his Badger Ranger notebook. He turned to the open flame burner in the center of the basket and adjusted it. This heated the air inside the giant bunny balloon that was carrying them across the sky.

Jordan smiled at his friend in action. "How did you learn to do all this stuff?"

Eldon looked up, a little surprised. "Did I not mention I'm a Badger Ranger?"

"C'mon. There can't be a Badger Badge for navigating a hot-air balloo—" Eldon stuck out his sash.

One badge had a tiny balloon on it. "Wow. That's actually impressive."

Jordan watched Eldon test all the knots along the side of the basket, then check each task in his notebook. It reminded him of his dad's to-do list. He wondered how his family was doing, and if his mom and dad missed him.

"Eldon, where's your family?"

Eldon stopped writing, and Jordan immediately felt like he shouldn't have asked. "Sorry," he said. "You don't have to tell me."

Eldon slipped his notebook into his shirt pocket. "It's just that no one's asked me about them in a long time." The two boys stood together looking out over the horizon. A warm southerly breeze gently nudged them toward the Gulf of Mexico. "I guess the short answer is, I'm an orphan."

"So your parents are, uh—"

"Yep. Died years ago. But I lost them long before that happened." Eldon glanced down at his uniform, flicked a speck of sand off his lapel, and straightened his bolo tie. "For as long as I can remember I wanted to be a Badger Ranger. As soon as I could walk, I became an honorary Junior Runt. I learned as much as I could, as fast as I could. And of course, I grew eager to apply what I'd learned. I'd sneak out, scaring my family half to death. They'd find me wandering the woods, sleeping in trees in the park, tracking and trapping neighbors' pets. They started locking me in my room at night. They were just trying to keep me safe, of course, but I didn't see it that way. I felt like a prisoner. So I ran away. I wanted to live outdoors, like a real Badger Ranger. Eventually I learned that being a Badger Ranger isn't about survival and adventure and living in the wild. It's about helping others."

"So you went back?"

"No. I couldn't face my parents after the pain I'd caused them. But I needed to go somewhere. I found a place—a home—filled with others like me, who had run away and couldn't go home."

"An orphanage?"

"Sort of. It was a broken down old house, rotting from the inside, run by a wretched old woman who didn't even own it. She moved in and took it over, then did the bare minimum to claim herself as a caretaker, so she could collect money from the government. The more of us she had living there, the more money she got."

"Some caretaker."

"I just liked that she didn't care enough to lock my door. So I snuck out a lot. I still dreamed of becoming a First-Class Badger Ranger, and living with so many people in need allowed me to work on my community badges. But I needed wilderness skills, too. And the location of the house was perfect for me to hone my survival-badge skills. It sat at the edge of a thick, overgrown swamp."

Jordan's eyes grew wide. *"The Okeeyucka-chokee? You lived in my grandfather's house!"*

"Your grandfather had long since abandoned it. But for many of my friends, it was the best life they'd ever had. At least, until I offered them a better one. The Okeeyuckachokee Swamp was my classroom. It's where I learned plant and animal classification, survival skills, hunting, gathering—and of course, the ancient art of spooring, which led me to the trail of the great Florida Skunk Ape."

"Bernard said my grandfather taught him how to trust you," Jordan said.

"That came later. I had to find him first. I'd pick up clues—a clump of fur here, a warm dropping there—but the trail always went cold, right at the same spot."

"Let me guess. The great lemon tree."

Eldon nodded. "Of course I'd heard all about your grandfather. Both he and Skunk Ape Summer were still a local punch line. But like you, I began to think maybe there was something real behind the jokes. Maybe your grandfather hadn't been crazy."

"You must have a badge in acting. You were such a jerk when I asked for your help, but you knew exactly how I felt."

"I had to test you. I wanted to be sure you were serious."

"So how did you find Bernard?"

"One night, a terrible rainstorm hit while I was out spooring. The swamp began to flood, and I nearly drowned as I made my way back to the house. I entered my usual way, through a broken basement window. It was flooded that night, and in the darkness I could hear water rushing *under the house*. My only concern was sneaking safely back to my room. I made my way up the rotting basement stairs. I quietly opened the door to the kitchen to find the old woman sitting up, guarding the refrigerator. She was afraid that in the noisy storm some of us might try to sneak downstairs to steal extra food. As I reached the top of the cellar stairs and opened the door, she lunged at me. But I was too quick for her, and ducked out of the way."

"She fell down the stairs?"

"She fell *through* them. She was swept away by the underground torrent rushing beneath the house. As much as I hated her, I had a duty as a Badger Ranger—especially one working toward his Citizen Hero Badge—and dived in after her. The water whisked me away from the house and under the swamp. The underground streams split off in ten different directions, and I was sure I'd drown. But I got lucky. I suddenly found myself careening down a mudslide, faster and faster, deeper into the earth. I shot out into an underground room, splashing and sputtering on the muddy floor, gasping for air like a catfish. And there he was—the great Florida Skunk Ape, surprised as I was that the floodwaters had dropped me smack-dab in the middle of your grandfather's lemon-tree lair."

"What happened to the awful caretaker?"

"I never saw that old lady again. As for Bernard, he was a proud creature, and not very happy when the annoying ranger kid he'd successfully dodged and evaded for so long belly flopped in the middle of his flooded-out living room. But he respected me as a worthy adversary, and decided not to toss me back out into the storm, or tear my limbs off."

"That was nice of him."

"He was lonely, and he saw a loneliness in me. For the first time in my life, I didn't want to run away. I felt like I was home. I wanted to stay down there forever. And soon after, Bernard invited me to do just that. He showed me what he and your grandfather had started, and wanted me to help him make it a reality. Bernard wanted to protect and hide the cryptids your grandfather had made contact with, but knew it was just a matter of time before they were discovered. He couldn't board an airplane or cruise across the sea to check on them. We both realized what I could bring to the operation, aside from my Badger Ranger skills, was the ability to pass in and out of both worlds. Together we could protect all the cryptids your grandfather had met. But we couldn't do it alone. We'd need helpers. Lots of them. We'd need a team."

"So you went back to the old house. For the others."

"With the old lady finally gone, there was no one left to care for them. Many of them were happy to follow me into the swamp. Those who weren't we helped take care of in other ways. But the ones eager to join this adventure were even more eager to get to work. They made it all happen. Your grandfather's dream of a secret society of Creature Keepers would've died without them. They all would've made him very proud."

"Not all of them," Jordan said. "I don't think Grampa Grimsley would be too happy with this Harvey Quisling kid."

Eldon shook his head. "I can't understand it. I helped trained Harvey myself. He's a good kid. Never in a million years would I have guessed he'd be capable of something like this. Still, I should've seen it. This is all my fault."

"Don't say that. You never know about people, what's really in their hearts. How could anyone guess someone who'd been abandoned himself could abandon the amazing creature he was supposed to care for? You told me how being a Creature Keeper is about keeping quiet and remaining unseen. I bet it can get boring. Maybe Harvey was offered a better job."

"Not a chance. Being a Creature Keeper is far niftier than being a zookeeper."

"Not just a zookeeper. A *crypto-zookeeper*." Jordan thought about this as he gazed out at the horizon. "Still, I can't connect Harvey to getting Nessie across the Atlantic."

"You saw the letter from that Gusto person. They had a deal."

"Exactly! Harvey's part of the bargain was to deliver Nessie. But it wasn't Harvey that Alistair saw that night; it was some old man—maybe even this Gusto himself. So if Gusto is paying for the zoo, *and* he's kidnapping Nessie himself, what's he need Harvey for?"

"Maybe Harvey just told Gusto where he could find her."

"I thought that, too, but it still doesn't compute. If Harvey wanted to open a crypto-zoo with Gusto, what's wrong with the cryptid he already had? I mean, he and his antler-headed, fluffy-tailed roommate live just a few states away from where the zoo's being built—why cross an entire ocean to try and bag a six-ton water lizard with an attitude, who you know will put up a fight the whole trip back from Scotland to Florida?"

"She can be a handful. Not to mention risking the wrath of Alistair . . ."

"Right! Meanwhile, all Harvey needs to do is jiggle some car keys and Peggy goes into screen-saver sleep mode. Load her onto a U-Haul, and you're open for business the next day. I'm telling you, something here still doesn't add up."

"Nessie's more famous," Eldon said. "She'd bring in bigger crowds."

"My dad has tossed us in that ugly car for a family road-trip vacation every year I've been alive. Believe me, anyone willing to pay good money to see a giant, captive water lizard will pay just as much to see a giant, captive jackalope. Nessie may have the name recognition. But after driving hundreds of miles with a carful of bored and whining kids, parents will pay whatever you ask, to see whatever you stick in front of them."

"You're right," Eldon said. "It doesn't make sense, unless—"

"*Unless* this Gusto person has another reason for wanting Nessie."

Eldon and Jordan looked down at the calm, blue waters of the Gulf of Mexico, rippling gently beneath them—the complete opposite of the violent, surging black waters of Loch Ness.

"Maybe it'll be all right," Jordan said. "According to Alistair, Nessie's too smart and too strong to let herself be caged up in some swamp zoo by an old fart and a crooked Keeper kid."

"Still," Eldon said, staring at the water below. "We have to find her before anyone else does."

22

"Abbie! Come in for dinner!" Mrs. Grimsley shouted down the sloping front yard, from the re-bricked front steps of the house. She turned and went back inside to set the table, shutting the freshly painted front door behind her. On the edge of the newly sodded lawn, Abbie sat with Mrs. Fritzler, watching the other residents finish their stickball game as the sun began to set over Waning Acres.

"That eyesore of a house is looking less like a lump of crud every day," Mrs. Fritzler said through a wrinkled frown. "I would've just bulldozed the dump, but if your fool parents wanna throw away good money, whatever toots in their boots, I suppose."

Abbie smiled. "Mrs. Fritzler, I wanna be just like you when I get old and ugly."

She smiled back. "I'll be dead and gone by then, so knock yourself out, kid. Tell ya what, I'll leave you the house your grandpa gave me. That should get you started. You can have my slippers and my dryer-lint collection, too. You'll be on your way to Fritzville."

"What house? My grampa gave you a house?"

Mrs. Fritzler stood and cracked her back. "Sure. He gave us all houses. Least he could do, disappearing on us like he did." She began shuffling off.

"What? When was this?"

She stopped and turned. "Open your ears. I just told you. Soon after he disappeared from the old folks' home, there."

Abbie looked up at her grandfather's house. "That was an old folks' home?"

"Sure. That dump was the original Waning Acres." She pointed from the old house to the newer neighborhood with its manicured lawns and smoothly paved road. "Long before any of this. He had all this built, just for us. Like I said, least he could do."

"So you, all of you, lived there together?"

"Most miserable I've ever been. And for me,

that's sayin' something. Your grandpa was fruitier than a jelly donut, always gabbin' about weird creatures. But he did one good thing—left us this land and plans for this community. So I guess his life wasn't a *total* waste." She mumbled to herself as she started shuffling away again. "Although what kind of fool wanders into a swamp in his pajamas to get eaten by an alligator, I'll never understand. . . ."

"Wait, how'd you get the houses *after* he disappeared and died?"

Mrs. Fritzler stopped once again. This was getting irritating. "You writing a book or something? I don't remember, some lawyer. *Needlepine, Nosenpooper . . . Noodlepen . . . C. E. Noodlepen.* Sent us the letters, deeds, and keys, easy as you please. Well, not *all* of us, mind you. Just the lucky ones, I guess. Although standing here getting harassed by you, I'm starting to wish I lived somewhere far away."

She glared at Abbie, who was suddenly lost in thought. Mrs. Fritzler shrugged and turned away again. "I see you're working on a new life plan. Well, it was flattering while it lasted. See ya tomorrow, kid. Unless I don't."

Abbie stood staring at the neat row of identical houses lining Waning Acres.

The sun began to set behind the bunny-shaped balloon, casting a golden glow on Florida's western coast. Eldon adjusted the flame in the center of the basket, causing the air inside the balloon to cool slightly. They began to descend, drifting low to the water toward the green tangle of the Everglades in the distance.

Gliding silently along the shoreline, Eldon gazed through the binoculars, identifying all the coves and bays as they made their way south. The farther down they traveled, the more unwelcoming the names sounded. Up near the accessible and populated Everglades Airport, the inlets were called Oyster Bay, Sweetwater, and Duck Rock Cove. Farther south into no-man's-land, it was Dismal Bay and Alligator Cove—if they had names at all.

"There!" Eldon pointed toward the coastline and handed Jordan the binoculars. "Just off the deepwater side of Lost Man's Cove."

Jordan took the binoculars and scanned the gnarled tree line for anything man-made. Something gleamed off the end of one edge of a large inlet, catching his eye. On the outer shore of the inlet stood a large, circular structure that looked to be constructed from thick eucalyptus trunks. What was strange was the enormous bubble dome perched

on top of it. Jordan lowered the binoculars.

"That's it?" he said. "That overgrown jungle hut is the crypto-zoo?"

"It has to be, although there's no way a structure like that could hold Nessie. Let's sail in for a closer look."

Except for the bubble dome, the building blended in perfectly with the surrounding swamp. Its tree trunk–camouflaged circular walls rose two stories high and were cut off at the top to form a narrow ledge that ran around the perimeter of the dome roof. The dome itself was opaque. It revealed nothing inside, while reflecting the overhanging trees and dusk-streaked sky above.

But the most suspicious and disturbing thing was how it sat on the far edge of Lost Man's Cove, just north of the Okeeyuckachokee Swamp. The next major inlet down was Ponce de Leon Bay. It was only a few short miles from there to the great lemon tree—and the Creature Keepers' secret swamp lair hidden beneath it.

"I don't like this," Eldon said. "We should go back to base and regroup."

But Jordan was already fanning the flame in the center of the basket, turning up the heat and making their airship rise. "What do you think you're doing?" Eldon said.

"We're going in." Jordan looked down at the tree line below. "Well, first we're going over. Then we're going on top. *Then* we're going in."

As night fell across the swamp, the bunny-shaped hot-air balloon descended along with it, slowly drifting down from above the surrounding trees. It gently touched down on top of the glass dome, and Eldon turned off the flame in the burner. As the air cooled, the big bunny drooped over its basket drowsily.

Slipping out of the basket, Jordan was surprised how warm the dome's surface felt, even through his sneakers. He leaned down and touched the glass. It felt like a toasty mug of Bernard's hot cocoa. He lay down on his stomach and cupped his hands around his eyes, trying to peer into the gray glass. It was dimly lit below, and he could barely make out large, dark shapes inside. The glass wasn't tinted after all—it was an actual fog, filling the dome. It reminded Jordan of something, but he couldn't put a finger on what it was.

"Excuse me, Jordan? I could use some assistance, here!"

Eldon had tiptoed too close to the slope of the dome, and was now on his butt, trying not to slide over the side. Jordan scurried over on his stomach, reached out, and grasped the back of Eldon's Badger Ranger bolo kerchief. He pulled with all his might, but the two of them continued to slide down the increasingly steep slope together. They picked up speed and went over the edge of the dome.

They landed not on the swampy ground, but rather on the ledge of the tree-stump wall supporting the perimeter of the dome. Eldon hit first, then had the pleasure of breaking Jordan's fall. "Would you kindly get off me so I can check if I've broken anything and am in need of first aid? Thank you."

Jordan rolled off Eldon and found himself facing a small, covered vent in the floor of the ledge. "Hey, give me your Badger Ranger buck knife," he said. He unfolded its small screwdriver, then removed the vent cover. A blast of humid air hit his face as he peered in. "Okay," he said excitedly. "You ready?"

"Entering like this could be dangerous. At the very least, it's trespassing on private property. I'd like to suggest a new plan. I say we balloon back to the lair, get reinforcements, and return during their regular business hours."

"What? Nessie could be in there. What if *she's* their business?"

"I told you, this place could never hold her. But it might yield more clues, or maybe the proprietors know something. We'll come back tomorrow. I'll bring a box of Badger Ranger Butterscotch Brownies. Technically, we're neighbors."

"Well, I say we pop in now and meet the neighbors." Jordan moved toward the vent, but Eldon blocked it.

"I can't condone breaking and entering. It's very poor citizenship. My Badger Ranger buck knife, if you please."

Jordan couldn't believe this. He sat back, gently

closed the knife, then tossed it to Eldon—just a little out of his reach. As Eldon moved to catch it, Jordan scrambled through the vent, faster than a desert jackalope burrowing under a rock, disappearing into the crypto-zoo.

23

It was a long drop to the floor, but the landing was surprisingly soft and smushy, just like the mossy ground of the swamp outside. Feeling the warm, moist cushion beneath him, Jordan realized that it didn't just *feel* mossy—it *was* mossy. Real moss, growing indoors. Jordan breathed in the soupy, humid air and started to stand up. *WUMP!* Eldon fell on top of him, flattening his face in the moss.

"Ow!"

"Good. You deserved that." Eldon rolled off him and stood up. "I can't believe you disobeyed my authority."

"I can't believe you wanted to wait until tomorrow. Besides, I don't think you technically have any authority over me." Jordan stood up. "I'm not a Badger Ranger or a Creature Keeper."

"With that attitude, you never will be." He peered through the foggy air. "What is this place? It's like a sweat lodge in here!"

Something wet hit the top of Jordan's head. The glass-domed ceiling was dripping with condensation. This reminded him even more of whatever it was that he couldn't quite remember.

"There's no way this place was designed for Nessie," Eldon said. "Some other creature, maybe, but not her. Not only could this bubble never hold her, it's providing the exact opposite of the environment that she needs. The humidity in here could kill her, never mind make her very cranky."

Humidity, Jordan thought.

Suddenly, a slow, slinking, slithering sound from just off to their right sent a chill up their sweaty backs. Worse, it was followed by a horrible squealing sound that echoed throughout the foggy dome.

Squeeeeeeee!

"What was that?" Eldon whispered.

"Remember what Alistair said? That Gusto guy who came to Nessie's cave had a vicious creature in a box! Maybe this is where Gusto keeps his monsters!"

They moved quickly away from the noise, feeling their way for an exit through the misty fog, along the rock formations jutting out of the floor.

Squeeeeeeee!

The creature's unnatural high-pitched cry bounced off the glass above them, muffling at the moss beneath their feet. Jordan inched closer to Eldon.

Squeeeeeeee!

WUMP. Eldon stopped short, causing Jordan to bump into him. "What is it?"

"It sounds like it's in pain," Eldon said.

"It's probably hungry. Keep moving!"

Squeeeeeeee!

"No," Eldon said. "We have to go back. We should try to help it."

"You didn't even want to come down here!"

"That was before I knew there was an animal in distress down here."

"It's not a kitty cat stuck in a tree, Eldon! We don't know what that thing is! I'm not gonna go rooting around in the darkness looking for it!"

A spotlight suddenly cut through the steamy fog, blinding them.

"Don't mind him," a raspy, high-pitched voice called out from behind the light. A blurry figure moved toward them, growing sharper as it approached. "He's just being a good little Creature Keeper. Isn't that right, Eldon?"

Out of the fog stepped a wrinkled little old man.

His skin was as white as the fog swirling around him. His pale scalp had a few scraggly hairs on it, and he was hunched over. He wore a shiny white jumpsuit, made of silky fur. They both recognized him from Alistair's fireside ghost story. But this was no ghost.

"So glad you came. You're also just the fella I wanted to see, hee-hee . . ."

Eldon studied him. "I don't think we've met. Señor Gusto, I presume?"

"Ha-ha-ha-ha-ha-ha!" The old man burst into a high-pitched, cackling fit of laughter. "Of course! You think I'm Gusto! Of course, of course! Yes! Perfect!" He reached into a sack hanging around his neck and pulled out something shiny and squirming, then flung it past them, into the fog.

Squeeeeeeeee!

Flopping and thumping noises were followed by the horrible sounds of the mashing and smashing of flesh and bone. It smelled very fishy.

"I suppose, since you're our first visitors, I should officially welcome you to *Quisling's Zoopendous Crypto-Zoo!*"

"So if you're not Gusto, then who are you? And where is Harvey Quisling? I would very much like to have a word with him."

"Yes, I bet you would, hee-hee. Who knows who is who is who is who?"

Jordan was preoccupied with the dark area where the munching sounds were coming from. "Hey, could we maybe, uh, take the crazy talk somewhere else?"

The old man looked at him. "You I *do not* know. Who are you, m'boy?"

"Grimsley," Jordan said. "Jordan Grimsley."

The old man's eyes widened slightly. He grinned at Eldon and then moved closer to Jordan, studying his face in the spotlight. "Yes, of course you are! Hee-hee! Come, into my office. It's hotter than a desert hole-in-the-ground, isn't it, hee-hee."

The old man led them toward a double-sealed pair of glass doors, which slid open. Jordan followed him through both, into a small office with a desk and a sewing machine in the corner, much like the one he'd seen in Peggy's burrow. Suddenly, the old man spun around and hit a button on a console on his desk. The inner sealed door closed, followed by the outer one, trapping Eldon between the two.

"Hey!" Jordan rushed toward the old man.

"Stop where you are," the old man said, standing over the console. "Or I'll gas him!"

Jordan froze. He looked back at Eldon, trapped in the small space between the two doors.

"Aw, heck. Let's gas him anyway." The old man hit the button. The chamber where Eldon was trapped suddenly filled with a thick, brown smoke.

"*No!*" Jordan rushed the glass door and tried to pry it open. He couldn't see Eldon, the smoke was so thick. He turned back to face the old man with fear and anger in his eyes. "If you harm him

in any way, I swear I'll—"

"Harm who?" He hit a button. *WHOOSH*—the door swept open. Jordan spun back around. The gas was gone. And so was Eldon.

24

"What have you done, you crazy old troll?" The old man had moved behind a small desk and stood before a panel filled with buttons. "What was that stuff?" Jordan demanded. "Where did he go? WHERE'S ELDON?"

"Relax," the old man said. "He's below. My new crypto-zoo has a surprisingly roomy basement. As for the gas, it's a natural extract from a swamp flower. A simple sleeping gas, perfectly harmless. He'll have a headache when he comes to in a day or so, but he'll be fine. Unless, of course, you're not cooperative."

"You get him back up here, NOW!" Jordan lurched toward him, fists clenched.

"Uh-uh." The old man laid a bony, white finger on a big, red button. "I wouldn't do that if I were you. This is a newly installed control system, and I'm still not sure which buttons do what. I'd hate for our old friend to get hurt down there."

"What do you want?" Jordan seethed.

"Ah! I thought you'd never ask, hee-hee!" The old man grinned at him. He squinted his beady little eyes. "Let's see. I want, I want, I want . . . the Puddle of Ripeness."

"What is that? What are you talking about?"

The old man's grin faded. "I thought you were a Grimsley."

"Yes. But I don't know about any ripening pool—"

"The Puddle of Ripeness! I know you've heard of it!" He slammed his wrinkled fist down on the console of buttons.

"Okay!" Jordan tried to think fast. He didn't want this nut to do anything reckless. "Puddle of Ripeness. Got it. I'll get it for you, I promise. Just let Eldon go and tell me where it is."

"I don't know where it is! That's why I need you to get it for me!" He eyed Jordan carefully. "Hmm . . . Not much like your grandfather, I can see that . . ."

Jordan quietly slipped his grandfather's ring off his finger and tucked it in his pocket. "You never knew my grandfather. He'd never befriend someone like you."

"Oh, no, he preferred his freaky little creature friends, didn't he? Hee-hee. But he never had a head for business. Never *capitalized* on what he had, *tsk tsk* . . ." The old man's eyes suddenly lit up. "I've got it! If you're palling around with Eldon, you must know his creature, no?" Jordan hesitated. He wasn't sure if he should answer this truthfully, but the old man raised a hand. "Come, come, or I start pressing buttons!"

"Yes, yes, okay!" Jordan shouted. "The Skunk Ape! I think I may have met him."

"Good. All you have to do is find that smelly creature and get him to take you to the Puddle of Ripeness. Legend has it the Skunk Ape is the guardian of its source. He'll refuse, of course. But you tell him if he doesn't cooperate, his beloved young Keeper will die a horrible death, blah, blah, blah." He looked down at his buttons. "I don't know which of these it is, but one of them will do the job, I'm sure. Any questions?"

Jordan tried to think of what Eldon would want him to do. He tried to think like a real Creature Keeper. And that led him to only one question.

"Yes," he said. "Tell me where the Loch Ness Monster is."

"Oopsie! Wrong question! You have exactly twelve hours to bring me the Puddle of Ripeness. Good luck!"

The old man covered his eyes and hit a button. The ceiling opened above Jordan's head as a panel beneath Jordan's feet suddenly catapulted him into the air.

"*Aaaaaaahhhh!*" Jordan flew far out over the bay, landing in the water with a *SPLASH!* Eager to find Eldon, he resurfaced and immediately swam toward the building he'd just been ejected from. As he got closer, he heard something off in the distance and stopped swimming. A horrible thrashing sound was coming from the nearby shore. The giant bunny balloon was lying lopsided in the shallows. It had obviously slipped off the roof of the dome, and was now being violently torn to shreds. Jordan assumed they were alligators, but as he treaded water in the twilight, he got a terrible sense that it was something worse.

Suddenly, the mauling stopped. A tall, dark silhouette popped up amid the torn material. This was definitely no alligator. It stood on two hind legs and lifted its thin head up, sniffing the moonlit air. It snapped its head in Jordan's direction, and Jordan plunged his head under the murky water, but not before he caught a glimpse of two shining red eyes, glowing in the darkness.

Jordan swam under the pitch-black water for as long as he could hold his breath, toward the opposite shore. Once safely on land, he looked back across the bay. The creature was gone, leaving the shards of white bunny balloon floating in the shallows. He turned to go, when a voice suddenly got his attention.

"WHERE IS HE?"

The voice barked from inside the camouflaged dome building. It was strong and deep, with a Latino accent. "Grimsley. Tell me where he is!"

The old man's answer drifted clearly across the still, humid air. "There *was* a Grimsley here! George Grimsley's grandson! But he's gone now! I sent him away to bring back the Puddle of Ripeness! I thought that's what you would've wanted, Señor Gusto!"

The old man isn't Señor Areck Gusto, Jordan thought to himself.

"Please tell me my *zookeeper* didn't just release a Grimsley back into the wild. . . ." The man's voice sounded calmer now, steadier. But somehow even more dangerous.

The old man's voice trembled as he spoke. "I—I just sent him to the Skunk Ape, to get us what we need! I ordered him to bring it directly to us. I thought it would save us the trouble—"

"You thought," Gusto snarled. "And as a retired brain-dead bunny sitter, tell me—what made you think you could think?" There was a long silence. "You'd better hope for your sake that Grimsley's 'grandson' does bring us the true Puddle of Ripeness," Gusto said. "In fact, we'll make sure it's real by testing it on him first."

"B-but, señor . . . I don't see what good that would do. . . . Besides, you promised we'd use it on *her*, so I could open my crypto-zoo. We had a deal, remember?"

"That was before you let Grimsley escape. We'll discuss it tomorrow."

The dark, domed building went silent. Jordan replayed everything he'd just heard in his head, but couldn't figure out what it meant. Whatever it was, it wasn't good. And his friend was caught in the middle of it. Jordan looked down, where Eldon was being held captive. He now owed it to him to get back to the great lemon tree as fast as he could, to ask Bernard and Creature Keeper central command for help, just like Eldon had suggested from the very start.

Jordan only wished he'd listened to his friend earlier.

25

Jordan slogged through the dark, mucky swamp for what felt like hours. He was exhausted, but didn't dare stop to rest. For one thing, he didn't want to waste a second while his friend was holed up in that horrible place. There was also the thought that wherever Nessie was, she might be in danger. Lastly, he couldn't shake the creepy feeling that if he stopped, even for a moment, there was a very good chance something might slink, slide, or slither up his leg. Or bite it clean off.

He knew if he kept the moon on his right, he'd eventually reach Ponce de Leon Bay, where he'd find the Creature Keepers' hidden dock and boathouse. From there he could make his way inland to the great lemon tree. The moon was playing peekaboo with him from behind the clouds—disappearing for a bit and casting him in darkness and then poking out again to splash the Okeeyuckachokee Swamp with silvery light, illuminating the stems, stumps, roots, and rocks that threatened to trip him underfoot.

He ran faster and more recklessly in the moonlight, leaping over logs and puddles of muck, ducking under low-hanging vines and briars. Only when the moon went back into hiding, casting darkness over the swamp, did he slow down, jogging along more carefully and catching his breath.

This went on for some time, until something struck him as odd. So odd, in fact, that Jordan stopped running altogether, just to stand in the darkness and listen. The swamp noises, all of them, had suddenly gone completely silent.

Jordan peered around in the darkness. The only sound was his own heart, which was beating faster than when he'd been running. He wished more than anything to hear the creepy swamp noises again. This silence was much worse.

CRACK!

A loud splintering of wood broke the silence, startling him. The moon came back out from behind the clouds, and Jordan spotted something moving far off in the distance. It lurched from shadow to shadow but was headed toward him very fast.

Jordan wasn't going to stick around to find out what it was. He broke into a sprint, with little regard for where he was going.

CRACK! CRUNCH! Another sound of splitting wood, louder and closer. A tree crashed to his left. He glanced back and caught a glimpse of the thing leaping from tree to tree like they were monkey bars. Terrified, Jordan suddenly thought of something. He managed to reach into his pocket as he ran, and slipped the ring Eldon had given him onto his finger. He glanced down as the glass object caught the moonlight, and pressed the ruby-red bead as hard as he could. He felt it sink into the ring, then something popped. It emitted a blast of vapor with a pungent odor. Jordan's eyes watered up at the awful, stinky mist that shot out of his ring. He wiped his eyes so he could see. What he saw, too late, was a large, thick branch, right in his path. *CRACK!* The sound of his head hitting solid wood was the last thing he heard before everything went black.

Jordan opened his eyes to see the sky through the treetops. He was lying flat on his back on the damp floor of the swamp, watching clouds catching and then releasing the moon, until its silver light was completely eclipsed—not by a cloud, but by something looming directly over him. It was the creature that had been chasing him. The same one he saw by the bay. The shape of its long muzzle and pointy ears was sharply outlined against the moonlit sky, and its eyes glowed red as they stared into his. It was panting through a mouthful of sharp, white

teeth, and it seemed to be studying him. It noticed the thick glass ring on his finger and lifted his hand in its claws. Its jowls pulled back into a horrible grin and it opened its terrible jaws. Just as it lowered its hungry mouth toward Jordan's neck, a heavy, thundering noise approached.

THUMP-THUMP-THUMP-WHAM!

A hulking shadow flew into Jordan's blurry field of vision, knocking the creature off him. Jordan heard snarling and grunting, snapped branches, and finally a loud *YELP!* It took all the strength Jordan could muster to lift his head and catch a glimpse of the doglike creature limping away, climbing back into the shadow of the trees. Jordan lowered his head onto the moss, and smiled. He recognized the sloppily shaven face looming over him, as well as the stinky smell that loomed with it. He shut his eyes and drifted off as he felt Bernard gather him up in his arms.

26

Jordan awoke to find himself in a cozy little bed. For a moment he thought he'd had a horrible nightmare. With some effort, he lifted his head and looked past his feet. He was in the library room, and it was packed with kids in their Badger Runt uniforms. They crowded around his bed, staring silently at him. Doris stepped forward, gently reached out toward his face—and jammed her thumb into his eye.

"Ow! Hey!" Jordan tried to pull his head away as Doris forced his eyelid open with her thumb and forefinger, but was stopped by a sharp, sudden throbbing pain behind his eyes. He suddenly remembered slamming his skull into a tree branch,

and he lowered his head back onto the pillow. It hurt too much for it to have been nightmare.

"Help me up. I need to see Bernard."

Doris didn't help him up. She reached down and placed a large, rubber hot-water bottle over his head. It smothered him in warmth, and felt nice for a second. But he tossed it off.

"Cut that out! Did you hear me? We need to save Eldon! Where's Bernard?"

Doris turned to the crowd. "He'll be okay."

"YEAAAAAAAHHHHH!" The entire Creature Keeper central-command crew erupted into cheers, hugging one another and enthusiastically shaking Doris's hand.

"All right, everyone. Back to your stations," Bernard's voice sounded from behind him. "Local team, keep eyes and ears on the perimeter and inner swamp. International team, keep me posted on the water levels of the Celtic Seas in the UK."

Everyone exited, smacking Jordan on the legs and giving thumbs-ups as they passed. Doris was the last to leave, but not before awkwardly leaning down and giving Jordan a peck on the cheek. "Glad you're feeling better, dearie." Then she ran out of the room.

Bernard stepped up to Jordan's bedside. He'd shed his tight-fitting Badger Ranger uniform, and his natty, black fur was already growing back in many places. He looked awful, and yet Jordan had never seen a more welcome sight.

"Bernard," he said. "Eldon's okay. He's being held hostage, but I don't think he's badly hurt—"

"I know," the Skunk Ape said. "You mumbled all about it on our walk home."

"Thank you for saving me from— What was that thing?"

"You can thank me by telling me how we can save Eldon—and what happened in Scotland."

"Nessie's gone. We're not sure where. Loch Ness is going crazy."

"Not just Loch Ness. It's spreading to surrounding waters, too. The Irish and Celtic Seas. Without her keeping things in balance, it could spread through the English Channel, out to the North Sea, even to the North Atlantic. By then, even she might not be able to make things right." Bernard sighed. He looked more worried and serious than Jordan had ever seen him. "There's not much time. We need to get Eldon back. He'll know what to do."

"They'll give him to us, but only in exchange for something called the Puddle of Ripeness. They said you'd know where I could find it."

Bernard's expression changed. "Who? Who asked you for this?"

"There's a mystery guy," Jordan said. "Gusto. Señor Areck Gusto. I never saw him, but he's clearly the leader. They're building a zoo, just up Ponce de Leon Bay. A zoo for cryptids."

"That doesn't sound so bad. I'd love to be able to visit a zoo."

"No, Bernard. Not a zoo for cryptids to visit—a zoo for cryptids to *be visited*."

"Oh. That's different. And explains why they'd take Nessie."

"The intruder who visited her cave the night she went missing, this crazy old man, left clues that led us back to the burrow of the giant jackalope. It seems Peggy's keeper, Harvey Quisling, has abandoned her. We don't know where he is, either."

"Quisling. I never liked that kid."

"We didn't find him. At this zoo it seems to be just the old man and this Gusto guy, along with some nasty creature they keep, probably for protection. As for Nessie, Eldon says the zoo is far too small to hold her. But it's a tricky place, with lots of surprises."

Jordan thought back to the look of fear on Eldon's face as he was engulfed in that brown smoke. "We're losing time. Can you get this Puddle of Ripeness they want or not?"

Bernard seemed lost in thought. Finally he said, "I can. But I can't."

"What does that mean? What are you talking about? Think about Eldon!"

"I am thinking about Eldon," Bernard said slowly. "I'm thinking about what he would do in this situation. We have to find another way."

Jordan couldn't believe his ears. But Bernard

seemed conflicted and very worried suddenly. Jordan thought for a moment. "What was that thing that attacked me?"

The Skunk Ape got up and pulled *A Field Guide to Cryptids* from the bookshelf. He opened it to the very first page and handed it to Jordan. There it was again—the Latin American Chupacabra, snarling at the camera. Jordan recognized its face instantly. He slammed it shut.

Bernard took the book and set it aside. "Remember how I told you your grandfather hadn't befriended all the cryptids he'd met over his lifetime?"

Jordan nodded.

"Well, there was only one that he actually feared. He never told me why, but after spending his whole life tracking cryptids, it seems that one of them was also hunting him."

"But my Grampa Grimsley is dead. What would the Chupacabra want now?"

"I don't know. But I know what it isn't going to get." Bernard put the book back on the shelf and pressed a panel, opening the bookcase door. "Rest up. When I return, we'll pull together a strike force. You're going to lead us—all of us—back to where this Gusto is holding Eldon hostage. There'll be no exchanges. We're going to break him out of there, and you're going to lead us into battle." The Florida Skunk Ape turned and lumbered out.

Jordan's mind was reeling, but one thing was perfectly clear to him—it was his fault that Eldon had been captured, and so it was his responsibility to free him, without putting anyone else's life in danger. To do that, he'd need this Puddle of Ripeness. And he had a feeling Bernard might lead him to it.

He threw off his covers and stood up. His head was throbbing. He looked down at the huge, rubber hot-water bottle on the floor. He squeezed the water out of it, folded it up, and walked to the bookcase. He thumped the panel and the bookcase opened.

Jordan snuck out of the Creature Keeper lair, finding his way up a winding staircase, through the knothole tree door, and finally out into the cool, swampy night air. He stopped and felt his finger. His grandfather's ring was gone. He thought about the last place he had it and shuddered. He closed his eyes, swallowed his fear, and breathed in deeply.

Sniff. Sniff-sniff.

Standing at the base of the great lemon tree, Jordan picked up a trace of—

"Skunk Ape." Jordan's nose pointed him in the

direction of the boathouse and Ponce de Leon Bay. With the empty rubber hot-water bottle under his arm, he began walking very carefully and very quietly, keeping his eyes on the lookout for the Chupacabra, and his nostrils on the sniffout for Bernard.

Jordan followed the Skunk Ape's odoriferous trail toward Ponce de Leon Bay, then farther inland. As the sky began to lighten, so did the scent, until it suddenly disappeared. Jordan stopped and sniffed in every direction, but couldn't pick it up again. All he could smell was the warm, woodsy fragrance of a nearby cypress-tree grove growing in a tight, circular cluster.

He tried to ignore the thick, piney smell the trees gave off as he sniffed around to pick up Bernard's scent. He was very tired and his head was still aching. He sat down at the base of one of the larger cypress trees. They were clustered together so tightly they formed a round wall. It reminded him of the base of the crypto-zoo.

He was about to stand and keep moving when he felt something shift behind him. The tree trunk he'd been leaning on was rotating. Jordan rolled behind a nearby bush and peeked out. The rotating tree turned to reveal a large, cutout doorway. Out of that doorway stepped Bernard. The Skunk Ape looked around, then lumbered off, back toward the Creature Keeper lair.

As the cypress-tree doorway began to rotate closed, Jordan had no time to think. He scurried over to the narrowing cutout and jumped through just before it disappeared. Once inside, the hollowed-out tree moved around him. When it stopped, the cutout was open again, but now facing the inner circle of the grove. There was a clear, circular path leading out from the doorway, walled by the clustered trees. The fragrant smell of cypress was overwhelming as he followed the coiled path. It led him farther and farther inward, until he came to a clearing in the hub of the cluster. He kneeled down at the edge of a small, green puddle of very stinky goo. "The Puddle of Ripeness," Jordan uttered. He studied the thick liquid. It looked perfectly still and harmless. He dabbed it with his fingertip. It felt oddly cool to the touch. Then he lifted his finger to his nose.

"*Ugh!*" He flung the nasty-smelling sample off like a booger.

Thanks to the cathedral-like ceiling of cypress branches intertwined above, both the Puddle of Ripeness and its awful odor were perfectly disguised to anyone walking by outside. But up close

the puddle definitely earned its name.

"It's just a nasty-smelling pool of stinky glop," he said to himself. "If that's what that weird old dude wants in exchange for Eldon, he can have it."

Jordan dipped the mouth of his hot-water bottle into the Puddle of Ripeness. *Glorp-glorp-glorp*— the green goo oozed into the large rubber container. Once it was filled, Jordan secured the top, then snuck back out of the cypress grove, and headed straight for the boathouse.

27

Jordan found both the old boathouse, as well as the boats inside, unlocked. The security system protecting the Creature Keepers' only modes of transportation appeared to be their appearance— both the glass-bottom tour boat and the rickety fan boat looked like death traps. No sane person would ever take them out on open water.

Moments later, zooming across Ponce de Leon Bay in the rattling fan boat, on his way to deliver a big rubber bag filled with smelly goo beneath his seat to a crazy old man who'd kidnapped his friend, Jordan thought to himself, *Yep. No sane person would ever do this.*

The fan boat was much faster than the Grimsley

Family Rambler, a lot louder than the old seaplane, and harder to control than a lassoed jackalope tearing across the desert sand.

Jordan knew he was disobeying Bernard. But he also knew that when he returned with Eldon at his side, he'd be welcomed as a hero. Of course, first he'd have to make the exchange. The old man was most definitely bonkers, and possibly dangerous. But his boss, this mysterious Gusto person, sounded worse. The old man wanted the Puddle of Ripeness, and Jordan was happy to give it to him in exchange for Eldon. But given what he'd overheard, Gusto wanted something more. Gusto was upset the old man had let Jordan go. Skimming across Ponce de Leon Bay, Jordan couldn't think why Gusto would want *him*. He'd have to be very careful.

He gunned the engine and tilted the mop handle joystick, steering the fan boat up the swampy coast toward Lost Man's Cove. The crypto-zoo sat in the distance, much more visible in the daylight but still camouflaged against the green background of the swamp.

As the side of the crypto-zoo loomed close, Jordan quickly realized something that had escaped his attention when he had quickly figured out how to operate a fan boat: *fan boats have no brakes.* He cut the engine and grabbed the stick with both hands. Shutting his eyes, he jerked it to the left with all his might. The fan boat fishtailed, nearly toppling over, spraying a wall of water as it skittered sideways, blasting the tall, green wall of the crypto-zoo with a wave of mucky mud before coming to a backward stop and slamming into the base of the building with a *wump*.

"So much for the element of surprise," he said to himself as he climbed off the boat and walked to front of the building.

BANG! BANG! BANG! Jordan pounded on the wall. After his noisy entrance, there was no point in being discreet. "Stinky goop delivery! Bring out Eldon and it's all yours!"

A hissing noise sounded from above his head and a drawbridge-like door lowered from the top of the wall, forming a ramp. Jordan entered what he assumed was the welcome lobby of this strange tourist attraction. At the foot of a short staircase was a glass display and gift shop showcasing Loch Ness Monster merchandise: little stuffed Nessie dolls, coffee mugs, T-shirts, snow globes, and novelty pens. Each item sported the *Quisling's Zoopendous Crypto-Zoo* logo. The sight of it made Jordan feel a little sick to his stomach. And very angry.

There were no other doors or stairs except for the short steps leading up to a sealed, vaultlike door with a fogged-up window. A sign read *AUTHO-RIZED ACCESS ONLY*. Jordan slowly turned the lock and pulled open the heavy door. *Hisssss . . .* Warm, moist air rushed out, and Jordan could immediately smell the mossy funk of the humid dome room inside. He knew this could be a trap. He knew there was a strange creature in there. But he also knew Eldon was in trouble. He stepped into the foggy mist.

Squeeeeeeeee . . . The high-pitched crying sounded less piercing than before. It was quieter—more like an animal suffering. He thought of Eldon and how he had wanted to go back and help it. Jordan stepped in the direction of the sound, his feet sinking slightly into the mossy floor.

The morning Florida sun was now baking the glass bubble dome, making the air trapped inside thick and sticky. Jordan suddenly realized what this place reminded him of—Chunk's molting tank, which Abbie used to help her pet iguana shed his skin. Maybe the strange creature kept in here was some kind of horrible lizard. A giant Gila monster, or Komodo dragon. If that was what ended up eating him, at least his sister would be impressed.

Squeeeeeeeee . . .

Whatever it was, the wheezing beast's cry now sounded more like a cry for help. And it was coming, quite clearly, from a shadowy rock formation Jordan could make out through the fog. The rocks formed a shallow cave, like in a lion or bear enclosure in a proper zoo. Jordan moved closer.

Squeeeeeeeee . . .

Clutching the large rubber pouch of goo, Jordan slowly rounded the rock. There was a heap of something at the base of the shallow cave, and it was sparkling in the sunlit dome. The twinkling was so powerful it cut through the fog, and Jordan thought the heap might be a pile of diamonds. Then the heap moved.

It was alive. It heaved with a *squeeeeeee*, then exhaled. It was roughly the size and body type of a sea lion, with flippers and a long tail, although Jordan couldn't see its head. As he stepped closer, its long, thin neck rose up, and it turned toward him.

Squeeeeeeee . . .

Jordan gasped. As impossible as it seemed, he immediately knew what this poor creature was. A miniature Loch Ness Monster.

He rushed toward her. Her skin was covered with sparkling scales, but it was hanging loosely off her body, like an oversized coat. Her half-lidded eyes strained to meet his before closing again. She drooped her head back down and slumped over lazily. She looked like she was dying.

"Beautiful, isn't it, Grimsley?"

Jordan recognized the deep, dark, Latino-accented voice behind him, and spun around. Leaning casually against a rock was a tall, thin man in a long, black trench coat. His black eyes flashed, reflecting the twinkling scales of the creature lying before them. "And it should make a

perfect fit, don't you think?"

Jordan stood between Gusto and the sick cryptid lying just inside the small cave. "What have you done to Nessie? And where's Eldon?" He held up the Puddle of Ripeness. "I brought what you asked for. Take it, and let me leave. With both of them."

"I don't recall asking you for anything." The strange man furrowed his brow. "As for the both of them, I have a better idea. You give me the Puddle of Ripeness, and I'll release *either* your friend—*or* the cryptid. Choose, Grimsley."

"No!" A voice rang out from inside the cave. The fur-suited crazy old man reached over Nessie, and snatched the satchel of goo from Jordan's hand. He held it over the sick creature lying at his feet. "We had a deal, Gusto!"

"Quisling, you idiot!" the dark Latino snarled. "What are you doing?"

Jordan's mind was racing. So the thin man was Areck Gusto, but why did he think this crazy old coot was thirteen-year-old Harvey Quisling?

"I'll tell you what I'm doing, you twisted goat! This is *my* cryptid, *my* zoo, and *my* chance to be somebody!"

"Listen to me very carefully," Gusto hissed. "She's nearly shed her coat. It's not part of her anymore. If you spill one drop, it'll be destroyed."

"I don't care! I spent years taking care of a cryptid!" The old man lifted the rubber water bottle over the creature's limp body. "It's high time a cryptid took care of me!"

Gusto suddenly grinned. "Harvey," he purred. "My friend, what are we doing? We're business partners, you and I. Let's negotiate. Give her a little longer. Once she's shed, I'll take her coat, and you can take the rest. You'll open your wonderful zoo— which I paid for, I'll humbly remind you—and you'll take one hundred percent of the profit. All of it, I insist."

Gusto waited for a moment as Harvey considered this. Then he leaned closer. "Or—you can follow through with this shortsighted plan and be left with nothing but the consequences of your actions. Don't do something we'll both regret, Harvey. Because I promise you this—spill a drop of that goo on my Hydro-Hide, and it'll be the last thing you ever do."

Señor Areck Gusto's eyes flashed as he glared at the wrinkled old man. Harvey's pale, bony hands trembled slightly. He glanced at Jordan, then slowly lowered the water bottle.

SWOOSH! Gusto pounced. In a blur, he had the Puddle of Ripeness in one of his clawlike hands, and Harvey's neck in the other.

"HOW DARE YOU TRY TO CROSS ME? I TOLD YOU—I DO THE THINKING AROUND HERE!" He hurled Harvey across the room, sending him tumbling in a fur-covered clump on the mossy floor. In the same swift movement, he had Jordan pinned by the neck against the wall. "And as for you, my old friend . . ." *Sniff. Sniff.* He tried to take in Jordan's scent, but picked up the nasty-smelling goo in his hand instead. He looked at the rubber sack in his other hand. *"Ugh.* This stuff had better not work as bad as it smells. Let's find out, shall we?" He lifted the bottle over Jordan's head.

"What are you doing?" Jordan exclaimed, squirming in Gusto's tight grip.

"Come now, Grimsley," Gusto said. "You didn't think I'd let you remain in the form of a child, did you? I'm not a monster." He chuckled to himself. "Did you think I'd be so easily fooled? I thought you knew me better than that, *Georgie boy*."

"What? George Grimsley is dead, you psycho! I'm his grandson!"

"Well, why don't we find out? You have, after all, conveniently brought me the very thing I need to remove your disguise, forever." Gusto tipped the bottle. Jordan struggled in his grip, straining his neck to look up and see the goo about to ooze out over his head. He shut his eyes.

SQUEEEEEEEEEE!

Nessie's pain-filled squeal interrupted them from below. Gusto stopped and looked down at her. Harvey limped up and peeked at the miniature cryptid from behind his master's trench coat. "It's happening, señor. She's molting!"

Gusto glared down at the writhing creature, then grinned as she began writhing on the mossy floor, squirming out of her shiny skin.

"No thanks to you!" Gusto shoved Harvey at Jordan, knocking them both to the ground. "We'll finish our game later, Grimsley," he said to Jordan. As Harvey scrambled to his feet, Gusto spoke to him, never taking his eyes off the dazzling coat of scales the creature was slithering free from. "Lock him up with his friend and leave me alone with the cryptid. NOW!"

Jordan moved toward Gusto. "I swear, if you hurt her—" He stopped short as Harvey stepped to Jordan, holding a small knife. Jordan decided not to fight the old man. If this was Harvey Quisling, could he change his age at will? He might be more dangerous than Jordan thought. Besides, by going along, he'd be able to make sure Eldon was all right. As Harvey marched him away from the cave and out of the molting dome, Jordan glanced back. The last thing he saw was Señor Areck Gusto grinning as he loomed over the helpless, terrified Loch Ness Monster.

28

Harvey marched Jordan into the chamber where Eldon was gassed, and then stepped through into his own office.

"What did you two do to her? If you really are a Creature Keeper, how could you?"

"No questions!" Harvey's hand was trembling as he reached for a button beside the door.

"Harvey, listen to me." Jordan stopped him from sealing off the chamber. "Gusto's using you. I don't know how you did it, but shrinking and kidnapping a cryptid isn't just bad, it's bad for business. No one will believe that sick, little, skinless reptile is the Loch Ness Monster, no matter how many T-shirts you make."

"You don't know what you're talking about!" Harvey rubbed his bald head.

Jordan glanced back to see if there was any movement through the window to the dome. "Think about it—there's no way Gusto will let Nessie live after he gets her coat. And I don't see why he'd keep us alive, either. Including you." Harvey looked at Jordan with fear in his eyes. Jordan stared back. "We can help you, Harvey. Just let me see Eldon. He'll know what to do."

Harvey was mumbling to himself nervously as he thought about this. He walked to the console of buttons on his desk. He rested a finger on a button and looked up at Jordan.

"You'll find Eldon below," he whispered. "He'll be coming around from the swamp-gas soon. Get him out of here."

"You know we can't leave here without Nessie."

"Don't be a fool! You don't know how powerful Gusto is! And now with the Hydro-Hide . . ." Harvey trailed off, mumbling to himself again. "You must go. And regroup. Then come back with everything and everyone you've got. I'll try to hold him off. But there isn't much time."

SLAM! Harvey hit the button on his desk, and Jordan dropped through the floor.

THUMP! Jordan fell, landing hard on a cold, metal surface. He stood to find himself on a large, oval platform. It was dark, but he could hear a sloshing sound. As his eyes adjusted to the darkness, he saw the platform was surrounded by water.

"*Unnnh . . .*"

Jordan spun around. Lying there on the platform a few yards away was Eldon, nearly conscious, but seemingly unhurt. Jordan rushed to his side.

"Eldon! Can you hear me?"

Eldon stirred, but didn't wake. Jordan looked

across the dark water surrounding their iron prison island, searching for a way out. Something caught his eye. Something moving in the water. A spiny shape surfaced and dived again. Then another. And another. "Alligators," Jordan said. "Why did it have to be alligators?"

A loud whir echoed through the watery chamber as a section of the wall tilted inward toward Jordan, cracking the darkness with a bright sliver of daylight. The reptiles thrashed below as the wall section lowered like a drawbridge, connecting to the platform and offering a straight path to the outside. "Looks like ol' Harvey figured out what some of those buttons are for," Jordan said. He lifted his unresponsive friend and carried him across the bridge, over the snapping reptiles.

A moment later he was at the fan boat, strapping Eldon in. He fired up the fan, then jammed the broomstick controller forward. The fan boat lurched in the shallow water before speeding out of Lost Man's Cove, away from the crypto-zoo.

Harvey Quisling took a deep breath before opening the hatch door to the humid molting dome. A million flashes of bright light met him as he pushed it open. He shielded his eyes, then refocused. Standing

before him was Señor Areck Gusto, holding Nessie's molted heap of sparkly, scaled skin. "Look at it, Quisling," he breathed. "It barely weighs anything and yet—" He moved it in his arms. The scales flipped in unison, reflecting the light and forming patterns that moved through the coat. "They're alive!"

He gently set the Hydro-Hide down and presented Harvey with a rolled-up parchment. "These are the exact specifications of what I want you to tailor for me. Do not make any mistakes or alterations, Creature Keeper, or I'll stick you right back under the rock where I found you."

"Yes, Señor Gusto."

"Do a good job and we'll forget about your recent insubordination. Now, where is Grimsley? I have some unfinished business to attend to."

Harvey swallowed hard. He took a deep breath and looked into Gusto's beady black eyes. "I . . . let him go. I let them both go."

"YOU WHAT?" In a flash, Gusto's long, bony, clawlike hands were an inch from Harvey's face, poised to tear him apart.

"We had a deal," Harvey said in a quivering voice. "I delivered what you wanted, and now you owe me the cryptid—alive, and in her proper proportion. Grimsley is my collateral. As long as we keep Nessie alive, Grimsley will come back for her. They all will. And when they do, I'll get the creature, and you'll get Grimsley."

Señor Gusto stepped back and observed the trembling old man. His lips spread, forming a thin grin across his bony face. "I may have underestimated you, Quisling. They *will* come. And when they do, I will get Grimsley. But I'll get much more. I'll get them all!"

"And I'll get Nessie," Harvey reminded him. "Per our original agreement."

Señor Areck Gusto's expression suddenly

darkened again as he gave Harvey a threatening glare. "For now, you'll get busy making my Hydro-Hide suit. I'll need it by nightfall. And it had better fit perfectly, Quisling. Or you and that doughy reptile in the other room will be gator bait."

29

Jordan carried Eldon through the Okeeyuckachokee Swamp, wishing he had his grandfather's ring to summon Bernard's assistance.

When he finally reached the site of the hidden Creature Keeper lair, he set Eldon down and pulled on the branch. The mossy trapdoor gave way beneath them and they dropped, sliding through the dark and landing at the furry feet of Bernard, who scooped them up and hugged them before Jordan knew what was happening. Through his fur, however, he heard the muffled cheers of a roomful of kids. When the smelly beast finally set them down, there were tears in his big green eyes. He pulled back and got a look at Eldon, slumped over and still

unconscious. Bernard let out a loud gasp—which was repeated by the dozens of young onlookers.

"He's okay, just swamp-gassed," Jordan said so they all could hear. "Still knocked out."

Doris rushed through the crowd wearing an old-timey doctor's stethoscope. The room fell silent as she placed it against Eldon's chest and listened. Then she pulled it off and started barking orders. "I need three of you to go up and get me some ingredients. I'll need black gum tree bark, hibiscus petals, greenbrier vine leaves—oh, and a bunch of Spanish moss. STAT!"

A few of the kids leaped into action, rushing from

the room, while a couple of the burlier ones carried Eldon to the little recovery bed. Jordan looked at Bernard, afraid of what was going to happen next. "Bernard, I know I disobeyed you, and I'm sorry—"

The giant Skunk Ape cut him off by bursting into tears. "I'm just so glad you're alive!" He scooped Jordan up in his arms again, sobbing into his hair. He set him down and wiped a snot bubble from his nose.

Jordan considered telling him about how he'd followed him to the Puddle of Ripeness and stolen from it, but decided it best not to upset the Skunk Ape further. Besides, what difference did it make, so long as Eldon was safely returned. And there was a new challenge at hand.

"They have Nessie," Jordan said. "And she's in a lot of danger. It's gonna take everything we've got to rescue her."

Bernard looked out over the wide-eyed central-command team, then back at Jordan. "We can be ready within the hour. Just tell us what you need."

As the entire base prepared for battle, Jordan debriefed Bernard from the head of the long table in the top secret secret room. He told the Skunk Ape all he knew about the fortress they were going to invade; about the strange old man who thought he was Harvey Quisling and could prove to be a reliable ally; about the powerful Señor Areck Gusto who was trying to hijack the Hydro-Hide; and most importantly about the likely whereabouts, health, and safety of Nessie.

"So she's . . . *little*?" Bernard said. "As in, she lost some weight?"

"Not exactly. She's been somehow . . . *shrunk*." He awkwardly held out his arms as wide as they could go, to illustrate just how small the mighty Loch Ness Monster had become.

"It doesn't make any sense," Bernard said. "How could this have happened?"

"It makes perfect sense, if you're willing to think the unthinkable." The voice from the doorway belonged to Eldon. He was a bit pale, with a thermometer dangling out of his mouth. Doris pulled the thermometer out, read it, and rushed out of the room.

Bernard practically leaped at Eldon and gave his Keeper a big hug. Eldon smiled at Jordan. "I believe I owe you a big Badger Ranger thank-you." He pulled one of his badges off his sash and pinned it on Jordan's shirt. It had on it a small, golden heart. "This is the highest Badger Badge there is. It's for bravery, loyalty, and friendship."

"Thank you," Jordan said, smiling down at the tiny badge. He looked up again. "What's unthinkable?"

"For a Creature Keeper to abandon his own cryptid, then put another one in danger . . . It's hard to imagine, but apparently that's exactly what Quisling's done."

"So that old man really is Harvey Quisling. But how is that possible? You said no Creature Keeper was ever over twelve or thirteen years old."

"No, I said no Creature Keeper was *currently* over twelve or thirteen years old. When your grandfather began his life's work, one of the first challenges he found was the cryptids' innate fear of men. In his travels to places where there were reported sightings, even to remote tribes and villages, he'd find it was often the children who would know where he could find them, and more importantly, how to approach them once he did. The cryptids sensed an openness in children, a curiosity and kindness that hadn't yet been corrupted. And while your grandfather possessed those traits himself, the cryptids wouldn't allow him to get close enough to sense them in him, because he was a grown man."

"So, he recruited kids?"

"Children need to be with their families," said Eldon, "not living with some Dingonek."

Bernard read Jordan's confusion. "Jungle Walrus. West African Congo," he whispered.

"Your grandfather needed to find helpers with a seemingly impossible combination—adults like himself, with a childlike wonder and openness to adventure—yet whose outward appearance matched their inner spirit. It's what brought him to this part of the world."

"He didn't come to Florida to find the Skunk Ape?" He glanced at Bernard, who shrugged.

"Your grandfather came searching for a mystery greater than any cryptid," Eldon said. "He came to find the Fountain of Youth."

Jordan's eyes grew wide.

"Unfortunately, he never found it."

"What?"

"Nope. He died before he could find the Fountain of Youth. Never found it."

"Wait, so . . . who did?"

"Me." Eldon smiled.

"You? How did you find the Fountain of Youth? Please don't say spooring."

"Your grandfather theorized that the ancient fountain most likely wouldn't be a fountain at all. Or a spring, or a pool. Not anymore, anyway. It would have been long since destroyed. He knew what would remain, if anything, would be some wellspring, maybe, deep underground. So he began studying and documenting the local plant life of the Okeeyuckachokee, looking for anything out of the ordinary."

"Like, say, a giant lemon tree growing in the middle of a swamp?"

"Bingo. He began tunneling beneath it, creating what would become this lair. But his tunneling weakened the already unstable soil system beneath the swamp. He caused sinkholes, erosion, and of course, subterranean rivers. When the heavy rains came, water would rush for miles underground, in any direction."

"One of which brought Eldon and I together," Bernard said sweetly.

"That's right. When I dived in after that old caretaker woman," Eldon continued, "it was one of your grandfather's accidental hidden rivers that carried me from his abandoned house to his underground lair."

"And into my flooded living room," Bernard added.

"Discovering a Skunk Ape in an underground

library room was a shock, but it wasn't the only secret I found there. I began reading your grandfather's writings. His records on the Okeeyuckachokee plant life, and his theories on the Fountain of Youth.

"So he discovered that the fountain was somewhere under the swamp?"

"He discovered that the fountain *was* the swamp. Its water was *everywhere*. A tiny bit in nearly every living thing that grows here. A drop squeezed from the lobed leaves of an oakleaf hydrangea, a molecule from the stamen of a swamp hibiscus flower. From the top of the highest cypress tree to the deepest root of—"

"A giant lemon tree." Jordan was catching on. "And in its lemons, too."

"That's right. All around us, hiding in plain sight. All we had to figure out was how to extract it. And as it happened . . ." Eldon pointed out another Badger Badge on his sash—a little cactus next to a drop of water.

"C'mon," Jordan said. "A Fountain of Youth badge? Really?"

"Water extraction. A fairly helpful survival skill, actually."

"So that's the elixir—the stuff those lab kids

squeeze out of the soil down here. You called it 'swamp medicine.' You said it helps the creatures stay hidden."

"And it does," Eldon said. "But it's not for the creatures. It's for the Keepers."

"They're old people? Made young?"

"Not just them. The dedicated workers here at headquarters, too. Jordan, you and I are the only people down here who aren't over eighty or ninety years old. Every member of our organization was left behind and alone—all forgotten souls living out their days in your grandfather's old, abandoned house. But they were young at heart, with lots of living left to do. They were the ones who deserved another go-around. So I asked them if they'd like to help."

"You said my grandfather's house had become an orphanage."

"You assumed that's what I meant, and I let you. It was an old folks' home, run by that awful woman. I squatted there, sneaking around to help them, working toward my Community Badge. It was an odd situation, but we were an odd family."

Jordan thought of everyone he'd met, all the dedicated "kids" he'd watched as they worked at Creature Keepers headquarters. Then he thought of something else. "So, Alistair . . . ?"

"In his late eighties, the old coot," Eldon said. "Harvey, too, until recently."

"How did that traitorous toad manage to grow old so quickly?" Bernard said.

"He must have stopped taking his elixir, aging as he stashed it away. Who knows how long it took him to revert to his proper age."

"Hope it was slow and painful," Bernard said.

"But why would he give up his youth?"

"Gosh, I guess for the reasons most grown-ups do. For stuff he considered more valuable. Wealth, success, fame."

"His crypto-zoo," Jordan said. "He somehow gave the elixir to Nessie that night in the cave. It's the only way he could've kidnapped her."

"It was incredibly reckless of him," Eldon said. "We're lucky she's alive. There's no telling how a cryptid might have reacted to the Fountain of Youth. It's never been done."

"And that's why he needed to get his hands on my Puddle of Ripeness," Bernard said.

Eldon stepped up and put his hand on his big friend's furry shoulder. "And you stayed true to your sacred duty to protect it, even in exchange for my freedom. I know how hard that must've been for you, old friend. But it was the right decision."

Jordan felt a sudden, sick feeling in his stomach.

"Sorry. Not to be a dimwit, but what *exactly* does this ripey puddle stuff do, again?"

"It doesn't matter, because Bernard kept them from getting hold of it," Eldon said. "Besides, we're running out of time. The latest reports we're getting in show that the North Sea is beginning to surge, causing flooding in ports of Rotterdam, Antwerp, and Hamburg. It hasn't hit the Atlantic . . . yet. Right now we need to save Nessie—as well as Harvey. He may be a turncoat, but he's still a Creature Keeper."

Jordan's stomach was doing belly flops. Things were happening too fast. He knew he should tell them about stealing from the Puddle of Ripeness. He opened his mouth, but Eldon spoke before he could find the words.

"Jordan—you know that fortress better than anyone. You're the only one who's met Gusto face-to-face. And you convinced Harvey to let you rescue me. You're our best hope for success. Will you lead us into battle and help us save the Loch Ness Monster?"

Jordan glanced down at the Badger Badge on his shirt. He felt neither brave nor loyal as he looked back up at the hopeful, confident faces of Eldon and Bernard.

He found the strength to say just one word.

"Yes."

30

When it was in operation, the S.S. *Peek-A-Boo* puttered around the perimeter of the swamp, her glass-bottom floor allowing tourists to stare past their flip-flops and sensible walking shoes at schools of fish or underwater plant life. But like the fan boat, it hadn't been taken out in years.

So it was a slight miracle when, after a few attempts and a sudden belch of black smoke, the S.S. *Peek-A-Boo* started up and slowly pulled out of the hidden boathouse on Ponce de Leon Bay. Bernard was captaining the boat, and crammed on board behind him was the entire Creature Keeper crew. Every last kid from the lemon-tree lair had come out on this rescue mission, and these passengers

were as battle ready as they could be, given the fact that they had no weapons, no fighting skills, and weren't used to being up past their bedtimes. It would be nightfall by the time they reached Lost Man's Cove to raid the crypto-zoo and save Nessie, and while that wasn't much to cling to, everyone hoped it would help a bit.

Jordan had explained the layout of the crypto-zoo to everyone on the dock before boarding. They had two more things going for them: greater numbers and the element of surprise. The only thing that worried Jordan was Harvey's console of buttons. He wasn't sure what tricks Harvey still had at his fingertips, or even whose side he was really on.

Harvey had helped Jordan once, but he wasn't going to count on his help again. The Keeper kids would circle the building, climb the structure, and surround it completely before anyone knew they were there. With nowhere for Gusto or Harvey to hide, they'd have to give up Nessie—hopefully without a fight.

Leading the way in the fan boat, Jordan sat atop the captain's tower, with Eldon standing beside him. As they approached Lost Man's Cove, Jordan cut the engine and coasted toward the crypto-zoo in the distance. Then they sat and waited along with the S.S. *Peek-A-Boo* for dark.

Eldon smiled at Jordan and closed his eyes, still

groggy from the effects of the gas. Jordan was anything but sleepy. He still couldn't shake his guilt about giving away the Puddle of Ripeness. After a couple of minutes, he just couldn't keep quiet anymore.

"Eldon," he began, trying to sound like he was making conversation to pass the time. "What would happen if, say, Harvey and Gusto ended up getting their hands on that puddle stuff?"

Eldon yawned. "Super-duper dangerous. Downright destructive. Good ol' Bernard. I don't envy him the choice he had to make. I'm really proud of him."

"Yeah. He sure came through for us." Jordan began to sweat, and chuckled nervously. "But let's just say, y'know, that we had given Harvey the puddle. What *exactly* could it do, exactly?"

"Jeez, Jordan," Eldon said, opening one eye. "Curiosity killed the cat, remember?"

Jordan smiled faintly at this horrible choice of phrase. Eldon continued, "It's basically the antidote to the Fountain of Youth. With a once-a-year dose of the youth elixir, we can de-age a person and keep them as young as they want for as long as they want. But just one drop of that nasty Puddle of Ripeness will violently and painfully restore a person to their proper chronological age—in a matter of minutes."

Jordan's mouth went dry. "Oh, no . . ." He looked across the water at the glass-bottom boat. It was growing dark, and he could just make out all the kids getting ready for action. Bernard waved to Jordan and pointed at the horizon. Jordan saw the setting sun casting a long shadow over the bay. "No, no, no, no!" Jordan waved back to Bernard.

"Jordan, what's wrong with you?"

"We have to get them out of here. This is a trap! We have to warn them!"

Jordan stood on the tower waving his arms wildly to Bernard on the other boat. Suddenly, a surge of water between the two crafts began bubbling beneath the surface.

Jordan turned to Eldon. "I didn't know. I had to save you. I didn't think it would matter."

"Jordan. What are you talking about?"

"I gave it to them. I gave them the Puddle of Ripeness."

"You *what?*"

WHOOOOOSH! The top-heavy fan boat teetered violently as something big suddenly rose from the water with a powerful surge between the two small crafts. It pushed the little fan boat toward the shore, tipping it over. Jordan and Eldon scrambled over the metal bars, leaning with all their weight to try to right the clunky vessel.

It was a submarine. Long and large, it breached the surface, sending waves out in every direction. It had bubble windows along the side and a large, oval, flat-topped turret on top. This was the oval platform Jordan and Eldon were trapped on beneath the crypto-zoo. The space beneath the crypto-zoo wasn't just a roomy basement, or even an alligator-infested water-dungeon. It was a submarine garage.

A hatch on top of the turret slammed open. All was silent as the water began to calm again. Señor Areck Gusto climbed out of the top of the sub. He stood grinning atop the platform, wrapped in

his long, black trench coat. He waved down to the glass-bottom boat, now drifting dangerously close to him.

From their near-beached and tipped-over fan boat, Jordan and Eldon could see both the submarine and the glass-bottom boat in the deeper water. Helplessly, Jordan watched as Gusto addressed the frightened, huddled Keeper kids on the S.S. *Peek-A-Boo*.

"Greetings, Creature Keepers!" Gusto called out. "You all look so excited to be out of your safe little swamp burrow for the first time in, what? Years? Decades? We'll soon find out!"

"What do you want?" Bernard yelled up at the

sub. The water had grown still again and the sound carried easily in the calm night air. Jordan could imagine Bernard's dilemma—wanting to leap onto the sub to throttle that skinny weasel, but not wanting to leave his crew behind. Eldon was trying to start the waterlogged engine but wasn't having any luck.

"I don't want anything to do with your putrid hide, Stink Monkey," Gusto sneered. "I'm interested in your passengers. I'd like to see who they really are!" He pulled from his trench-coat pocket a green, glowing orb, the same vile color as the Puddle of Ripeness. He held up the ball and smiled down on them. "You're outside getting some fresh air; whaddya say we play some catch, kids! It's such a fun game for everyone—*young and old*!"

He reached back and hurled the sphere at the S.S. *Peek-A-Boo. POOM!* It exploded into a ball of thick, green gas. Laughing a horrible laugh, he threw another. *POOM!* It burst at the other end of the glass-bottom boat, engulfing everyone on board in the thick, putrid smoke.

"NO!" Jordan yelled over the screams and explosions. He looked down at Eldon, who was staring across the water, frozen in shock. "We've got to do something!"

Eldon looked back at the crypto-zoo. "Nessie might still be in there somewhere. Quisling, too."

"Okay. You go for them, I'll swim out toward the others. But Eldon—" The two boys looked each other in the eye. "Just promise me you'll save Nessie first."

Eldon dived toward the shore. Jordan hit the water and began swimming toward the S.S. *Peek-A-Boo. POOM!* Another ripeness bomb went off. *POOM! POOM!*

"HA-HA-HA!" Gusto's laughter echoed over the still water. Even swimming as fast as he could, Jordan felt like he was getting no closer at all to the horrible scene. But he could make out the tall Latino's lanky body atop the submarine, looking down on his victims.

He could hear him, too. And what he heard sent a chill down his spine. "Now, then," Gusto snarled. "I'm looking for George Grimsley. One of you has to be my old friend, but I'm afraid you old folk all look the same to me. C'mon, George, don't be a coward! Show yourself and I'll spare your crewmates any more suffering!" He snapped his clawlike fingers as he thought of something. "Ooh! I know what's got you so shy, Georgie boy! You want me to show my new skin, too, is that it? Fair enough!"

Jordan stopped swimming. He stared up and

across the water as Gusto threw off his trench coat. A blinding light shot out—twinkling and sparkling from his body in every direction. It was dizzying to stare at, and yet Jordan couldn't look away. He was wearing Nessie's Hydro-Hide. It had been fashioned into a tight-fitting body suit, like a second skin.

Gusto posed for a moment, grinning down at the glass-bottom boat. "Well? You still won't show yourself and spare your friends, Grimsley? Very well. Because of your cowardice, they'll suffer your fate, as well."

"*NO!*" Jordan's cry from the water went unheard as Gusto suddenly leaped into the air, twenty, thirty, forty feet, then—*SPLASH!*—hit the water like a comet crashing into the Earth. His body of light plunged deep into the cove. The water around the submarine and the S.S. *Peek-A-Boo* immediately began to swirl. Round and round, faster and faster, it formed a giant whirlpool. Both the submarine and the glass-bottom boat were pulled into a crazy circle, drawing closer to the center.

Jordan was also swept up and could hear the cries onboard the *Peek-A-Boo*. They were not the cries of children. They were the moans of elderly people.

FLOOOOOOSSSHHHH!

The descending whirlpool suddenly reversed course, acting like a massive water cannon. It blasted a solid funnel of water straight up into the air. The glass-bottom boat was nearly upended by the huge spout. Jordan was tossed and tumbled by the sudden blast. Dancing high atop the gushing geyser, in his sparkling Hydro-Hide suit, was Señor Areck Gusto, looking like a fallen angel.

31

"NOW WILL YOU SHOW YOURSELF, GEORGE GRIMSLEY?"

Gusto's voice bellowed across Lost Man's Cove from his watery perch as the S.S. *Peek-A-Boo* floated silently below. Gusto saw his submarine had been tipped onto its side from the deluge, and was beginning to sink. The scales on his Hydro-Hide flickered and shimmered, and he leaped into the air. The moment he broke contact with the spout, it collapsed, cascading to the surface. Gusto dived alongside it, racing the falling water back into the bay.

SPLOOOSH! As soon as he plunged into the cove, a large wave rose up like a great liquid fist, lifting the submarine high above the waterline and crashing it back down. Now upright, the sub bobbed in its own wake for a moment. Gusto appeared from inside again, slamming open the hatch as before, and stepping out onto the deck. He was carrying something large in his arms.

Squeeeeeee! The tiny Nessie's soft, new skin looked slick and raw in the moonlight. She seemed dangerously vulnerable without her scales, especially in the clutches of such a powerful kidnapper. Gusto lifted her above his head and addressed them again.

"I offer you one last chance, George Grimsley! Come and sacrifice yourself in the Hall of the Chupacabra! I trust your old and feeble memory can still guide you there. If you do not come and lay yourself at my feet before the next full moon, your cowardice will cost you that which you have vowed to protect!"

Squeeeeeee!

"No!" Jordan yelled out. "I'm here! I'm the one you want!" His cries went unheard, drowned out by Gusto's booming bellow:

"CANNONBALL!"

With Nessie in his arms, Gusto leaped from his perch and plunged into the water. For a moment everything was calm. Suddenly, a strong undertow pulled out to sea, as if Gusto was dragging the water away with him. Jordan had seen this before. He knew what came next.

"Get down! Take cover!" He looked back at the shoreline. The water was quickly drawing out to sea, just like Loch Ness, pulling him, the sub, and the glass-bottom boat out with it. He looked back toward the horizon. A massive mountain of water was rearing up at the entrance to Lost Man's Cove. It rose higher and higher above them. Just as it was about to topple, Jordan dived as deep as he could

under the surface of the water.

KERRRRRSPLOOOOOSSSSHHH! The avalanche of water crashed down, tossing all three vessels like they were toys. It violently pounded the shore, demolishing the crypto-zoo, uprooting its cypress stilts, and flooding the coastline.

Jordan was tossed around underwater like a sock monkey in a washing machine. When he finally came up for air, it took him a moment to get his bearings. He spotted the S.S. *Peek-A-Boo* on shore, upended in the flooded inland area of the swamp. The glass-bottom boat leaned awkwardly on its side against a thick cypress tree.

Jordan swam, then waded, straight toward it. The boat's see-through floor faced him like a large glass wall. He feared the worst, until he saw some shadows moving through the muddy glass. The figures were huddled together, some helping others. The thick, muck-covered glass seemed to distort their features: their bodies appeared more hunched, their bellies thicker, their faces sagging. Of course, Jordan knew this was no distortion.

A hulking, black shape suddenly stepped up behind them. Bernard's thick arms pushed the boat toward Jordan, off the tree. *SPLASH!* The S.S. *Peek-A-Boo* hit the shallow floodwater, soaking

Jordan and revealing the shockingly transformed Keeper crew.

Not one of them appeared younger than eighty. Many were bald or balding, and the ones who weren't had heads of gray, thinning hair. They stood hunched over in wet, undersized clothing, and stared at Jordan with wrinkled, saggy faces. He stared back, feeling as bad as he'd ever felt.

He opened his mouth to say something, but was suddenly interrupted by a loud, whirring motor. The fan boat drifted across the shallow floodwaters up to the S.S. *Peek-A-Boo*. Eldon scanned the sad, old faces. But rather than show sympathy, he was very businesslike, like a true troop leader after a fiercely lost battle.

"Is everyone accounted for?" he asked Bernard. "Anyone hurt?"

"It's a miracle, but we all made it," Bernard said. "A few bumps and bruises, but everyone's in good shape. Relatively speaking."

"Okay, then let's figure our next move," Eldon said. "We've got to get out of this area. There was a Chupacabra sighting the other night—"

The elderly people gasped as they scanned the trees and shadows. Eldon did his best to calm them down. "I'm sure he's not in the area after the

drubbing Bernard gave him, but we can't be too safe. Bernard, I need you to get everyone back to the base immediately." He looked at their sad and frightened faces. "I know this is scary and painful. The aftereffects of the Puddle of Ripeness aren't pleasant, but I promise you the worst is over. When you get back to base, Bernard will give you each a full dose of elixir, but no more. Your bodies are older now. You have to ease back into this. It will take some time, but we'll get you all young again."

Bernard began helping the elderly back onto the S.S. *Peek-A-Boo* as Eldon checked the fuel on the fan boat. Jordan waded over to him but before he could speak, Eldon hollered over his head. "Bernard, I have enough gas to make it up the coast. I'm going to take it as far as I can, then find some way to head north."

"North?" Bernard asked. "Where are you going?"

"To get us some backup. We're gonna need muscle, as well as airpower."

"Oh, no. Not those two . . . ," Bernard said.

"I've never asked anything of them before. But then, we've never been in a situation like this before. Harvey Quisling did the unthinkable—giving Nessie the elixir could've killed her. I don't know what the effect will be, or how much time we have. We have to move fast and find her."

Jordan waded toward the fan boat. "Where is Quisling? Did you find him?"

Eldon answered Jordan without looking him in the eye. "He was tied to the outside of the building. I released him just in time. But when the floodwaters hit, I couldn't hold on to him. He was swept away. I don't know if he survived or not."

Jordan had a horrible feeling in his stomach. "What can I do? Bernard's got the others. I could come with you."

Eldon looked at him with an expression that seemed genuinely surprised. "You've done enough, Jordan. I think it'd be best if you went back to your family." He climbed into the captain's chair and revved the engine. He zoomed off, leaving Jordan feeling worse than he did even a minute ago.

He looked up sadly and found Bernard's big, friendly face. The Skunk Ape nodded toward the boat, and Jordan sloshed over and climbed aboard. He sat down, ignoring the angry glares. Some refused to look at him. Others stared off with shocked or sad looks in their eyes. But not one of them spoke.

As Bernard began to push the boat through the shallow waters of the flooded swamp toward their home beneath the lemon tree, Jordan shut his eyes and tried not to cry.

"How's your head feel, dearie?"

Jordan popped open his eyes. He'd fallen asleep, but only for a minute. Cypress trees and swamp plants were drifting by as they floated through the inner swamp. He heard a rhythmic sloshing behind him, Bernard wading through the flooded Okeeyuckachokee as he pushed them along. Sitting beside Jordan was a very old woman. She took his hand and smiled at him. She turned his hand so it was palm up. Then she suddenly poked it with a sharp stick.

"Ow!"

She put her other hand on Jordan's forehead. "No nerve damage; vital signs seem normal. I was worried with your recent concussion, and then being thrashed underwater . . . well, anyway, you seem fine."

She stood with some effort and turned to shuffle away, stopping when she heard Jordan utter her name. "Doris?" The old woman turned back and he looked her in the eye. "It is you," he said, his eyes tearing up. "I—I'm so sorry."

Doris sat down beside him again and took his hand. "It's okay, dearie," she said. "I'm just glad everyone's alive, and still together. That's all that matters."

Jordan didn't feel any better. He kept thinking about Eldon. "You've known Eldon for a long time. Do you think he'll ever forgive me?"

"I suppose if he could forgive me, he can forgive anyone."

"What do you mean?"

"Let's just say, when we first met, I wasn't very nice to him." She gestured toward the others on the boat. "To any of them. And I got what I had comin' to me. I would've throttled him that night, if I'd gotten my hands on him. Instead, I fell through those cellar stairs to what should've been a well-deserved, proper drowning. But after all the horrible things I'd done, he dived right in after me. And everyone thinks I'm the weird one."

"You're the caretaker! Eldon told me he never saw you again!"

"Well, in a way, I suppose that's true. That was the last time anyone saw this wrinkly old prune of a face. 'Til tonight, anyway. I swallowed a lot of water when I got sucked under that house and flushed beneath that swamp. And when I popped out the other side, well, let's just say the near-death experience took years off my life."

"The Fountain of Youth."

"When Eldon found me, he didn't just see that I'd gotten younger on the outside. He recognized something good in me, on the inside. He saved me that night, but not by diving in after me. He saved me by forgiving me, and offering me a second chance."

The old, gray, balding heads began to turn around to listen to the two of them. Doris looked up at them. "Truth is," she said, "he saved all of us."

32

SLLLUUURRP! As the sunrise began to paint the morning sky pink overhead, the loud, draining sound was the first clue that something wasn't right. That, and how the waters were getting shallower as the S.S. *Peek-A-Boo* began picking up speed.

Bernard was suddenly working harder pulling on the boat he'd been pushing all night. He dug in his feet, but the boat began drifting faster, as if being pulled by some invisible force toward the great lemon tree.

A moment later, they were faced with a horrible sight. The lemon tree was gone. Where the massive trunk once stood was now a gigantic sinkhole, draining the entire swamp. The floodwaters that

began with Gusto's big exit had drained to this spot, and were rapidly swirling to form a wide whirlpool, as if someone had pulled the lemon tree out of the ground like a plug in the bottom of a bathtub. What was even worse to consider was where all that water was draining.

"HOLD ON, EVERYONE!" Bernard yelled from outside the rear of the boat. He clutched the back rail as they got caught up in the churning rapids and rounded the outer rim of the massive suckhole. The Skunk Ape looked around frantically for something to grab on to. He knew the swamp like the fur on the front of his hand—where every tree, vine, and shrub should be—but everything he knew had been submerged, swept away, or sucked down the sinkhole.

Each time they rounded the swirling spiral, they picked up speed and drew closer to the deadly center. It was impossible to imagine the destruction all of that water was doing below, and there was no time for Jordan to mourn the loss of Grampa Grimsley's creation and the artifacts it held. They were out of control and about to be flushed into a swirling vortex—something had to be done.

Jordan jumped onto the back of his seat and leaped from the boat, grabbing a vine hanging from the high branch of a cypress tree on the edge of the whirlpool. The other passengers, assuming he was abandoning them to save himself, began yelling very unpleasant things, calling him all sorts of inappropriate names.

Jordan swung overhead, examining the tree holding his vine. He yelled down to Bernard, who had climbed up onto the back of the boat. "Bernard!

Up here! Grab the vine!"

Bernard shook his head. "No! A captain always goes down with his ship!"

Captain? Bernard was choosing the worst time ever to pull rank on him, while failing to see the genius of Jordan's plan. The boat sped around the whirlpool again, dipping closer to the center. He had one shot at this—by the next go-round, Bernard would be out of reach. Moving quickly, Jordan tied the end of the vine into a lasso, thankful that he paid attention to Eldon's handiwork on their bunny-balloon ride. As the S.S. *Peek-A-Boo* came around, Jordan hurled the vine lasso straight at the cryptid's burly neck. *SPROING!* It caught him around his thick, furry mane, and Bernard instinctively grabbed the vine above him to keep from choking as he was lifted off the deck.

As the boat made its final pass before it would be sucked down the center of the drain hole, Bernard's massive weight and crazed flailing began to pull on the tree trunk. It leaned inward with a loud *CREEEEEAAAAAK.* . . . Then it fell. "TIMBER!" Jordan shouted.

KER-SPLASH! The tall tree fell across the center of the whirlpool, forming a bridge as its top reached the other side. *WHUMP!* The boat came around and slammed against the tree, jammed by the force of the water. Beneath the boat, Jordan and Bernard hung from the vine, dangling over the gaping mouth of the sinkhole. Jordan was above Bernard, and could see Doris helping the others off the boat, across the tree-trunk bridge and onto safe land.

Jordan climbed up the vine and reached the trunk just as the last of them stepped to safety. He heard another loud *CREEEEAAAAAK!* The glass-bottom boat was beginning to crack from the force of the water pushing it against the tree trunk. He jumped out of the way just as the boat broke in half and slipped under the tree, disappearing down the hole. Bernard swung out on the vine just in time to miss getting slammed by the S.S. *Peek-A-Boo*. Then he began trying to pull himself up the fraying vine.

"C'mon, Bernard!" Jordan cried out. "You can do it!" Jordan lay flat on the tree trunk, pulling on the vine with all his might. As Bernard got closer, Jordan stretched out his arm as far as he could. Bernard raised his paw toward Jordan's hand. They reached closer . . . closer . . . *SNAP!*

The vine gave way. Bernard dropped, swallowed up by the vortex. He was gone.

"Noooooooooo!" Jordan screamed. He stared into the abyss where his friend had disappeared. He couldn't believe it. *CREEEAAAAAK!* The tree shifted as it started to give way, snapping him out of his trance. Through tear-filled eyes he saw Doris and the others yelling from the edge of the whirl-pool, frantically waving at him to cross. Glancing down once more into the swirling crater that took his friend, Jordan forced himself to stand. He ran across the trunk and dived onto the marshy swamp floor, just as the base of the tree slipped into the whirlpool.

Jordan sat at the edge and stared at the center of the whirlpool for a long time, watching the water slow to a gentle, circular current. It finally stopped, leaving his grandfather's underground lair filled to the brim, forming a calm, tranquil pool where the great lemon tree once stood. For Jordan, it was a sad but peaceful resting place for his dear friend, Bernard.

After a while, Doris sat down next to him. She put a gentle hand on his shoulder. "I'm so sorry, dearie," she said softly. "He was a great friend. To all of us."

"I was his Creature Keeper while Eldon was away. He was my responsibility."

"The two of you saved us. Wherever he is, he's happy we're all still here."

Jordan turned. Standing behind him, soaking and shivering, were the fifty elderly survivors of the tragic sinking of the S.S. *Peek-A-Boo*. Many of them were crying softly, and Jordan realized he wasn't the only one who would miss Bernard. He also realized that sitting there feeling sorry for himself was just the opposite of what his giant, smelly friend would do.

He stood up. "C'mon, everyone. Let's go."

"Where are we going?" Doris asked.

"You're going home."

Mr. and Mrs. Grimsley stood arm in arm in the front hall, admiring the refinished wooden staircase, the freshly painted hallway, and the completely made-over living room. "I have to hand it to us, Betsy," Mr. Grimsley said. "In just a little over one short week, we transformed a run-down, beat-up, abandoned fixer-upper into a beautiful home. We really tackled this challenge . . . together."

Mrs. Grimsley grinned at her husband. "It's more beautiful than I ever could've imagined," she said. "Now all it needs are visitors, to come and enjoy the fruits of our labor!"

Ding-dong! The newly installed, two-toned harmonious door chime in the key of G major soothingly alerted them that someone was at the door. They opened it, together.

Standing on the front step was Jordan—worn, wet, and ragged. Behind him were fifty or so very soggy senior citizens, looking not much better.

"Hi, Mom and Dad. Place looks great. Got any long-term vacancies available?"

33

Jordan stood in the sun-filled backyard. The grass was perfectly manicured, the flower patch was colorful and vibrant, and the freshly painted garden gnome stood watch over a robust herb garden by

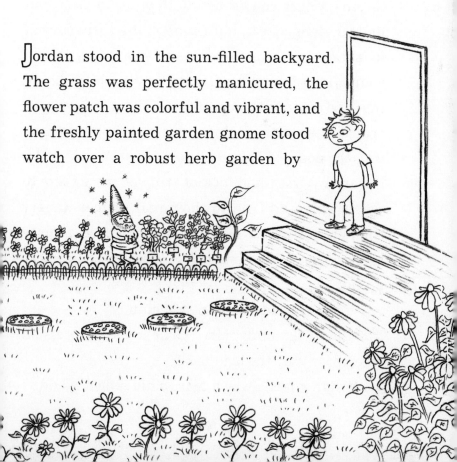

the kitchen door. This was not the same backyard Jordan stepped into just a week ago.

His attention drifted to a small, bubbling fountain installed near the wall separating the yard from the Okeeyuckachokee Swamp. He stared at the gurgling water sadly.

"Hey there, pal!" Jordan jumped at the sound of his father, who was suddenly standing right next to him. "Sorry if I startled ya—I just wanted to say how proud I am of you. Not only for tackling the challenges you needed to in order to pass your Badger Ranger test, but for applying them so well in a real-life situation. Thank heavens you and your fellow Rangers on that Badgeroobilee heard the distress call from that sinking retirement cruise ship! With all this rogue-wave madness hitting the coast of Europe, those old folks are lucky it wasn't worse—and luckier still you were there to save them! And then to show real Badger Ranger community-service skills by offering them a place to stay here? Your mom and I couldn't be more proud."

"Thanks, Dad," Jordan said glumly.

"Hey, champ." Mr. Grimsley's expression changed. "Why the long face?"

Jordan wiped away a tear so his father wouldn't

see. "It's . . . a friend of mine. He . . . didn't make it, Dad."

"Oh, no." Mr. Grimsley put an arm around Jordan. "That must be hard, son." He hesitated a moment. "But not everyone can become a Badger Ranger. I'm sure your friend's happy you made it through Badger training. And I'll bet he's proud to have a friend who's such a shining example of everything a Badger Ranger stands for: bravery, community—and friendship."

Jordan looked at the Badger Badge on his shirt.

"Besides," his father continued. "There's always next year. Your friend can try out again then!" Mr. Grimsley held up his to-do clipboard and beamed. "Now, then. Don't know if you noticed, but your mom and I have been busy taking care of business."

"Yeah, I noticed. The place looks really awesome, Dad."

Mr. Grimsley flipped through the reams of checked-off chores. "Don't worry, though. I didn't forget *our* project. See?" He flipped to a page and found the only chore that wasn't crossed out: *CUT BACK SWAMP ON BACKYARD WALL.*

"I promised you we'd tackle this challenge togeth—" Mr. Grimsley was looking at the far wall.

He turned to Jordan. "You tackled it all by yourself! That's the Grimsley in ya!"

Mr. Grimsley dramatically crossed the item off his list, slapped Jordan on the back, and marched inside. Jordan looked at the wall. His father was right—the snarled, weedy swamp growth that had been creeping over it like a giant squid was completely gone. Jordan knew he hadn't cut all that swamp growth off the backyard wall. And if his parents hadn't done it, who had?

"Hey, you brainless guppie." Jordan spun around to find Abbie glaring at him, arms crossed and eyebrows furrowed. "We need to talk."

"Sure. Hey, did you trim the weeds back here?"

"What? No. I've been in charge of your lemonade stand, remember?"

"Oh, right. You'll be happy to hear that you won't have to do that anymore."

Abbie's expression suddenly flashed a hint of disappointment, which she quickly tried to cover. "Oh. Well, I've been doing it all week. So I might as well finish doing it the last few days of our cruddy vacation." Jordan gave her a strange look. "What?" she snapped. "It's not like I like doing it. I'm doing you a favor. Don't forget that."

"Okay . . . but I'm afraid you *can't* do it anymore.

The lemons are . . . gone."

"Well, get some more." Abbie seemed more than a little irked about the thought of losing her lemonade-stand duties.

"I can't. They weren't just any lemons. They were, uh, *extra*-organic."

"Ha! I knew it! I knew there was something about those lemons! They're vitamin boosted, or enchanted, or biologically mutated somehow, aren't they? Every day you were gone, a bag of those supercharged lemons mysteriously showed up on our doorstep. And every day I used 'em, following your dorky friend's dorky instructions—and the old people went crazy on the stuff!"

"Crazy? Crazy how?"

"Like, they had all this energy, like they were young even though they were old, which was actually cool because they weren't boring like normal old people. They were actually interesting and had the best stories, like when Mr. Truitt told me about his time in the circus, after the war, when he—" Abbie stopped herself. Jordan narrowed his eyes at Abbie's oversharing. Abbie never overshared. Abbie never regular-shared.

Embarrassed, she grabbed Jordan's collar. "Tell me what's going on—now."

Jordan smiled. For the first time, he wasn't afraid of her. He'd been chased through a swamp at night by a Chupacabra—what could she do to him? She let go and looked at him closer. "You seem less twerpy. It's like you've . . . changed."

"Yeah, there's been a lot of that going around. C'mon. I wanna show you something."

34

Jordan helped Abbie through the opening in the wall and led her into the Okeeyuckachokee Swamp. As she took it all in, he noticed something was different. The vegetation seemed smaller. He spun around and looked back at the wall separating the swamp from his backyard. Sure enough, the plants *had shrunk*. He crouched down at the base of the wall. The thick, overgrown tangle of vines that had once climbed up and over the wall had regressed, turning back into little sprouts.

"All that elixir that was kept in the lemon tree lair," he said. "It was wiped out by the floodwaters and must've been reabsorbed into the soil."

"Stop that," Abbie said. "Stop being weirder than me."

Jordan dashed past his sister, running as fast as he could, deeper into the swamp. *"Hey!"* she shouted, and chased after him.

They reached the small, tranquil lake left by the whirlpool, where the lemon tree once stood. Abbie was frantically catching her breath as she tried her best to yell at him. "What's your problem, you spaz?"

"That's it," he said, pointing out to the middle of the pool. "When the lair flooded, the Fountain of Youth elixir must've shrunk the great lemon tree!"

"You just said, 'lair,' 'Fountain of Youth,' and 'elixir' in the same sentence. You know who talks like that? Wizards and weirdos. And you're no wizard."

"You said yourself there was something special about those lemons. Well, you were right. And this is where they came from."

"A big puddle?"

"There was a massive lemon tree here. Its roots soaked up the Fountain of Youth water in the soil; then it released tiny amounts into each of its lemons. The lemonade you made from those lemons had just enough of the Fountain of Youth water in them to keep the residents of Waning Acres active and healthy."

"So where'd this lemon tree of youth go?"

"It must've been *de-aged*. There were millions of bottles of the elixir stored underground. When the flood waters came crashing in and spilled them, all that elixir returned to the soil. The tree, the vines, any vegetation that soaked it up have shrunk back into seeds or saplings."

"Or . . . this is just a normal little pond, and you're totally messing with me."

Bloop! A bubble burped from the center of the still water. What looked like a leafy bundle of sticks emerged from the depths. Jordan grabbed a long branch from the shore and pulled it to the edge. It was the lemon tree sapling, downsized and uprooted. A few green leaves and budding flowers were on it, as well as a couple of marble-sized lemons. He showed it to his sister.

"Okay, so you're *elaborately* messing with me. I'm slightly impressed but not amused."

Bloop! Another bubble. A rectangular object floated toward the shore. Abbie pulled it out by its handle. "Wait. I've seen this before." She set the suitcase on the muddy shore and opened it up. She pulled out Grampa Grimsley's black, furry Skunk

Ape mask and looked at Jordan. "I don't understand," she said, looking back at the suitcase, a bit dazed by all of this. "How did you— How did this . . . get down there?"

"*Down there* is Grampa Grimsley's lair. He created it years ago. It was the home of the Creature Keepers—protectors of the cryptids of the world. Dedicated to help, hide, and hoax."

"*Cryptids?*" Abbie looked down at the Skunk Ape mask in her hand. "Okay. I don't know how you planned all of this. But Mom said cryptids aren't real."

"Pff! Your *mom* ain't real!" A gruff voice from above startled the two of them, forcing them to look up. Hanging upside down from a high tree branch was a red wad of muscles. The creature also had black, beady eyes, horns on its head, little pointed ears, and a pointed tail. It let go of the branch with its hooved legs and flipped right-side up. Two small, black, batlike wings unfolded and fluttered frantically, barely delivering the bulky, muscle-bound creature to the ground. It landed awkwardly but recovered with attitude, glaring at Abbie. "Drink me in, sweet stuff. I'm about as real as it gets."

Abbie screamed. Jordan ran to her, crouching down between his sister and the red demon-creature.

He still had the lemon tree sapling in his hand, and was waving it around ridiculously as if it were a weapon. *"Stay back! You hear me?"*

"HAW-HAW!" The creature laughed, its quivering red lips flashing a row of tiny, daggerlike, sharp teeth. It turned and yelled to the base of the tree it had just alighted from. "Yo, Eldon! I thought you said this kid was a Grimsley!"

Eldon stepped out from behind the tree. Its trunk cast a thick shadow, and for a second Abbie thought she saw something else stir within it.

"He is a Grimsley, Lou," Eldon said. "More than

anyone here, it turns out." He reached down and helped Jordan up. "I heard what you did for the others."

"Then you must've heard about Bernard, too," Jordan said sadly. "He's gone."

Eldon nodded, then scratched his head, as if trying to remember something. "Although . . . if Bernard's gone, then who was it that told me what you did?"

"Wasn't me, boss," the red creature said, picking something out of his teeth. Abbie was staring at him with a look of slightly disgusted horror on her face.

"Gosh, how rude of me." Eldon gestured toward her. "Lou, I'd like to introduce Abigail Grimsley. And this is her brother, Jordan Grimsley, grandkids of the great George Grimsley. Guys, this is Lou. The Jersey Devil."

"Sorry if I got too real back there. That's kinda my thing. Keepin' it real, I mean."

Jordan remembered his first encounter with a real, live cryptid and hoped he didn't look as stupid then as Abbie did now. He looked at Eldon. "Hey, what did you mean when you said—"

Bloop! BRAAAP!

They all turned to the pool. This time the burping bubbles revealed a shiny, golden object. At first

Jordan thought it might be his grandfather's urn. He heard it again. *BRAAAP!* It didn't sound like an urn. He knew that sound.

It was a tuba. Specifically, it was Bernard's tuba. And it was rising out of the water. And it was being played—horribly. There was only one Skunk Ape Jordan knew who played as horribly as that. *BRAAAAAAP!* Jordan dived into the water.

"Bernard!" The Skunk Ape moved the tuba to reveal he was wearing his diver's mask and scuba tank. Jordan swam up to him and hugged him. He was so happy he didn't even notice that the only thing smellier than a Skunk Ape was a wet Skunk Ape.

"You're alive!" he yelled. "I can't believe it! How did you survive down there?"

Bernard smiled back at him. "Skunk Apes can hold their breath for a really long time," he said. "Kind of a helpful skill to have when you smell like we do."

Jordan hugged him again, and Bernard lifted Jordan out of the pool and set him down on the shore. Then he turned to greet Abbie, who was suddenly having a very complicated day. "Hello again," Bernard said, extending a wet paw. "We met a week or so ago. I was clean-shaven, in disguise, and not wearing flippers, so I understand if you don't recall us being introduced."

"No," Abbie whispered. She looked paler than usual. "I—I remember. Nice to, uh—hi."

They walked through the damp swamp as the twilight shadows grew long. Eldon told Jordan of his adventures up North, and how he felt when he found the great lemon tree replaced by a big watering hole. He feared the worst, assuming Gusto must have attacked again, until a very out-of-breath Skunk Ape suddenly emerged from the waters. After telling Eldon what had happened, Bernard began deep well diving to try to salvage what he could from Grampa Grimsley's underground (now underwater) lair. There wasn't much left.

"What about the field guide?" Jordan asked as they reached the wall to Waning Acres.

"I'm afraid not," Bernard said. "The entire library room is completely caved in."

As this sunk in, Eldon pulled two Badger Ranger hats out of his backpack and turned to Jordan and Abbie. "Okay, you guys are clear on the plan, right? Tell your folks you're going on one last Badger Ranger outing, and you'll be back in a coupla days."

Lou chuckled. "The 'last outing' part's true. Dunno about the 'coming back' part."

"That's quite enough, Lou," Bernard said.

"Just keepin' it real," the red cryptid shot back.

"Real *dumb*."

"You wanna piece of this, stinky?"

"Knock it off, you two," Eldon said. He took the suitcase from Lou and handed it to Jordan. "We won't be needing this. Might as well hide it back where you found it."

"I don't know if I can. I think my parents turned the attic into a tearoom."

"Get Doris to help you. She knows every inch of that house, and might even remember a secret hiding spot. Bring it to her. She'll know what to do with it. Okay. You guys know where and when to meet, right?"

"Boathouse. At dawn," Jordan said. Abbie was distracted, staring off into the swamp behind them. Both boys noticed.

"Abbie. You okay?"

"Yeah, I just . . . I keep thinking something's in the shadows, following us."

"Very perceptive," Eldon said. "That's Kriss. The Mothman. He's shy, but sooner or later he'll come out of his cocoon. Or, he won't. Either way, good eye, Abbie. Glad you're on board."

He offered her a Badger Ranger hat. She looked at it. "Like I'd ever wear that." She ducked through the swamp wall. Jordan shrugged, then shoved the suitcase through. He went to follow her but stopped, turned back, and gave Bernard a very big hug.

The old Grimsley place was a beehive of activity—
if the hive were a huge, beautifully refinished house,
and the bees were giggly, overexcited eighty-year-
olds. Jordan's parents were running from room to
room to room delivering hot tea and fresh cookies,
spreading blankets, filling heating pads, fluffing
up pillows, and telling bedtime stories. And their
children couldn't remember ever seeing them
happier.

Jordan was happy, too, with all the Creature
Keeper crew easing so comfortably into a forced and
rather violently sudden retirement. He knew they'd
want the latest news on the plan to save Nessie, and
of course would be eager to hear that Bernard was

alive. So Jordan and his sister made their rounds, too, dropping by each bedroom to whisper into hairy old ears what was happening. Jordan was especially surprised at how Abbie seemed to enjoy spending time with the old folks—but decided it was probably best not to point that out to her.

The last room Jordan visited belonged to Doris, on the very top floor. He lugged the old suitcase to the end of the hall, just before the attic stairs. Setting it down outside her door, he entered and offered her a cup of hot cocoa.

"It's an ancient Skunk Ape recipe." Jordan smiled. "From an old friend."

"Thank goodness he's all right. He gave us all quite a scare." She smiled and took a sip. "Eldon told me it was your fine detective work in Nessie's cave that led you to her kidnapper. Any clue where she's being held now?"

"The Hall of the Chupacabra is in Mexico, but Eldon says its exact location died with my Grampa Grimsley. That evil madman thinks I'm my grand-father, and so assumes I know where to find them."

"You're a wonderful boy." Doris chuckled. "And you're clearly a Grimsley. But dearie, you're not your grandfather."

"I wish I was. I'd lead everyone straight to the

Chupacabra's front door, bang it down, and get Nessie out of there. Gusto must've promised that horrible beast he could deliver my grandfather in return for something."

"Trust me, that cryptid doesn't work with anyone. It's always been a loner."

"I saw it lurking outside the crypto-zoo the night I overheard Gusto talking to Harvey. There's gotta be a connection, or Gusto wouldn't have chosen the Mexican location as a trap. But I'm not my grandfather, so I don't have a clue where they are."

"I wish there was something I could do to help."

Jordan remembered something. "You can help me with this." He got up and carried the suitcase in to her and placed it on the bed.

Doris sat up. She seemed startled. "Where did you get that?"

"Up in the attic. But I need a new place to stash it. Its old hiding place has been taken over by loveseats and tea cozies. Any ideas?"

She stared at the case. "Y'know, I was caretaker of this place for years. Including the night your grandfather died."

"But he died in the swamp."

"That stormy night, he showed up in soaking wet pajamas, frightened, saying how he was going to be taken away, wouldn't be able to continue his life's work. I'd heard what he'd done, how he was responsible for Skunk Ape Summer, and that he'd been arrested in Leisureville." She closed her eyes. "I ordered him to leave. He told me that this was his house. That scared me. No one knew but me that I didn't rightfully own this house. I couldn't afford him getting me in any trouble. I couldn't have him here." A tear ran down her cheek. "So I turned him away. I turned a frightened old man away from his own home."

"Oh, Doris."

"I'm so sorry. I can't undo what I did then. But I can help you now." She placed her bony fingers on the case. "He had this with him. He didn't want to stay or even hide here. He just wanted me to keep this case. To hide it." She clicked open the latches. "He showed me what was inside of it. Everything that was inside of it." She pulled out the Skunk Ape costume, the foot-on-a-stick, the newspaper clippings, setting them aside without looking at them. "He told me if I hid this case, and kept its secret to myself, someday someone who needed it very badly would come. And they would give me something very valuable in exchange for what was hidden inside."

Her hand slid along the inner lining of the empty suitcase. There was a lump that Jordan hadn't noticed before. She slowly pulled the fabric from the corner, tearing open the lining. A thin diary tumbled out, followed by a faded old piece of parchment paper.

Jordan looked up at Doris. "Who? Who did he say would come?"

"A boy." She smiled. "A Grimsley boy. And here you are."

Awestruck, Jordan lifted the parchment and carefully unfolded it. On it was a hand-drawn map of a mountain, located outside of Mexico City.

There were hand-scribbled notes and directions, including what looked like instructions on how and where to enter the mountain. At the bottom of the map, written in large letters, it said, *HALL OF CHUPACABRA. POPOCATÉPETL VOLCANO. MEXICO. STAY AWAY!*

Jordan looked back at Doris. Her eyes were welled up with tears, but she was now smiling through them. "Doris," he said quietly. "I have nothing valuable to give you."

She handed Jordan the diary. "You brought me home. That's pretty valuable."

The next morning Jordan and Abbie got up before dawn and crept down the stairs. They didn't have to worry about being too quiet, since the snoring roar of the old people was louder than a parade of monster trucks filled with hungry walruses.

The sun began to rise as they entered the swamp and made their way to the boathouse. Out of the corner of her eye, Abbie kept catching a glimpse of movement within the shadows as before. She glanced behind her, then leaned forward to whisper to Jordan. "*Psst* . . . I think that Moth thing might be following us again. . . ."

"Uh-huh." Jordan was studying the Mexico map

as he walked, barely listening to her. Abbie looked back again. She was met with two giant, purple eyes, right behind her.

"Aaaaahhh!"

A tall, gray, slightly furry creature with enormous wings was gliding along with them. Jordan spun around. The shadowy creature wrapped its wings around itself like a cocoon. It stood in one spot, completely frozen.

"Kriss!" It was Eldon, who'd come running from the boathouse dock at the sound of Abigail's scream. "We've talked about this! You can't just sidle up to people like that!"

"Not cool, bro," Lou the Jersey Devil said, fluttering awkwardly a few feet off the ground with his too-small wings. "You creep people out. You need to own that."

Eldon sighed and quickly introduced Jordan and Abbie to the thin, gray husk before them. "Kriss, this is Jordan and Abbie. Guys, this is Kriss. Otherwise known as Mothman." Eldon began walking back to the dock, with Lou fluttering alongside him. "C'mon, Rangers. Lots to do. Let's focus up."

Jordan followed, and Abbie glanced back at Kriss. She was rewarded with a beautiful glowing purple eye that peeked out at her. She smiled slightly, and—*WHOOSH!*—the Mothman shot straight up in the air with one mighty flap of his wings.

On the dock, Jordan and Abbie were introduced to two others, who looked, Abbie was thankful to see, relatively human. Paco, Mothman's Creature Keeper, was a tall, slender, well-dressed, bookish-looking boy. As soon as he heard his cryptid had gone into cocoon mode, he ran off in the direction of the incident, muttering, "Not again!"

Lou's Keeper, Mike, was a lot like the Jersey Devil he was in charge of: brash, bulky, and a bit of a knucklehead. He wore a tank-top shirt under a red velour tracksuit, with gold chains around his neck. He had a bit of a potbelly, and looked like he could be related to Lou, if not for the fact that he didn't have horns, hooves, or a pointy tail.

"Hey, good to meetcha," Mike said, grabbing Jordan's hand a little too hard. "My first time down here in swamptown. Yo, you guys got a deli around here? I'm starvin'."

"COWABUNGA!" Lou the Jersey Devil suddenly galloped past them down the dock, dived into the water, and began swimming out to the center of the cove. Mike suddenly ran to the end of the dock and egged him on like a gym trainer. "Let's go! Push it! Feel the burn! You got this!"

Reaching the deep water, Lou dived down. His
pointy red tail followed his kicking hooves.

Jordan looked at Eldon. "What's he doing?"

"Giving Bernard a hand. Badger Ranger rule
forty-seven: 'Nothin' works like teamwork works!'"

There was a great churning in the water as a
familiar oval platform rose out above the surface. It
was Gusto's submarine, and it was moving toward
the dock. "I hate that thing," Jordan muttered.

"Well, you might want to start liking it," Eldon
said. "'Cause it's all we've got."

The sub rose out of the water, followed by Bernard and Lou. They had it propped on their big
shoulders, straining to guide it into the boathouse.
They were having a harder time as they got closer

into the shallows, and the submarine began to tilt dangerously toward the dock.

WHOOSH! A gray streak suddenly flew in behind them, slamming into the sub and pushing it back up on the two creatures' shoulders, saving the humans from being squashed like swamp bugs against the foot of the dock. Kriss hovered watchfully as Bernard and Lou gently parked it in the boathouse, then swooped over to the dock and landed silently beside the others.

"See?" Eldon said to Jordan. "What'd I tell ya? 'Nothin' works like teamwork works!'"

Abbie stared up at the Mothman, wondering if he was into reptiles.

36

The main cabin of Gusto's submarine was equipped with more than enough space to comfortably fit a full-grown Skunk Ape, a Jersey Devil, and a Mothman, along with their five human traveling companions. Once aboard, they all began excitedly exploring the vessel that would take them out of the Everglades, across and beneath the Gulf of Mexico.

The cockpit was a dizzying array of buttons, gauges, dials, levers, and screens. There were two seats, and Eldon immediately plopped himself into one of them, where he began fiddling with a computerized navigational system he clearly didn't understand. Jordan sat down beside him. "Finally!" he exclaimed. "Something built after the nineteenth

century! Look at all this stuff! I bet this thing's equipped with an internal navigation system!" He was marveling at the displays laid out before him, then noticed Eldon, tapping on a screen, trying to get it to wake up.

"What are you doing? Don't do that."

Eldon slumped back in the chair. "How are we going to get it to go? Where are the stick shifts and pulleys? Where's the On switch?"

"Listen. Spooring, knot-tying, Swiss Army knives—that's your thing. But this—" He waved his arms over the blinking dashboard. "This is *my* thing." Jordan studied the panel laid out before him. "What we have here is your basic diesel submarine, which uses a simple compression ignition system." He hit some switches, and the submarine shuddered to life. Jordan pointed to a gauge. "And it looks like our host was kind enough to leave us with enough fuel for the generators. Once our battery bank is recharged, we'll be free to submerge. Easy peasy, lemon squeezy."

He smiled at Eldon, who stared vacantly for a moment, then sadly looked down at his Badger Badge sash. Feeling badly for him, Jordan pointed to one he hadn't seen before. "Hey! Look at that one there! What's that one?"

"Uh, Cartography. See, there's a little map on it, and a compass, and . . ." He trailed off.

"That's perfect!" Jordan opened his backpack and pulled out the map Doris had helped him find. "You need to be in charge of this."

Eldon took the old parchment map and opened it. His face lit up immediately. "This is fantastic!" He pored over the notes and transcriptions. "Where'd you find it?"

"It was hidden in the lining of my grandfather's suitcase." He smiled. "Think it'll help?"

"You betcha! It not only shows us where the hall is, it provides entranceways, caverns, and passages! But first things first—" He reached into the Badger

Ranger Travel Pouch on his belt and pulled out a small, old-looking book. "I'll cross-reference this map with my atlas and figure out where on the Mexican coast we should aim for."

"Hold on." Jordan turned back to the console. The computer screen glowed to life. "If I can access the memory bank of the navigation system, I should be able to get the sub to recalculate and reverse its own past position, orientation, and velocity . . . bingo!"

Eldon's jaw fell open as a soothing, female voice spoke from the computer.

"*Departure history cache accessed. Recent coordinates now uploading for display. Please stand by. . . .*" *Bing!*

Only one coordinate number appeared on the screen, with the name of the location beneath it: Veracruz, Mexico. Jordan clicked on the coordinate and hit Enter again.

"*New destination coordinate accepted. Autopilot engaged. Preparing to disembark. Please stand by. . . .*" *Bing!*

"Yes!" Jordan grinned. "Well, you heard the nice computerized lady–voice. The sub is now programmed to take us precisely back to the last place it traveled from."

Eldon blinked at Jordan.

Jordan smiled. "Now let's go back and take a look at that map."

Eldon and Jordan stepped out of the cockpit and made their way through the submarine. "Okay, team," Eldon addressed the crew. "We're on our way. Kriss, I need you to fly ahead and meet us there, after making a quick detour. I'll give you your instructions and our destination."

He and Kriss huddled by the main hatch as the others prepared for departure. Abbie pretended not to watch as Eldon and Kriss climbed up and out of the hatch.

Up on the oval platform, Eldon showed the Mothman the map, and then opened his atlas to point out another stop. He wished him well, and watched as the furry gray cryptid zoomed into the air.

Back inside, Abbie ran to the port window. She caught a glimpse of Kriss streaking across the sky just before the murky waters of Ponce de Leon Bay sloshed over the outer glass as the submarine dived beneath the surface.

Hours into the voyage, Bernard was sitting in the cockpit, pretending to be a narwhal. Abbie was studying the map, actively ignoring Lou and Mike's push-up contest, and Jordan was quietly reading his grandfather's worn diary. Eldon sat down next to Abbie. "Say, are you interested in cartography, Abbie?"

She looked at him like he was from another planet, and he continued. "Because I sure am. In fact, I earned a Badger Badge for it. See? It's right here, next to my—"

"She doesn't care," Jordan said without looking up from the diary.

Abbie shot Jordan a look, then slid the map over to share with Eldon. "I've been wondering about these markings. Grampa Grimsley put in a lot of detail about the Chupacabra's lair."

"He should have," Jordan said. "According to this, he was held captive in it for days." They both looked up at him. "It's his journal. It was hidden in the suitcase, along with the map."

"He writes how Chupacabra was the first cryptid he ever saw, when he was a young man traveling through Latin America. He was so excited he went out and bought the best camera he could afford, and began his hunt. He got his picture, and sold it to a local paper. It caused a panic and spread like wildfire. It soon became a national pastime of many Latin American countries to hunt the Chupacabra."

"I thought our grandfather was all about protecting cryptids," Abbie said.

"Maybe he didn't know any better at the time," Eldon said.

"That's what I think, too," Jordan said. "I think seeing what he'd done to Chupacabra made him change his philosophy about cryptids."

"And made him an enemy for life," Abbie said.

Jordan skimmed the pages. "It's true. According to some of the stories in here, Chupacabra was pretty good at holding a grudge, among other lovely qualities. Like controlling fire."

"So why does this Gusto guy think you're Grampa Grimsley?" Abbie asked.

"I don't know. That grouchy lady at the lemonade stand said we look alike."

"The question isn't why he thinks Jordan is Grampa Grimsley," Eldon said. "What I'm curious about is why does he think your grandfather is alive at all?"

"It doesn't matter," Jordan said. "So long as he believes it, we can use it." They all looked at him. "I'm the one he wants. I mean, I'm not *the* one he wants, but he thinks I'm the one he wants, so I may as well pretend to be the one he wants. And that will help us get what we want. Get it?"

"No," said Abbie. "No one got that."

Eldon got it. He looked at Jordan with concern in his eyes.

"Land ho!" Paco yelled from the periscope. "El Mexico, dead ahead!"

They had traveled all through the night, so it was nearly daybreak as they approached the coast, which was a few hundred yards away. Through the periscope they could see a touristy little beach area with a deep dock and a waterfront boardwalk. There weren't many people on the beach, just a few vendors setting up their stands and food trucks for the tourists.

Jordan stationed the sub just past the end of the dock, and breached just enough for the turret to rise above the surface. Then he and the other four humans onboard—Eldon, Abbie, Paco, and Mike— dived into the warm gulf water, and swam to shore.

Once on the beach, Eldon and Paco looked around. They were searching for something. "Now we see if your creature did his job," Eldon said.

"Don't worry about Kriss," Paco said. "He's very reliable."

Abbie pricked up her ears at this. "Kriss? Is he here somewhere?" Jordan stared at his sister as she frantically squeezed the water out of her hair, then tried to comb it with an old Popsicle stick she found in the sand.

"Well, I don't know about you guys," Mike said. "But I'm starving. I'm gonna hit that food truck up there. Love to get me a hoagie, but I guess some of that hare haggis will have to do the trick. When in Mexico, right?"

Eldon and Paco glanced at each other. Jordan joined them in looking up at the boardwalk. *Hare haggis?* Parked there among the other concession stands and T-shirt shacks was a very odd-looking

food truck. Actually, it was a bus. A sky-blue bus. And sitting on top of its roof was a giant bunny. With antlers. And Mike was jogging straight for it.

The three of them burst into a sprint to catch up to Mike, who was having trouble finding the order window. Seeing none, he started banging on the side of the bus.

CLANG! CLANG! CLANG! "Hola! Anybody in there? Los bunny burritos, por favoray?"

A Scottish voice called out from the driver's seat of the bus. "Oi! Stop all that racket! Yer gonna wake my creature, ya eel-brained git!" The driver's-side window slid open and a shock of red hair stuck out. Alistair MacAlister was frantically pointing up at the roof.

On the top of the bus, the giant jackalope blinked, sniffed, and shook her head out of a deep sleep. Jordan knew what was coming. She was gonna bolt.

"Alistair! Jingle jangle!" Jordan yelled. The young Scot tossed the bus keys out the window to Jordan. *WHOOOSH!* A gray blur swooped by and snagged them out of midair. A second later, Kriss was hovering directly in front of Peggy, dangling the keys in front of her face. The big, antlered bunny's eyes glazed over, and she slipped back into her catatonic state.

Mike smiled, impressed. "Nice work! Let's hear it for Mothra, there! Hip, hip, HOO—" *SLAM!* Before he could finish his loud cheer—one that surely would have reawoken Peggy—a wet, black, furry lump shot out from behind a nearby palm thicket and tackled him to the ground. The next second, Bernard was sitting on Mike's chest. Mike made a face as he got a noseful of Bernard's bouquet, and his eyes scanned the faces above him, landing on Lou.

37

Alistair veered the bus off Federal Highway 150 onto a bumpy dirt road, toward the base of the Popocatépetl volcano. Jordan sat in the front passenger seat, chatting with the Creature Keeper. He knew Alistair had to be concerned for Nessie, and Jordan figured the least he could do as they made the journey was to keep his mind on something else.

"Your hare allergies seem better. I noticed you haven't sneezed once."

Alistair reached into the pocket of his kilt and pulled out a package of allergy tablets. "These help. Also, I got out of that awful hole in the ground whenever I could. Midnight walks into that little town did wonders for my head in more ways than one.

Kept me from goin' cuckoo, like ol' Harebrained Harvey."

"What about Milo and Bertha? They didn't mind you taking their bus?"

The chubby Scot shrugged at Jordan from behind the wheel. "They went on vacation. Left her parked in the desert. So they don't exactly know they've lent it to me. But when they come back nice and relaxed, I'm bettin' they'll be all right with it."

Jordan smiled at his redheaded friend, who wasn't doing a good job of hiding his worry. "It's gonna be okay," Jordan said. "We're gonna find her."

"I just hope we find her in time. I hear the waters are really starting to act up without her there to tame 'em. Lotta folks could get hurt."

Behind Jordan, the others members of the team kept occupied. Mike and Lou were arm wrestling on the floor near the back. Kriss was looking straight ahead uncomfortably as Abbie animatedly showed him pictures of her iguana, Chunk, on her smartphone.

Eldon and Paco studied the map of the Popocaté-petl volcano, until the real thing suddenly appeared on the horizon outside their window. A hush fell over the bus as everyone gazed at it.

Although Popocatépetl was an active volcano,

it hadn't erupted in over fifty years. Still, it never let anyone living within a hundred-mile radius forget it was there. Day and night, a steady stream of white, smoky ash rose from its central crater, like a Skunk Ape's stripe running up the middle of the sky. As Abbie gawked at it with the others, Jordan borrowed her smartphone and quickly accessed the internet to read as much information as he could on the volcano.

He learned that over the last decade or so, the

area around the foothills of Popocatépetl had been abandoned because of large, unpredictable blasts of ash, chunks of hot rock, and burps of lava that it would occasionally spit out. Reading about the volcano, Jordan was reminded a lot of the man who'd lured them to it—unpredictable, unstable, and very dangerous.

Because it was so isolated, there was no chance of being spotted. Lou and Mike made quick work of the barbed-wire fence marked *¡PELIGROSO!* that surrounded the perimeter. Soon the bus was parked outside the cavernous entrance to the Popocatépetl volcano, which Grampa Grimsley had drawn on his map.

"This entrance is supposed to be blocked," Eldon said, looking at the map. "Someone's put out the welcome mat for us."

KABOOM! An explosion suddenly sprayed ash into the sky. It was so loud it jerked Peggy out of her trance. She jumped straight up a hundred feet, landing beside the bus. Her fluffy head jerked this way and that as she frantically searched for the safest direction to flee. Before she could, Kriss swooped into action, flying up to her twitching face, staring into her eyes with his purple orbs, and whispering into her enormous floppy ears. He calmed her, then led her to the shade of the bus, where she dug a shallow hole and lay in the cool dirt.

Abbie smiled. Lou mumbled something about the bunny whisperer.

Alistair looked even more rattled than Peggy. He walked over to the hole where Kriss was petting Peggy, and climbed in beside her. The Mothman gently took the Scot's hand and placed it on Peggy's fuzzy nose. As Alistair gently began to pet the giant jackalope, Kriss got up and walked away, leaving them in peace.

Eldon and Jordan glanced at each other with a look of concern, then quietly approached the Scot. "Alistair," Eldon said. "It's time. Let's go get your creature."

"She's scared," Alistair said. "I can tell. I've grown pretty close to this critter. Nothing like my connection with Haggis-Breath, of course, but . . ." He trailed off. Jordan saw the worry on his friend's face and glanced at Eldon.

"Hey, what's the protocol for a cryptid's stand-in Keeper in a case like this?" He asked so that Alistair could hear. "Wouldn't he or she be the best one to comfort and protect a creature who might stay behind? Just wondering."

Eldon smiled slightly. "Y'know, come to think of

it, that is the rule. And we all know Badger Ranger rule number three twenty-six: *A rule is a rule.* Alistair, I'm afraid you'd better stay here."

Alistair looked up at them with a grateful smile. "Sure, laddies. Wouldn't want to endanger the mission by having a part of the team in there who's all nervous and jumpy."

Eldon gave him a quick Badger claw salute, then went to check on the others. "Thanks, mate," Alistair said to Jordan.

Jordan crouched down beside him. "Alistair, I'm gonna promise you two things. First, if Nessie's in there, we're gonna get her out."

"What's the second?"

"She's in there."

Both Grampa Grimsley's map and his diary were old, but fortunately Popocatépetl hadn't changed since he'd written them. All the twists, turns, tunnels, caverns, and caves were just as he described.

It grew hotter the farther Jordan, Eldon, Abbie, Bernard, Lou, Mike, Paco, and Kriss ventured into the heart of the volcano. It also grew darker, until they got closer to Popocatépetl's core. Soon an eerie orange light from deep within the volcano illuminated their path. They continued along the rocky terrain, carefully stepping over the crevices. Through the cracked rock they could feel the hot vapor and sometimes even see glowing orange magma oozing far below.

They came to a large, eerie cavern with open splits in the floor filled with boiling rock. The glow of the fiery lava against the misshapen rocks jutting from the ground cast weird shadows throughout. Bernard immediately stopped. "Does anyone hear that?" There was a deep, raspy breathing sound echoing faintly throughout the cavern. It was hard to pinpoint where it was coming from, until Eldon glanced up.

Directly overhead, clinging to the craggy ceiling high above them was the Chupacabra, staring down with its glowing red eyes.

It let out a horrible snarl and dropped to the floor. In an instant, Eldon grabbed Jordan and dived out of the way as Paco and Mike rolled behind a rock. Kriss scooped Abbie up in his arms and swooped to a nearby ledge. Bernard and Lou held their ground and faced the creature. *SLAM!* The Chupacabra crashed into them, immediately knocking Lou into a deep crevice. "No!" Mike cried out and tried to run toward the glowing fissure, but Paco somehow held him back.

Bernard and the Chupacabra wrestled across the cavern floor, clawing, punching, gnashing, and gnawing at each other. "Run!" Bernard managed to yell to the others. "I'll hold this thing off! Go and find Nessie!"

No one moved. They stood frozen in their hiding places, watching the fierce battle between the two massive cryptids. Kriss left Abbie on the high rock ledge and swooped down, dive-bombing the Chupacabra, scratching at it with his long claws as he passed. The horrible cryptid cried out in pain, but its rage seemed to make it stronger. It kicked Bernard off with its powerfully lanky legs, then pounced. Eldon and Jordan gasped as the evil creature was suddenly holding the Skunk Ape's head over the fiery crevice where Lou had disappeared.

"No!" Jordan cried out. "We have to do something! He's going to die!"

FOOOM! Suddenly, a red blaze rose out of the deadly fissure like a phoenix, knocking the

Chupacabra in the chin and sending it scrambling across the floor. Lou fluttered overhead, engulfed in dripping lava. "You leave my stinky bro alone!" He flicked some lava off his shoulder, then dived straight at the Chupacabra.

As they tumbled horn over tail into the back cavern wall, the others scrambled out of their hiding spots and helped Bernard up. His thick fur was singed, but otherwise he seemed all right.

Screeeeeeecccchhh! They all looked up to see Lou holding the wiry Chupacabra over his head. It squirmed and writhed in his grip as he lumbered over to the furnace-like fissure in the cavern floor. "Let's see how you like it, ya overgrown rat!" Lou threw the beast down into the fire pit with all his might. *FOOOOM!* A blast of fire shot straight up out of the crack, scorching the ceiling. Then it was quiet.

Lou shrugged to the others. "Fire, brimstone, it's my thing." They crowded the devil-cryptid, thanking and congratulating him. The celebration was quickly cut short as the cavern began to rumble and shake, and the floor beneath them started to crack and split, exposing more lava beneath their feet.

"Quick! Everyone, up here!" Abbie was still perched on the rock where Kriss had set her down.

Bernard scrambled up the wall to join her, while Kriss lifted Jordan and Eldon and flew them to safety. Lou grabbed hold of his Keeper as well as Paco, and they all huddled together on Abbie's perch, looking down as the cavern floor gave way, falling in chunks into the red-hot pool of lava below.

The wall behind them began to crack. As the lava rose, they pushed closer against it. Finally, Bernard pulled back and slammed his fists against it. The wall broke free, sending them tumbling down a dark, craggy decline, and into another cavern. They stood up and looked around. There were strange markings scraped into the stone, and Jordan recognized one of them immediately. It was a crudely carved Creature Keeper shield. "My grandfather was here!" he shouted.

Eldon looked down at the map and found what he was looking for. "It's a marker," he said. "We're near the center of the volcano. Chupacabra's lair."

"HA-HA-HA-HA-HA-HA-HA-HAAAA!"

Chillingly familiar laughter echoed from an archway on the other side of the cavern. "Grimsley!" Gusto's voice boomed from inside the adjoining lair. "You've accepted my invitation! But I have a very good sense of smell, and I'm picking up a foul stench—you brought that horrid skunk creature, as well as others. Such a shame you didn't have the courage or honor to come alone! Now your innocent friends will have to die with you!"

They all huddled together, unsure of what to do.

"I'M WAITING, GEORGE GRIMSLEY! And so is your miserable sea cow! You'd better hurry—this dry volcanic air really isn't good for her."

"That's it." Jordan stepped forward. "I'm going in. Alone. He wants my grandfather, and he thinks I'm him. If I can trick him into believing I'm George Grimsley, maybe he'll let Nessie go—along with all of you." He looked at Eldon. "It's the ultimate hoax."

"Jordan, no." Abbie had tears in her eyes.

Eldon stepped forward. "I'm not going to let you. He'll kill you."

"It's the only way to save her. And isn't that the sworn duty of a Creature Keeper?"

Eldon thought for a moment. "Yes, it is." The others gasped. "Except for one thing." Eldon stepped between Jordan and the archway. "You're not a Creature Keeper, Jordan. You never were."

Jordan's face dropped. He looked at the faces of the others. He pulled the Badger Badge Eldon had given him off his shirt. "Well, I suppose I'm not a Badger Ranger, either. And that means you don't have any real authority over me." He tossed the tiny heart badge to Eldon—a little to his right. Eldon moved to catch it, and Jordan rushed past him, diving through the archway.

38

Jordan tumbled into a large, circular room of volcanic rock. The walls here were smooth and glassy, as if they'd been glazed by extreme heat. Dead center, churning and bubbling, was a massive pool of hot lava. White steam rose from the boiling cauldron of flame and molten rock, drifting up to a cathedral-like ceiling that formed a more narrow cone leading to the peak of the volcano, thousands of feet above.

High above the pool of lava hung a net suspended by ropes bolted to the glassy sidewalls of this volcanic great room. And it was moving.

Jordan felt a cold chill despite the boiling heat in the room. Hanging there in the large net was Nessie.

Small and soft, she appeared orange from the glow of the molten rock below. She let out a tiny, pain-filled *squeeeeee.* . . .

"Well, well, well . . . ," an evil voice said. "Welcome back, Georgie. It's been awhile, no?"

Jordan spun around. Gusto was sitting on a throne of solid rock, looking down at him from a stone stage above the chamber floor and its pit of bubbling lava. He wore the Hydro-Hide, and grinned at Jordan through the steam.

"You made the honorable decision to come in on your own, rather than jeopardize your friends' lives by trying to ambush me." He pointed a long finger at Nessie overhead. "A wise choice considering, as you can see, the life of your precious cryptid literally hangs in the balance."

"Let her down, NOW! Who are you? Why would you do all of this?"

"Let's just say I'm an international businessman, Georgie. I have all the treasure and riches I need—even my own submarine! But what I want is true power." He stretched out his sleeves to admire the sparkling scales on his Hydro-Hide as they twinkled in the orange light. "And now, I have the power to control all the oceans and seas of the world! All it took was fooling your simple-minded bunnysitter

344

into helping me. I merely offered Quisling something you never think to offer any of those Creature Keeping *slaves* of yours . . . an early retirement."

"You don't know anything," Jordan said. "Not about me, not about the Creature Keepers." Jordan was trying to think fast. It was sheer luck that Gusto didn't know Chupacabra had been killed. If he did, or if he found out that Jordan wasn't actually George Grimsley, this final, crucial hoax would fail. Jordan couldn't let that happen. He took a deep breath. The hot air felt like fire in his lungs. "All right, if you're a businessman, then let's get down to business. Let my friends leave here with her, and you can do whatever you want with George Grimsley. Who is me. Because I'm him."

"I told you, Grimsley, you're no good to me while you're hiding in the body of a child. Chupacabra has waited a long time for its revenge, and wants to kill the man who turned it into a hunted animal. Luckily, that's an easy fix." Gusto pulled out a glowing, green Puddle of Ripeness ball and tossed it playfully into the air. "I honestly don't know how you managed to escape my Puddle of Ripeness bomb attack the other night. But I saved one, just for you." He reared back, ready to throw. "Time for you to become the pathetic, old coward of a man you always were, George Grimsley."

"WAIT!" A voice from the archway echoed through the chamber. Eldon entered.

"Eldon, what are you doing?" Jordan cried out. "Stay back!"

Eldon stood beside Jordan. "If that's your only stink bomb, Gusto, you might want to think before you throw it at him. Because he's not George Grimsley . . . I am."

Gusto peered confusedly at the Badger Ranger, then back at Jordan. Then another voice caught his attention as it echoed through the chamber. "So am I," Paco said. He entered and stepped up to join them.

"No, I am," Mike said, joining the line.

"Actually, I'm George Grimsley," Abbie said, stepping out and lining up with the boys.

"Enough of this," Gusto said. "Now you're *REALLY ANNOYING ME!*"

"Well, then you ain't gonna like this," Lou said. The Jersey Devil stood alongside the others. "'Cause it turns out I'm George Grimsley, too."

WHOOSH! The Mothman zipped along the floor, landing softly beside Paco, startling Gusto so much he nearly dropped the Puddle of Ripeness ball in his hand. Kriss whispered in Paco's ear. Paco nodded and looked up at Gusto. "He says he's also George Grimsley."

"You're all mistaken," a calm voice spoke out. Bernard entered last, defiantly taking his place on the other side of Jordan. "If anyone here is George Grimsley, it's me."

Señor Areck Gusto stared at this group of humans and cryptids, then looked down at the stink bomb in his hand. "This is all very endearing," he said. "Of course, there's enough gas in this ball to engulf you all with one shot, no matter who I throw it at."

"Then throw it at all of us," Jordan said, staring bravely at Gusto. "But before you do, you'd better understand something. No *one* of us is George Grimsley, because *all* of us are. Unfortunately for you, the man you promised you could deliver to that evil beast is dead and gone. He was my grandfather."

"Mine, too," Abbie added.

"I never got to know him when he was alive," Jordan continued. "But I feel like I know him now— thanks to everyone I've met who carries out his life's work. Helping, hiding, hoaxing—whatever it takes, wherever it takes them. They protect cryptids everywhere from men like you. That's what they do."

"That's what *we* do," Eldon said, putting a hand on Jordan's shoulder. "We're *all* Creature Keepers."

Gusto studied them a moment, then slowly grinned directly at Jordan. "Ooh . . . nice try. But if you're not George Grimsley, then how is it that you ended up in possession of *this*." Gusto held up a long, thin finger. A clear, thick band twinkled in the light. It was George Grimsley's ring.

"Give that back—it belongs to me!"

"Precisely my point, George. Thank you for making it so succinctly. I do sometimes tend to go on a bit."

Eldon's eyes were wide. He turned to Jordan. "How did he get that?"

Gusto sneered. "Let's just say a business acquaintance picked it up for me while out for an evening stroll in the swamp. A bonus to our transaction, for destroying his enemy's life's work. Really goes well with the outfit, don't you think?"

Lou stepped forward. "Let me get it back. I'll tear off his fingers, one by one."

"STOP!" Gusto shouted. His voice boomed through the hall. "Now, this has all been quite the dramatic showing of camaraderie. I've always worked alone, you see, which does have its drawbacks. For example, I realize that when I throw this at you, George, your colleagues here will no doubt see that they have nothing to lose. Then they'll attack, which may not work out too well for me."

"You got that right," the Jersey Devil said, inching closer.

"Easy, Lou," Eldon cautioned. "He's got something up his sleeve."

"What I have, George Grimsley, is a strong sense that our paths will soon cross again. I also have other business transactions I need to attend to. Being pummeled by your cryptid henchmen would be quite inconvenient."

"What are you saying?" Jordan said. "Are you letting us go?"

"What I'm saying, dear old Georgie, is that if the Chupacabra has waited this long, he can wait a bit longer. And I'm saying that unfortunately for you, I've got much bigger fish to fry."

Gusto reared back . . . and lofted the last Puddle of Ripeness stink bomb straight at Nessie. *POOM!* The orb exploded in the net overhead, engulfing its prisoner in the thick, green gas. *Squeeeeee! SqueeeeeEEEEE! SQUEEEEEEEE!* Her screams grew louder. And deeper. They rumbled the walls of the cavern. Nessie was getting larger. Much larger.

SQUEEEEEEEEOOOOOOOO! The smoke and

vapor rising from the lava pit carried the green haze up the volcanic tube, revealing the net—and the incredible creature within it. Jordan stared wide-eyed as Nessie doubled in size, then doubled again, writhing and thrashing about, shredding the weak fabric that held her over the bubbling lava.

Kriss and Lou leaped into the air, flying straight toward her. The two flying cryptids grabbed her front dorsal fins. In her panic, she flicked Kriss away. Abbie screamed as the Mothman was tossed against the wall. He bounced off it and flew right back in to grab Nessie again.

SNAP! The shards of net gave way. Nessie dropped, but not far. She was now awkwardly hovering over the bubbling lava as Kriss and Lou strained to hold her. Her great girth began to win out, and she slipped from their grip, falling fast toward the pit.

SLAM! Bernard leaped from a running start, side tackling her and knocking her off course. Nessie belly flopped onto the smooth rock floor along with Bernard, Kriss, and Lou, and slid on her slick, scaleless skin, banging into the far wall.

Eldon, Abbie, Mike, and Paco rushed to them. Jordan scanned the cavern. He spotted what he was looking for—Gusto was sneaking away along the

inside wall of the volcano, trying to escape unnoticed in all the chaos.

CRACK! *"Oweeeeeooo!"* Gusto was struck by something in the back of the head. He howled and spun around to see Jordan standing with his slingshot.

Jordan ran toward him and hurled himself at Gusto, tackling him to the floor. The two of them rolled, but Gusto was much bigger. He threw Jordan off and stood ominously before him, his clawlike fingers reaching for Jordan's neck.

"I tried to let you go, Grimsley. But now you will feel Chupacabra's revenge!"

"Jordan!" Eldon's voice called out to him. He looked over and caught the small hunk of metal flying at him. Jordan unfolded the blade and jumped to his feet just as Gusto moved in to strike. Jordan pointed Eldon's Badger Ranger buck knife at Gusto's throat.

The dazed Latino blinked at Jordan and grinned. "You are *certainly* a Grimsley."

"Yeah. I get that a lot." Jordan could feel the anger in him start to take over. He gripped the knife in his hand and took a step closer. "Any last words?"

Gusto backed up to the rocky overhang. He looked behind him at the bubbling cauldron of melting magma. When he turned back, there was a horrible grin on his face.

"Just one." He whispered, "Cannonball."

Gusto leaped into a backflip, tucked into a tight ball, and plunged into the boiling magma. A sickening, sizzling splash echoed throughout the cavern. Jordan ran to the edge and looked down in disbelief. He glanced through the superheated air at the others, who were staring up at him.

RRRRUUUUMMMMMBLLLLLE . . . The lava pool began to churn and thrash around, spilling like a kettle boiling over. The liquid sank into the pit, retracting as if it were being drained from its center. Jordan had seen this before. "I hate his cannonballs."

"RUN! GET NESSIE UP! THIS PLACE IS GONNA BLOW!" Jordan leaped to help them get Nessie out the archway. *RUMBLE!* The lava was being drawn deeper into the depths of Popocatépetl, and was causing the entire cavern to tremble. *CRASH!* Huge sheaths of rock broke loose from the walls, and stalactites dropped down like massive daggers.

They got Nessie close to the archway entrance just as another rumbling shook the hall. Rock rained down in front of them, sealing the door and trapping them inside. The pool of lava was now churning violently. The volcano was about to erupt for the first time in fifty years, and they all had front row seats.

Suddenly, another lower rumble shook from behind them. Panicking, they moved away as rock came loose from the wall. Abbie grabbed Jordan's hand, and they prepared for the worst.

CRASH! The wall suddenly crumbled. Peggy came leaping through, with Alistair on her back. "You lot look like ya need a lift home again!" The Scot spurred Peggy, who quickly hopped over to Nessie, lowered her head, and gently scooped the

limp water creature in her antlers.

"Well? You comin' or aren't ya?" Everyone climbed on Peggy's back and she pounced out through the same tunnel she'd burrowed to get in.

KABLOOOOSSSSSHHHH! The magma pool blasted molten rock in every direction. Lava shot through the cone, leading up, up, up to the top of the volcano.

Outside, Peggy bounded to a safe distance from the erupting Popocatépetl volcano and let everyone off. As MacAlister rushed to Nessie, a burst of orange blasted high into the sky. In the blaze that shot out of the top of the volcano, Jordan and Eldon spotted a tiny, sparkling object launch away from the eruption. The two boys watched it arc across the sky like a shooting star, until it disappeared somewhere in the jungle hills of central Mexico.

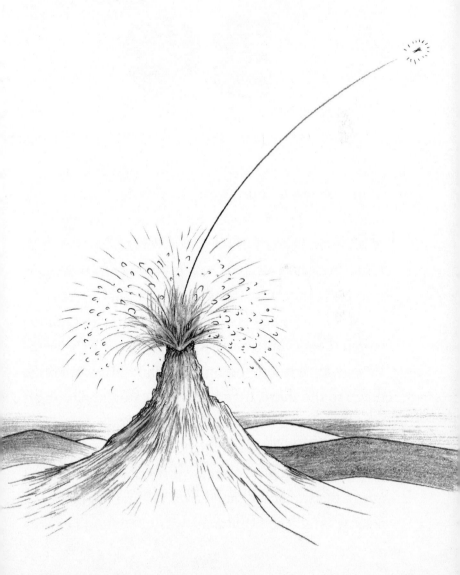

39

The sky-blue, bunnyless bus pulled up to the boardwalk by the beach and let out a weary crew of humans. Jordan, Eldon, and Abbie looked around for witnesses. The coast was pretty clear—just a few couples wandering around near the shore.

Mike and Paco stepped off the bus next. Eldon called them over to make a plan for getting the cryptids away without being seen, but Mike sprinted down to the shore, dived into the water, and took off through the surf. Lou could be heard yelling from the bus, "Feel the burn, bro!"

Mike swam out to the oval platform jutting just above the surface, opened a hatch, and hopped in. A minute later, the submarine was breaching near the shore. The few people present gawked at it, missing completely the giant Skunk Ape, Jersey Devil, and Mothman who stepped off the bus behind them and snuck into the water a bit farther down the beach.

Once the cryptids boarded the submarine, they were joined by the rest of the Creature Keepers. Everyone was happy to be submerged in water, far away from volcanoes and molten lava. They were also very happy to be heading home. But there were a few more passengers to pick up, and the sub rounded a bend to a secluded cove tucked beneath a steep dune. They opened the hatch and waited, staring at the dune wall. Some sand began to trickle down as the small cliff began to shudder and shake. Suddenly it exploded, blasting the area with sand.

Peggy erupted first, shook out her antlers,

bounced onto the beach, and froze in her tracks, mesmerized by the sparkling water. Next was Alistair MacAlister, riding on Nessie's smooth back. The full-sized Loch Ness Monster lumbered out of the tunnel. Seeing the water, she bucked her Keeper off with a flick of her tail and let out a happy *SQUONNNNNK!* as she bounded ecstatically into the surf.

The submarine passengers cheered Nessie on as she dived and frolicked in the water. Jordan looked toward the shoreline and saw Alistair sitting on the sand, chuckling heartily, tears rolling down his chubby red cheeks. Then the happy Scot turned to his other keep, put his fingers in his mouth, and let out a loud whistle. Peggy snapped out of her trance and looked at him. Alistair made a hand gesture toward the sub. Peggy tapped her foot and leaped into the air.

"Incoming!" Jordan ordered everyone inside the sub, and they all scurried into the hatch, slamming it closed just as—*WHAM!* Peggy stuck her landing atop the oval platform. Alistair whistled again. Nessie came swimming over and lowered her head. He stepped off the beach and onto her neck, and she delivered him, high and dry, onto the submarine deck. Alistair climbed up and gave Peggy a nice rub on her nose. "Atta bunny," he said as she fell into a half-lidded trance.

SPLOOSH! A stream of water blasted MacAlister, soaking him. He looked off the side of the submarine. Nessie was giving him serious stink eye.

"Oh, don't be such a jealous drama queen, Haggis-Breath," he said. "I'm just helping her get settled in for the ride home, that's all." Nessie snorted and dived under the water as Alistair turned back to Peggy. "Stay," he said, adding in a low whisper, "That's my girl." He patted her one more time, then joined the others below.

Jordan plugged the reverse coordinates into the

navigational system, and Bernard pretended to steer the submarine out into the gulf. They moved full speed ahead, careful to cruise near the surface so as not to drown the hypnotized Giant Desert Jackalope riding on the roof, just above the waterline.

Once they were underway, Jordan sat in the captain's seat and stared out the front window. As Nessie swam figure eights ahead of the sub, Jordan grinned in amazement, happy to be watching what he considered to be his first real sighting of the Loch Ness Monster.

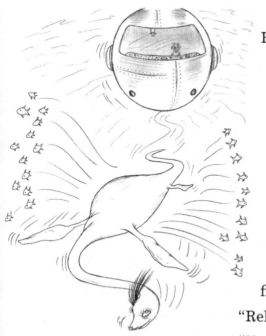

Bertha stood on the lido deck of the cruise ship *Serenity* with a big, fruity drink in one hand and a pair of binoculars in the other. Milo came up and gave her a kiss on the cheek. "How's my pretty little desert flower feelin'," he asked. "Relaxed?"

"You were so right, Milo. This is exactly what I needed. Out here on the open water, no desert heat, no stolen balloons, no demon bunnies."

"Gonna be another beautiful Mexican sunset, darlin'. You watch that peaceful horizon, and I'll go wrangle us up some more of that all-you-can-eat shrimp."

Bertha smiled as she raised the binoculars to her eyes. Scanning the horizon, she suddenly froze. *Crash!* Her big, fruity drink hit the lido deck. "M-M-Milo . . . ? MILO!"

Bertha spun around and slipped on the icy fruit smoothie spilled on the freshly swabbed lido deck. She slid down some steps, hit another railing, and went flying overboard. Milo and a bunch of nearby crew members scrambled to fish her out of the water with a big net, while throwing life preservers and ropes at her. Not one of her rescuers happened to look up and notice gliding along the horizon a giant, white, fluffy bunny rabbit. With antlers.

40

Mrs. Grimsley hauled the last of the suitcases out of her beautiful house and down to the driveway, where she loaded it into the Grimsley Family Rambler.

Inside, Mr. Grimsley reviewed his multipaged, color-coded, fully tabbed and footnoted to-do list with Doris one more time. There could be no confusion on how to properly run and manage the Grimsley House for Surprisingly Active Retirees.

"Mr. Nausbaum takes his chamomile tea with a drop of honey in the morning, but a cube of sugar before bed."

Doris smiled. "I won't forget, dearie. But thank you for the reminder."

"I know you'll keep things shipshape 'til we return this summer, Doris!"

"You can count on me. There's just one thing, if I may make a suggestion."

"Sure, Doris. I'm all ears."

"Well, some of us feel the 'Grimsley House for Surprisingly Active Retirees' is a mouthful."

"Oh. What'd you all have in mind?"

Doris whistled. Two retirees carried a large, beautiful wooden sign into the room. It was carved, painted, and ready for installation. It read, quite simply: *Eternal Acres.*

Mr. Grimsley looked at it, more taken with the handiwork than the new name. "Did you guys make this?"

"We have some very handy residents here," Doris said. "You wouldn't believe what they can accomplish."

"Well," Mr. Grimsley said, trying to hide his amazement. "I suppose we could live with it for a while, and see how it works."

As they excitedly dragged their heavy handiwork outside, Mr. Grimsley took one last look around. "To-do list, totally to-done." He glanced at his watch and yelled up the stairs. "Jordan! Abbie! Let's get ramblin'!"

"I'll find them and let them know it's time," Doris said, ushering Mr. Grimsley out.

She shuffled to the basement stairs at the end of the long hallway. About halfway down the steps, she stopped and turned, standing at the exact place where she fell through all those years ago. She reached under the banister and pressed a hidden button. A section of the staircase dropped down and flattened, sending her sliding beneath the stairs. As soon as she disappeared, the stairs sprung back into place.

"Whoooo-hooo-hoo!" Doris's ride was short, depositing her deep beneath the house in what was now an underground construction site. Many of the Eternal Acres residents were buzzing about in yellow hard hats, putting down flooring, putting up wall paneling, running wires, and installing pipes. Doris walked over to a temporary intercom call box. She stuck her yarn moustache to her upper lip, then pressed a button. It crackled to life. *Frzzzzt!*

"Denmother Doris here," she said in a deep, burry voice into the intercom. "Come in, Boathouse."

Frzzzzt. "Boathouse here, Double-D," a Scottish brogue crackled back.

"Tell Grandkid One and Grandkid Two that Poppa Bear is looking to ramble on out. Over."

In the boathouse, Alistair MacAlister spoke into
an identical intercom.

Frzzt. "Roger that, Den Mother. I'll let 'em know.
Over and out." He stepped outside and watched as
Lou and Mike were giving unnecessarily strong hugs
to Jordan and Abbie. The submarine was parked at
the end of the dock, and after the hug fest, the Jersey
Devil and his Keeper raced each other into the hatch.

Next, Jordan and Abbie said good-bye to Paco, who quietly and neatly boarded the sub. Jordan tried to shake the Mothman's hand, but Kriss kept turning away shyly. "That's okay," Jordan said. "I know we didn't talk much, but I want you to know that without your help we never would've gotten Nessie back. So thank you." Kriss stared at his feet. Jordan stepped away awkwardly.

He and Alistair pretended not to watch as Abbie and Kriss stared out at the water together. Abbie reached out and took his hand. Kriss pulled it away, but gave her a quick smile. *WHOOSH*. He took flight, disappearing in the sky. Only then did Alistair and Jordan approach Abbie. She had a goofy smile on her face, but Jordan decided not to point it out to her.

"Your mum and dad are looking for you two," Alistair said. "And I gotta be shovin' off meself, so . . ." Abbie gave Alistair a big hug, then walked up the dock. Jordan faced his Scottish mate and held out his hand. Alistair's arms wrapped around Jordan and squeezed him almost as tightly as Bernard. "Thank you," he said. "For keepin' yer promise."

He let go and the two of them looked out at the bay. Nessie suddenly came blasting out of the water. She leaped over the submarine, her scales glistening and sparkling like diamonds. Jordan's eyes popped.

"She's grown her Hydro-Hide back!"

"Aye, with the help of Bernard's secret stinky stash of Ripeness."

SKRONK! Nessie's head popped out of the water and barked at Alistair. He chuckled. "All right, Haggis-Breath! Hold yer water horses, I'm comin'!" He looked at Jordan. "We got a lotta work to do. She's anxious to get out there and start repairin' the seas."

Jordan pulled something out of his back pocket.

It was Alistair's slingshot. Alistair shook his head. "Nah. You keep it. Something tells me you might need it again real soon." He winked at him, then climbed the sub, closing the hatch behind him.

Jordan and Abbie watched the submarine pull out into Ponce de Leon Bay, escorted by a frolicking Loch Ness Monster. Then they made their way back through the swamp, passing the pool where the lemon tree used to stand. A homemade sign stuck in the ground read, *Eldon Pecone's All-Natural Spring & Swimmin' Hole*. They continued through the swamp, past the wall, and up to the house.

Inside, Jordan and Abbie made their way through a line of the new residents of Eternal Acres, who thanked them and wished them well. Doris finally led them to the door and gave them both big hugs. "Thank you," she said to Jordan. "For saving me."

"I think you saved me a lot more than I saved you."

"You're probably right about that. But I had an advantage. You needed a lot more saving than I did."

"I still don't believe I'm the Grimsley boy my grandfather said would come for his case. I mean, how could I be?"

"You might be right about that, too. We'll see. But for now, you're close enough."

A minute later, the Grimsley Family Rambler rambled past the rows of identical houses Jordan's grandfather had built and given away.

"Hey, Dad, could you stop the car, please?"

Jordan and Abbie hopped out and ran up to Eldon, dutifully manning his stand. It had a new sign, just like the one in the swamp: *Eldon Pecone's All-Natural Spring & Swimmin' Hole.* On the counter were stacks of fresh, clean towels. A number of bathing suit–clad elderly neighbors lined up, wearing nose plugs, rubber bathing caps, and arm floaties.

Jordan chuckled. "I think this new business is gonna do quite well."

"I'm not in it for money," Eldon said. "Just helping out the community."

Clunk. A rather large cherry pie was suddenly plopped down on the counter.

"Mrs. Fritzler!" Abbie said. "I'm glad I got to see you before I left."

"I hate baking," she said. "But apparently I have to check out this natural spring bath everybody's gabbin' about. And I don't take nothin' for free, so, pie."

Abbie suddenly did something she'd only done to Chunk. She leaned in and gave Mrs. Fritzler a kiss on the cheek. Then she ran into the car.

"Okay then, bye, Abbie . . . ," Eldon weakly called to her.

"Well?" Mrs. Fritzler said. "Do we gotta wait for glaciers to melt to fill up this idiot pool of yours, or what?"

Eldon handed her a towel and pointed her to a group of bathers gathered by a tree. "I should probably go," he said to Jordan. "Pretty big group."

"Have you seen Bernard or Peggy? I wanted to say good-bye."

Eldon shook his head. "Those two are kinda hard to miss, though."

"I have a feeling I'm gonna miss a lot of things around here." He lifted his fingers in the shape of a clenched monkey paw and gave his friend the official Badger claw salute. "See you this summer, First-Class Badger Ranger Pecone."

Eldon saluted back. "You betcha, Badger Runt Grimsley."

Jordan walked back to his dad's 1972 Pontiac Grand Safari and hopped in. He turned to his sister, but she already had her skull-shaped headphones on and was reading a new book: *The Fascinating World of Moths*.

Jordan sank back in his seat and stared out the window as the Grimsley Family Rambler pulled out

of Waning Acres and headed east on the Ingraham
Highway. For a second he thought he saw a flash
of something black and furry moving through the
trees, but he knew it was probably his mind playing tricks on him. Bernard was fast, but not that
fast.

Then he noticed something else. Every few seconds, Bernard's head would pop up over the trees.
Jordan rubbed his eyes and stared out the window.

WUMP! The Family Rambler suddenly jerked.
Then it hit something. Hard. *Scrreeech!* It skidded
to a stop in the middle of the highway. "Not again,"
Mrs. Grimsley said.

The Grimsley family all slowly turned around

in their seats and looked out the enormous back window. Something big, black, and furry was lying about fifty yards back in the middle of the Ingraham Highway, just like before.

SLAM! SLAM! Before their parents could say anything, Jordan and Abbie were running back to the black clump of fur lying in the middle of the road. As soon as they reached it, they saw that they'd been hoaxed. Having spent a good amount of time with an actual Skunk Ape, this clump was not nearly large enough—or smelly enough—to be the real deal. They both smiled. Crumpled in the street was Grampa Grimsley's Skunk Ape costume.

"Jordan!" Mr. Grimsley called out. "What is it?"

"Nothing, Dad!" Abbie yelled loudly toward the tree line. "Just somebody's idea of a joke!"

They looked into the thick tangle of trees. Nothing stirred. They gathered up the empty costume and walked back to the car.

As the Grimsley Family Rambler headed down the highway, Jordan stared into the empty eyes of the Skunk Ape mask. He picked it up, and something fell out. It was a note. Abbie looked up from her book as Jordan held up the paper. It read:

Congratulations.
You are official
CREATURE KEEPERS.
You will be
instructed on your
next mission at the
appropriate time.
Be ready— to
Help, Hide, and Hoax.

They both grinned. Abbie slipped her headphones back on and opened her book. Jordan read the note again, until a strange sense overcame him. He sat up, turned around, and looked out the back window. A few hundred yards back, a black, furry Florida Skunk Ape sat like a cowboy atop a Giant Desert Jackalope. The fluffy steed rose up on its hind legs, and the reeky rider waved a Badger Ranger hat in the air.

Jordan Grimsley faced forward. He opened his window all the way, shut his eyes, and let the wonderfully moist, sticky swampy air wash over his smiling face.

WORMHOLE THINGY, COOL FUTURISTIC STUFF,
AND SUPER-FREAKY ALIENS
TRYING TO TAKE OVER THE WORLD.

HOW AWESOME IS THAT?

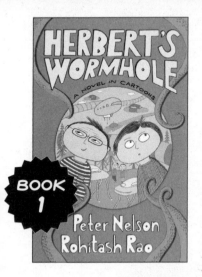

BOOK 1

BOOK 2

BOOK 3